The FOOL'S CIRCUS

Lost Pup

An imprint of Dani Rei LLC

www.danireiofficial.com
© Copyright 2021 by Dani Rei LLC

ISBN:
978-1-7367246-2-0 (Hardcover)
978-1-7367246-3-7 (Paperback)
978-1-7367246-1-3 (eBook)

LCCN:
2021904189

Developmental Edit by: Nicole Fegan
Copy Edit by: Joel Pierson
Proofread by: Caroline Barnhill
Cover design by: Weave – www.weave.design

The
FOOL'S
CIRCUS
Lost Pup

Book one of The Fools' Circus
Trilogy

Dani Rei

Dani Rei LLC

Acknowledgements

To my mother, Shakira, and my brother, Andre, for always believing in me, and supporting all of the wacky things I wanted to learn growing up.

To my Aunt Erika and my grandmother, Blanca, who always encouraged my creativity and helped it flourish in new ways.

To my son, Jacobi. While I'm the one raising you, you're showing me a side of myself that I never would've found otherwise. Being your mother is the best thing I've ever done with my life.

To my partner, Christian, for not only being supportive, but for giving me that gentle nudge outside my comfort zone to achieve my goals and continue to grow.

To my closest friends, Jacob, Lyn, and Evan. You've been more helpful and inspirational than you can imagine. Thank you for sticking by me all these years.

To the flow arts community, for welcoming and accepting me for who I am, supporting me, and making me feel less alone in this world.

To all the friends and family I didn't mention by name. There are so many I could fill an entire book with my thanks. I am eternally grateful to have each and every one of you in my life. Thank you for being your wonderful selves.

To my son. May you always be foolish enough to
chase your dreams.

"Go forth, ye fool. Continue to believe that what
awaits you in the end is applause."

-Jay Hickman, *Kaleido Star*

Prologue

I *remember the first time I attended The Fools'*
Circus. I was ten years old, watching a teenage boy
called the Blades Master juggle knives. A younger
boy wore cat ears and did leaps and somersaults on
trampolines. A little girl did tricks and jumped on a
trapeze, while another around my age danced with
flames.

Every time we went, my mom would ask me, "Wouldn't
it be cool to perform like that?"

She likely said it as a fun thought, but watching those
young performers made me believe I could do anything.

Soon, joining them became a dream of mine, and she encouraged me to try.

I taught myself to juggle, hoping to join the other kids on stage. When I was thirteen, my mom died in a car accident. I was adopted months later by a successful business couple, and they hated the circus. I missed the show that year, and it tore me apart inside.

The year after, I went with a friend and his parents, and the next year, I went alone. I brought dates in my late teens, but their passion didn't match mine. The point is, I never missed a show again, and I never stopped juggling, hoping I could perform on stage with the others.

I have to join. My mother's spirit is pushing me. I can't stay in the audience forever.

Chapter 1

Applause roars from behind the temporary fences that keep the patrons in line. Three clubs fly into the air, two landing in tanned hands, the third standing on its handle on Blake's forehead. He wobbles around to balance it as more cheers and whistles rise from the crowd. A few drivers honk or cheer from the window as they drive by. The ends of his brown waves tickle his eyes, but he does his best to hold the pose for a bit longer.

He flops his head forward to toss the club into his hand and takes a bow. Even passersby on the sidewalk have stopped to watch him, and the resulting applause sends chills over his skin and plasters a grin on his face.

He takes a second to gaze at the convention center, where The Fools' Circus is about to perform. His eyes scan the windows for a sign, some hint that someone in there is watching him. He didn't get this sign on Friday or Saturday, but tonight—Sunday night—is their last show and his last chance until next year.

Stuffing his backpack with his clubs and tossing it over his shoulder, he makes his way toward the back of the line.

Along the way, he thanks many people for their various compliments and words of encouragement. A few of them even reach out to shake his hand.

"Hey!" shouts an old man from the line. His white hair hangs at his shoulders under a gray fedora that matches his suit. His voice is raspy, but has a soothing air to it. "You're not part of The Fools' Circus, are you?"

"No sir." Blake stops with a smile. "I can't find a way of contacting them, so I just juggle here and hope they see me."

"Ah. So you'd like to join?"

"Yeah, but it looks like juggling won't be enough. I'll have to try harder this time."

"Where are you going then? Not staying for the show?"

"I am, but I already have my ticket, so I don't mind going to the back of the line. It's not like my assigned seat is going anywhere."

The old man lets out a small grumble and takes a step back to gesture at a space in front of him with his wooden cane. "Just hop the fence and get in here. You're only one guy. Fuck 'em if they get mad."

Blake chuckles and stumbles over the fence to take his spot in front of the old man, grateful that no one protests. "Thanks, Gramps. Can I call you Gramps?"

"You can call me Shit Head—I like long walks on the beach, and I hate people who clean the grease off their pizza."

Blake laughs as the line takes its first inch forward. "I like you, Shit Head. My name's Blake. Are you here alone?"

"Yeah, I planned to bring my daughter, but she's been in and out of the hospital for a long time now. And what about you? A handsome young man like you isn't here with a girlfriend? Boyfriend, maybe?"

"Nope. Single life isn't so bad. I like being able to focus on work and hobbies."

"Smart kid. How old are you anyway?"

"Twenty-three."

Shit Head purses his wrinkled old lips under his white stubble and nods. "Still young. No reason to rush it."

The line takes its first step forward as Shit Head raves on about his years of gymnastics experience, and how marvelous it would be to perform at such a show.

While Blake is enjoying the conversation and good company, his heart is pounding against his ribs, begging for the line to hurry so he can see the show and take his chance.

The light in the old man's eyes as he reminisces of his younger days only motivates Blake more and more.

Each step happens in slow motion until the entrance comes into view. A surge of energy pulses through Blake's veins as he reviews his plan. When the show ends, he'll find out if there is a place for him on stage.

It has to be today. I need to have an answer before I go home.

★ ★ ★

5

THE RINGLEADER TAKES HIS place on stage, donning a black suit with purple embellishments along his pants and jacket sleeves. The tailcoats on his blazer whip about with every movement, and a purple button-up lines his neck. When he turns to address the audience behind him, a purple embroidered lion roars on his back. He lifts his gloved hands, one of them holding a cane, as his voice booms over the cheering audience.

"Fans, fiends, and comrades! We thank you for joining us this evening! Our story begins a long time ago, with a little girl who lives with a wicked stepmother and two evil stepsisters."

The ringleader's voice trails off as his spotlight dims and others illuminate the rest of the stage.

A blonde woman dressed in rags dances on the stage floor while three other performers in pastel leap and bound on the surrounding trampolines in a violent display. Cinderella drops her broom to juggle a feather duster, a cleaning sponge, and a teapot.

Blake remembers her name from being announced in previous shows. She doesn't have a title like the Blades Master or Fire Goddess; her name is Axel. Her portrayal as Cinderella is sweet and elegant, with an air of innocence that makes the audience, including Blake, fall in love.

Everything falls around Cinderella, and one sister pulls her onto the trampoline. She's thrown around, each sister ripping parts of her dress and shoving her to the other, before they leave her on the stage floor and disappear.

The fairy godmother appears with a floating wand, each end engulfed in fire, as she dances around, her short, strawberry-red hair whipping in all directions.

Cinderella climbs up and twirls her body into a pink wall of silks. The fairy godmother uses her magic to seal

6

her in a cocoon while she dances around the stage with a man wearing cat ears. At the music's cue, Cinderella bursts from the wall of silks in her ball attire, making the audience boom into applause, before disappearing from the stage.

The lights go out, and intermission is called. Blake leans forward in his seat, trying to navigate the distance between the stage and the back of the building in his mind. His leg bounces in its place as people around him make their way to the concession stands and restrooms. A group of clowns take the stage and amuse the dwindling crowd.

Blake has never been so eager for the show to end before; he can't carry out his mission while the show is going on. Even if he could, he wouldn't dare miss it.

It feels like an eternity is going by; he's tempted to leave now but takes a deep breath to remind himself that the cast and crew won't be going anywhere in the middle of a show.

The clowns leave the stage, and the lights grow dim as the stadium seats fill themselves up again.

Finally.

The stage lights up in a tranquil blue hue. Couples perform on aerial hoops around the stage. The blond prince pulls Cinderella onto the trapeze to leap and hang in romantic poses as they whoosh through the air. The audience roars at their display, and Blake's heart stops.

The magic on stage is calling him again, begging him to join, but he stays put.

The performers land on the platform, and the prince holds out a fist. When he opens it, a bouquet of flowers grows from his palm. Cinderella is about to take them, when suddenly the lights turn purple and ominous music fills the stage as the bell tolls.

She leaps back onto the trapeze and swings to the next to get away from him. The prince tries to follow, but before he can reach the second swing, one stepsister snatches him from the air by his ankles. She pulls him onto her swing while he struggles; the dispute stays in tune with the music, and their poses make the audience go wild.

Stage lights change to sunrise colors, and soldiers soar through the air on trampolines. When they find Cinderella, the prince pulls her into a pair of white silks, while they twist and bend and their chemistry heats up the stadium.

The hours take their time inching by, and Blake's anxiety, coupled with fascination, create a confusing whirl in his mind. He hasn't even thought of what he will say or do if he actually gets the chance to talk to someone. He probably should, but the show is demanding every bit of his attention.

It all ends too soon, but not soon enough. The performers gather in a circle around the stage. Each of them is holding hands with the next as the ringleader sends additional thanks to the crew members before thanking the audience.

Wait, something's changed. Blake leans in to examine the changes on stage. There are fewer aerial rigs now than there were before. *Is the crew putting them away already?*

He leaps from his seat as the audience bursts into a standing ovation. He rushes out of the stadium and into the cold night air. An icy breeze makes him shiver and zip his black jacket before he hurries around the building, keeping his eye out for guards, police, or (in the best-case scenario) a clown to point him in the right direction.

Around the back, he finds a group of people moving equipment into the back of a white truck. At first, he isn't

8

sure if they're the right people, but one man is carrying aerial hoops, and that's all the evidence he needs.

"Excuse me!" Blake calls, running over without thinking. One of them, a dark-skinned man with short hair, stops to look at him with his eyebrows raised in attention.

"What's up, man?"

"Are you guys with the circus?" Blake asks.

"Yeah, but we don't perform."

"That's fine, I just have a question. How does someone get to be part of it? I looked everywhere online, and I couldn't find anything."

"We're not hiring," the man says as he turns around to get back to his work. "Sorry."

"No, wait, please." Blake gives the man's arm a gentle tug to stop him. "Please, can you give me some way to contact your boss?"

"Our hiring process doesn't work that way. There are plenty of other circuses you can try."

"There's nothing I can do? No one I can talk to?"

The man shrugs as he shakes his head. "I'm sorry. We just don't work like that."

"How *does* it work?"

"I can't tell you. Word spreads, jobs open, and suddenly sacred ground becomes another capitalist hotspot. Go try somewhere else."

The truck's trailer closes, and the man's coworkers gather behind him, furrowing their brows at their conversation. One of them pats the man on the shoulder. "We're ready when you are, Ronan."

Ronan nods them off, signaling them to give him one more minute with the curious stranger. They go back to their work, but not without glancing back and whispering amongst themselves.

9

"Please?" Blake asks, his heart sinking in his chest.

"I can't," Ronan says. "Look, it's nothing personal, all right? Tell you what, I can talk to some of my guys and get you a free souvenir. Maybe a DVD of tonight's show, yeah?"

"No, that's okay. Thanks, though."

Ronan holds out his hand. "Like I said, it's nothing personal. No hard feelings?"

Blake gives Ronan's hand a reluctant shake, forcing a smile to disguise the lump in his throat.

Ronan climbs into the passenger seat of the truck with one of the men while the other two make their way back into the building. His eyes lock on to Blake's as the truck drives off.

With a heavy breath, Blake turns to make his way back to the street. His heart is so heavy that he slouches, eyes glazing over as he watches the ground beneath his feet.

So, there it is. I wanted an answer, and I got it.

Or did I?

He stops in his tracks and turns back around to face the building again. He runs back to the doors and knocks, doing his best not to sound too angry or violent.

No answer. They must be gathering the rest of the equipment. Blake drops onto the cold cement, his back to the wall, his mind already reminiscing about the show. He closes his eyes and quietly begs in his heart that Ronan is wrong, praying to whatever higher power is watching that there is room for him somewhere on that stage.

He'd been attending the circus every year since childhood, watching kids his age perform incredible talents. They gave him something to aim for, something he could achieve if he only tried hard enough. The smile his birth mother had when he learned a new juggling pattern flashes into his mind and lights a fire in his chest. He won't give up just because one member said no.

The door opens, prompting Blake to scuttle to the side as he stands up. Two men lug a large case and set it against the wall while a third person holds it open. None of them seem to notice Blake as they continue.

"Lance, sit with it until Ronan gets back, will ya?"

"Hell no, it's freezing and my sweater's inside! One of you can wait out here!"

"You freakin' wuss!" calls a third burly voice. "It's only September! What, are you going to hibernate all winter?"

"I'll do it," a fourth gentler voice says.

"Mishkin?" says the burly voice. "Why aren't you with the others?"

"I need some fresh air. I can watch your stuff."

The three voices all seem to agree as a thin man in a sleeveless shirt, black pants, and cat ears steps out, the door closing behind him. He turns to face Blake with hazel eyes and a caramel-colored face. Three dermal piercings sit on each cheek as he raises a thick brow.

"So," Mishkin says, "you're still here."

"What?" says Blake. "Do you know me?"

"Kinda hard not to notice a guy who puts on his own show in front of a big name like ours."

"I'm sorry," says Blake. "I didn't mean anything by it. Well, I guess I sort of did, but nothing bad. I just …" Blake's voice trails off as he stares at the ground, embarrassed to be confessing his hopes and dreams to a man who was just on stage living them.

"You want to join, right? I heard the guys talking about you. Ronan told you off."

"Was he right? Is there really no way for me to join?"

11

"There are dozens of other circuses." Mishkin crosses his arms. "Many have names bigger than ours. Tell me, what makes ours so special?"

Blake tenses, and his eyes drop to the ground. "I, uh...I guess I don't know. It wasn't something I thought about; it was just something I had to do. I always thought I had to become part of it. For Mom."

"And when you join us and realize that we aren't as glamorous as you think, then what?"

Blake's lips form a tight line. "I guess I run screaming in the other direction and go to trauma counseling. Is that what you want to hear?"

Mishkin narrows his eyes and takes a step closer to Blake, whose heart is now racing in his chest. *Damn it, Blake. We're supposed to be begging here. You're going to get your ass kicked!*

Mishkin hunches over as laughter escapes his chest. His grinning lips reveal sharpened canines that make Blake's heart jump. He shudders at the thought of teeth being sanded.

"You're ballsy! I like you! But look, even if I want you to join, there's nothing I can do. It's not up to me."

"I don't understand, why is this so difficult?"

"Hey, kitty cat!" calls a voice from around the corner. "I see you've met my new friend."

Blake's eyes widen as a familiar old face approaches them with a cane and a cigarette.

"Shit Head!" Blake calls.

"What?" Mishkin yelps.

"So, Blake here wants to join, right?"

"No one can join without Rex's approval."

"Rex will approve. He's talented enough. Besides, a machine can't function if it's missing a piece, can it?

12

Letting Blake join could move things along. Hell, you can even tell Rex that this was my suggestion."

Mishkin puts a pensive hand over his chin as he stares back at Blake. Shit Head takes another puff of his cigarette, and Blake is frozen in his spot.

Mishkin runs his fingers through his black hair, his cheeks puffing as he huffs out his thoughts. "You still haven't told me what you're planning, old man. Care to explain?"

A grin slithers onto Shit Head's wrinkled face as cigarette smoke wafts into the air.

"Fine, useless schemer." Mishkin holds out a hand. "Who has a pen?"

Blake grabs his backpack from his shoulders and pulls one from the front pocket. Mishkin grabs the pen in one hand and Blake's wrist in the other, pulling him in so quickly that Blake's face almost collides with the back of his head. The cat ears block the view of his arm.

Blake's sleeve is shoved roughly up his arm, and the cold tip of the pen stabs his skin in rapid lines and curves. He clenches his teeth to avoid grunting in pain.

The back door opens again, and the crew members step out, each holding rigs and ropes in their arms. Mishkin turns around and leans his forehead against Blake's with a grin, putting the pen back in his hand.

"Don't say another word. I'll see you tomorrow."

"But—"

Mishkin shoves Blake toward Shit Head, who quickly grabs Blake's arm, and walks away from the two men before they can notice what's happening.

"You pesky boy!" Shit Head chuckles at an obnoxious volume, paying no mind to Blake's stumbling. "You got your autograph, now get out of here!"

"Autograph?" Blake mutters as Shit Head leads him around the building. "Gramps, what is going on?"

"I told you, call me Shit Head. The look on Mishkin's face was priceless!" He laughs, loosening his grip on Blake now that they're at the front of the building. "I should pay you for it!"

"Okay but, did he actually..." Blake stops to process the writing on his arm. An autograph? No, an address.

It's an appointment.

Chapter 2

Blake stares at the mansion with a slack jaw as he opens the front gate, surprised to find it unlocked. He figured The Fools' Circus must have an office space *somewhere*, but he never imagined it'd be in his own state. Newport isn't the shortest bus ride, but it's nice that he didn't need a plane ticket.

The gravel path cuts through a luscious green lawn, decorated with evergreen trees and bushes trimmed down to perfect raindrops and cubes. The mansion towers over the property with white paneling, black rooftops, and large windows everywhere, almost as big as a private school.

Is this where the circus owner lives? Or maybe it's where they come to practice?

He reaches the large, roofed porch, grateful to be out of the sun. A small jester hangs from enormous doors, smiling at him with bells on his colorful hat. Ribbons of gold and purple create a wreath with small white pom poms scattered around it. He's seen this jester all over the circus merch and has a T-shirt of it from that one time he was able to splurge on a souvenir.

He clears his throat and stands tall—as if the jester were able to smell his fear—and rings the doorbell. He takes a few deep breaths, willing his heartbeat to slow down and his nerves to relax.

He glances down at himself and wonders if his blue polo shirt and black pants are appropriate for a meeting with a circus. *Would they call this overdressed or underdressed?*

Images of the night before flash through Blake's mind: the old man, the Cat, and some secret reason for giving him a chance. He grabs at his backpack to make sure it's still there, trying to ignore the doubts in his mind.

The door opens, and his heart jumps, but he's relieved to see a familiar face.

"Oh good, you made it!"

"Yeah. Hi, Mishkin," says Blake.

"Follow me. I've already made you an appointment with the Keeper."

Blake steps in and eases the front door closed, as if it could break with the wrong amount of pressure. He looks around at the cream-colored walls as he and Mishkin make their way down the main hall. A few scattered paintings hang just above reach, and below them are benches and end tables. Beanbag chairs and sofas with worn spots and tears in the fabric line the walls.

Their footsteps echo through the empty halls, and Blake swallows hard, doing his best to focus on Mishkin instead of the haunting silence.

"What do you mean by *Keeper*?" he asks.

"The Fools' Keeper handles the paperwork," says Mishkin. "He'll get a feel for your personality, and then Rex will make the final decision."

"So Rex is the boss, then?"

"To put it in Fools' terms, he's our King, but you've got the right idea. The naming just makes it feel like we're part of our own little world, and it's kind of nice after all we've been through."

"*We? So you live here with the King?*"

"We all do. All forty-seven of us."

"Forty-seven!" Blake shoots his gaze around the mansion again. "But where is everyone? It's like a ghost town in here. It's freakin' creepy!"

"We just finished touring; We're exhausted. Breakfast is being delayed too, so no one is leaving their rooms anytime soon. You're lucky the old man showed up. I could be in bed, cuddling with my love right now, but nooo…"

"Sorry. Who is that old guy, anyway? And what did he mean by 'getting things moving?'"

The two reach a door with a frosted glass window. Mishkin opens it without knocking and steps aside to usher Blake in. "He's here."

A plump man in gray flannel lifts his head from his papers. A brown moustache with a few silver streaks blocks his upper lip, and his brown eyes peer through his glasses at the stranger in front of him.

Beside him stands a tall, slender man with long blond hair falling past his shoulders to his torso, covered by a white button-up tucked into black pants and a purple

17

blazer hanging off his shoulders. He gestures at the chair on the other side of the office desk, rings glistening in the sunlight from the large window behind him. "Sit."

Blake does as he's told, his heartbeat speeding up again. Mishkin shuts the office door and stands behind the chair, giving Blake's shoulder a comforting pat. Blake looks up at him, and Mishkin winks back, which doesn't help Blake feel any better.

"My name is Victor," says the plump man. "I'm the Keeper of Fools."

"And I am Rex," says the tall blond. "The King of Fools."

"Tell us," says Victor, crossing his arms, "what makes you think you belong in our circus?"

"Well—" Blake clears his throat, making every attempt to hide his frazzled nerves. "I've been watching you guys since I was a kid, and you all inspired me to juggle. In fact, circus days with my mom are some of the happiest memories I have. She never pushed me to perform, but she planted the idea in my mind, and it flourished after that. Then she died, and I never found anything that felt as fulfilling as performing does."

Victor and Rex shoot a glance at each other before Victor shakes his head. "Sorry, kid. You don't belong here."

"What?" Blake exclaims, straightening in his seat. "But you haven't seen what I can do yet!"

"Every child you saw on that stage was homeless when they joined. *Homeless*. No family. No hope. As children. We helped them because they couldn't help themselves. You are a grown man. I did my checking up on you, and I know you were adopted by a successful business couple. You also have a full-time job and managed to move out, right? You aren't homeless. You aren't helpless. You can stand on your own. Hartman asked me to give you a chance. I gave it to you, now I'm saying no."

Blake leans forward in his seat. "Is that how this works? You scout out homeless kids for a circus? Is that even legal?"

"Our process is top secret. I'm not explaining anything further, and I'm not letting you join."

"Hold on," says Rex. All eyes dart over to him as he rubs a pensive finger along his chin, eyeing Blake with a smirk. "Victor, please elaborate on your thoughts. How would you describe his desire to join our circus?"

"I'd say it's stupid," Victor scoffs.

"Would you say it's…foolish?" Rex grins at Victor, who throws his head to the side, huffing to himself.

"My dear boy," says Rex, sending a soft smile toward Blake, "do you know why we call ourselves The Fools' Circus?"

Blake hesitates, shifting his eyes to the ground, before shaking his head.

"All throughout history, we've had creators, explorers, remarkable individuals who changed the world. The world called these people fools. They faced their adversities and grew from them. They believed in their visions and led the world's greatest changes. Shakespeare himself acknowledged the fool as someone who sees the truth and dares to speak it, even to royalty.

"Even now, the Fool card in a tarot deck is the card of opportunity—a chance to fly for those foolish enough to take the leap."

"Wow." Blake drops his gaze to the patterned carpet beneath him. When he'd thought of fools before, he'd always pictured clowns and jesters.

If what Victor says about the kids is true, it would add new meaning to the name he'd dreamt about for so long.

19

"Look," he says. "I don't want to sound selfish, or anything. But the kids you adopted are adults, now. Would it really be so weird to hire someone their own age? It's not like I'm asking to join a fourth-grade art club, here. Hiring me won't take any opportunities away from the others."

"Perhaps not" Rex responds. "But you still haven't given us a good reason to hire you. I've seen you juggle, but what else can you offer?"

Blake sinks in his seat. "I guess I don't have much else. Juggling has always been my favorite. But I'm willing to learn other things, too. I can learn to swing on a trapeze or flip on a trampoline. I don't even care if I never get a lead role. I just want to perform alongside my childhood heroes."

"Is that so?" A tiny smirk curls the side of Rex's lips. "Then tell me, is the title of 'Fool' one you can wear with pride?"

"Of course." Blake responds. "I'd be even prouder to wear it now that I know what it really means."

"Then I suppose you deserve one chance," Rex smiles as he steps out from behind the desk. "Victor, get his paperwork started. I have an appointment to get to. Don't let your guard down, boy. The fool will always suffer before he rises."

Rex pats Blake's head as he leaves the office. Blake doesn't breathe until he closes the door behind him.

Is that it? I'm accepted just like that?

"Victor," says Mishkin, "there's something else. I didn't mention this part to Rex, but Hartman said letting him join would get things moving. Whatever that means."

Victor groans and leans his elbow on his desk. He takes off his glasses with one hand and rubs the bridge of his nose with the other. Blake's mind flashes back to Shit Head, unsure of whether to thank him or curse him.

"That crooked geezer is going to be the death of me," Victor sighs, picking up his pen and shifting through some files in one of his desk drawers.

"Um, please, sir," Blake says, leaning forward in his seat. "Who is Hartman, exactly? I met him yesterday, but he didn't tell me his name."

"He's our biggest investor. Rex hates taking orders, but we need Hartman's money, so we're stuck under his thumb. He's the only reason we're saying yes. In fact, *I* said no because I thought Rex would follow along and decide the money wasn't worth it. I guess I was wrong. But make no mistake, you won't be accepted by the others so easily. I suggest you choose your words and actions *very* carefully."

He places a sheet of paper on the desk. "Fill out this form at home and bring it back with your ID and social security card. I'll expect you back on the second of October, and you'll be with us for one year. We'll decide later to renew or terminate. You can tell your parents you're taking a trip or that you started school, or whatever you want, but you can't tell them you're here."

"What? Why not?"

"We keep our information under wraps for the safety of the cast and crew. It's a big part of why we don't allow people to audition. We don't need word spreading that The Fools' Circus is taking in a lost pup. The rules will explain everything. Just read them very closely before you sign."

Blake furrows his brow at Mishkin, then turns back to Victor. "Wait, but two weeks—I can't just quit my job."

"Why not?" Victor asks. "Two weeks is the standard notice for most jobs. Just give yourself time to pack up whatever you want to bring with you. We'll get a room ready with a new bed and empty dresser."

More objections, questions, and anxieties whirl through Blake's mind, but Victor puts his glasses back on and returns his attention to the work on his desk. Mishkin taps his shoulder and nods his head toward the door.

He follows the prompt, plucking the application from the desk and staring at it as Mishkin walks him out in silence.

Blake's dream of joining The Fools' Circus is about to come true.

So why does his heart feel heavy?

Chapter 3

"**Y**ou're wasting valuable time."
      The familiar voice can send chills even through the phone. He hoped putting her on speaker and keeping it a foot away would be easier on his ears. Nope, they're still burning with her disdain. "Time that can be spent on better things."

"Sure, Ma," Blake groans as he takes another bite of the shepherd's pie she brought him yesterday. He turns up his nose at the lack of flavor and quietly sprinkles salt and pepper over the top. Not that its blandness is anything new.

He takes another bite as her disapproving rant continues. His eyes wander around the pantry, passively scanning the floral wallpaper stained with oil spots and lifting at the edges. The nutty smell of pests fills the air, and he catches one of them crawling along the wall before its slick, brown body darts into a small crack in the cupboard.

With a silent scowl, he holds out his plate and lets the rest of his food drop into the trash. He forgot to wash the already clean dishes before he ate. Microwaved roach shit is probably the only seasoning he won't eat. Right along with the rat piss in the stew pots under the counter.

"We didn't adopt you so that you could quit college and goof off," his father chimes in, voice as forceful as ever. "What do you hope to achieve by driving around with your friends for an entire year?"

He shrugs to himself. "Experiences, maybe?"

It was the wrong response, and Blake deflates over the counter as they yell, assaulting his ears with the usual arguments. "Experiences don't pay bills," and "think ahead," and *blah blah blah*. He's grateful they can't see him rolling his eyes and grabbing a small bag of chips to replace his dinner.

Their lectures don't end soon enough. They finish the call with reminders of how much they love him and want the best for him. He promises to never become a delinquent and that he'll find a way to make ends meet, minding his words to avoid any mention of the circus. He spoke to them about wanting to join before, but they mocked the performers' very existence; patronized them as if performing were a low-intelligence career.

Finally, he can hang up, and he lets out a heavy breath, head falling back. The peeling paint on the ceiling reminds him to keep his mouth closed, in case of falling paint chips. He trudges to his room and closes the door behind him.

24

A fire lights in his chest when his eyes land on his backpack. The application—his ticket to freedom—is right inside, waiting to be filled out.

But first, juggling!

Blake pulls the clubs from his backpack, setting the application on his desk to wait for him.

He tosses the clubs from one hand to another, controlling the patterns and shapes with a simple flick of his wrist. Images of Shit Head—no, Hartman—flood his mind, along with the faces of Victor and Mishkin, as he replays the most confusing interview of his life.

And Rex.

The last club falls past his hands, and Blake sets out his foot to catch it and balance it on his ankle until he kicks it up to his hand. He drops his hands to the side and lets out a heavy breath as he stares at the popcorn texture of his ceiling.

So that's the ringleader. Rex's piercing blue eyes have etched themselves into his memory. He dresses like a modern-day king. He speaks like a king. He walks with his head held high and moves with confidence, as if no one can touch him.

The fool must always suffer before he rises. The fool must always suffer. Rex's voice rings in his ears, and a chill runs down his spine. He'd read stories and watched movies about circus performers being rude or self-centered. Maybe there's some truth to it, but he swallows down the anxiety and continues to toss his clubs around, allowing the swirling patterns to hypnotize his thoughts and calm his heart.

Rex makes it sound like he expects Blake to slay a dragon or something. Of course, joining a circus won't be easy. The rest of the cast is likely to brush him off until they see what he can do. Pranks and harsh words wouldn't be much different from middle school. None of that could be worse than roaches, junk-food dinners, and minimum wage.

A woman's moan rings through his bedroom wall, muffled, and his roommate breathes some vulgar sweet talk he didn't need to hear. Cringing, he rustles through his backpack, exchanging the clubs for a pair of earbuds. He sits at his desk, pretending he doesn't see the wall moving from the corner of his eye, and grabs a pen from the drawer with music on full blast.

No amount of childish bullying can be worse than that.

Before he begins writing, his eyes scan the first page. It looks pretty standard. Name, birthdate, address, nothing out of the ordinary. He flips to the second.

Rule #1 - Never stop improving. The fool gets nowhere by sitting comfortably.
Rule #2 – Never reveal your location. This is a precaution for everyone, including yourself.
Rule #3 - Never protest the Fools' King. And never lose his favor.

These are your rules for joining The Fools' Circus. Failure to abide by these rules will lead to contract termination or worse. By signing, you agree to live under Rex's command, at the mercy of the stage.

Blake puffs out his cheeks as he fidgets with the pen in his hand, glaring at the page. Victor told him the rules would explain everything, but it doesn't explain anything. *Tell no one where you are*? It sounds suspicious, but if everyone had been adopted as children, it might be safer that way after all.

The song in his headphones ends abruptly just in time for Blake to hear the woman's climax against the wall, and he growls to himself, scribbling his signature as quickly as possible. He flips back to the first page and proceeds with the boring part of any application.

It's a circus, after all. What could happen?

HOW HAS IT ONLY BEEN TWO DAYS? I want to live at the mansion now!

"I hate to see you go, Blake," says his boss, a hefty man with a brown mustache and short matching hair. "But I think a road trip will be good for you. Call me when you get home, and I'll see if I can squeeze you back in somehow."

"Great. Thanks, Terry."

Blake leaves the office and lets out a sigh of relief. It's not that Terry is an intimidating boss, but this is Blake's first time giving two weeks' notice. That was much easier than he expected. The department store has kept him for a solid five years and was happy to switch him to full time when he dropped out of college.

He slides his gaze around the store, at the clothes on the racks and signs that label the activewear, dresses, and other clothing categories. Memories of interesting customers and mocking the rude ones with his coworkers flood his mind. Leaving retail is a dream come true, but he never imagined he'd miss it so much, especially not at the very beginning of his last two weeks.

"Hey, stranger!" calls a sweet voice as Blake takes his place at the register. "How was your weekend off?"

27

"It was great," Blake responds with a smile. Judy is a longtime friend and coworker, and it makes him feel a little guilty that he can't tell her the good news. "I went to see the circus."

"You mean The Fools' Circus?"

"Yeah, and it inspired me to take a road trip with some friends of mine. I'd like to perform one day, so I should travel the country and see what I'm up against, don't you think? I already put in my two weeks' notice."

Judy's eyes grow wide, and her lips frown. "Why would you go to see *that* circus?"

Blake furrows his brow at her.

"I'm guessing you didn't know," says Judy, glancing around for anyone within earshot. "There are rumors about that circus—terrible ones. They say the children were kidnapped and forced to perform for profit. Some say they service pedophiles, and that the owner works with politicians to keep it all quiet. I mean, why else would they hide so much information about themselves?"

Blake shifts his lower jaw to process her words. "It'd be pretty stupid to put missing children on display like that, don't you think?"

"You don't know what a person in power is capable of."

"Oh, I know. I was there for the 2016 election. Besides, you make it sound like I'm joining them. I'm just going on a road trip to check out other plays, circuses, and street performers. I just want to enjoy life for a little bit and see if I have a shot. You can relax. The circus is leaving town anyway."

Judy looks a little relieved, but an elderly customer interrupts before she can speak, looking for a dress. Judy leaps to her aid with her best customer-service smile, leaving Blake to clean out the fitting room.

He knew of those rumors, of course, having been a longtime patron, but hearing them from Judy makes his mind race.

Tell no one where you are.

What if those rumors are based in truth, and that's why Blake can't tell anyone where *he* is? He shakes his head. No, that can't be true, Victor said they were all adopted from nothing. *He could've been lying. It could be a trap.*

Blake takes in a deep breath, trying to push out these terrifying thoughts to no avail. Those rumors came from somewhere. What exactly is he getting himself into?

Maybe some dreams are better left unlived.

Chapter 4

"My precious fools! I'd like you all to welcome Blake to our home!"

Rex's voice booms over the cast and crew gathered in the lobby. Blake's heart races in his chest. The thought of leaving this dream unlived was a genuine option, but not one he could follow through with. *Sorry, Judy.*

"He's a juggler with impressive skill," Rex continues. "But he must learn our ways before we can let him on stage. So, who needs a partner? An extra? Who would like to help this lost pup find his way to the stage?"

Eyes shift back and forth while whispers of confusion and rejection creep around the room. This is exactly what he expected. Even so, his stomach is still churning from it. He breathes slow to hide his trembling as his eyes scan the crowd, looking for some sign of friendliness or a hint of acceptance.

"Ian," Rex calls, "you juggle your knives. Why not take over this young man's learning curve?"

A bald man scoffs in response, sitting on the floor against the lobby wall with gray sweatpants. A tattoo of a red dragon tearing through his skin covers his left pec. He uses a pocketknife to clean dirt from under his nails.

"To be honest, Rex, it's a little upsetting that you would expect your own children to deal with someone like him. I will if I must, but it doesn't make sense to me. He's not one of yours, so why should we care?"

Nods of agreement and shrugs of apathy scatter among the crowd. Blake huffs, no longer bothering to hide his discomfort.

"It's okay," he says to Rex, projecting his voice so everyone can hear. "I'm sure I can figure things out on my own."

"Don't be absurd," Rex replies. "You have a lot to learn, and you should work with someone you can relate to. Where is Inez?"

"She's not here, sir." Mishkin frowns from his spot on a bench. "You only called this meeting for *your* children."

"Right, how silly of me," says Rex, patting Blake's shoulder. "Well, Blake, it appears you'll be working with our beloved Fire Goddess."

"I'll introduce you," Mishkin volunteers, lighting up with energy. He grabs Blake's arm with a smile and pulls Blake away from Rex without another word.

Blake barely keeps his footing as they rush up the stairs. Even after begging to slow down, Mishkin doesn't give way.

31

At the top of the staircase, Mishkin drops his grip, and Blake rests his hands on his knees to catch his breath before he takes in the view.

The second floor is a wide hall with doors along either side. Each bears a name or two on a gold plaque. At the far wall, there's another staircase curving to a third floor above them. The ceilings are high, with paintings of circus animals emerging from open cages in scenes of inspired chaos. Gold trim wraps the tops of the pillars, bleeding onto the ceiling. Matching trim adorns the bottom, spreading the same patterns into the lower wall. Large windows light the corners, their curtains spread to allow the golden sunset to burst through.

"There you are, Grump Face!" Mishkin calls to the young woman waiting for them with crossed arms just a few feet from the stairs. Her brown eyes narrow under her short, bottle-red hair, the shade of a strawberry.

"I know you heard the announcement. Say hello to our newest fool!"

Blake smiles at Inez, and another surge of excitement runs through him. "It's nice to meet you! I loved your Fairy Godmother role in *Cinderella*! You were amazing!"

"I know you," says Inez. "You're that guy who juggles before the show. Just what are you trying to pull by coming here?"

Blake's smile disappears as quickly as it came, prompting him to scramble through his mind for words, any words, to explain himself. He looks around at the other members going to their rooms or hesitating on the stairs. All eyes are on the trio, filling the halls with giggles and whispers.

"It was Hartman's suggestion," Mishkin says, taking a step in front of Blake. "He thinks Blake would be an excellent addition. And frankly, Miss Ice Queen, I agree with him."

Inez glares at Blake again before she takes a deep breath and gives Mishkin a soft smile. He isn't sure why, but this is more discomfiting than her glare.

"Mishkin, leave us alone for a second. If I'm going to mentor this guy, he should get to know me a little better."

Blake swallows thickly as he quietly begs Mishkin not to leave. He shudders when Mishkin walks off with a grin.

"Go easy on him."

Blake can almost hear each second ticking by as Mishkin disappears down the stairs. Inez grabs the front of his shirt and pulls him closer. Her searing gaze has already burned itself into Blake's nightmares, and though she's about half a foot shorter than him, he can swear she grew at least three feet taller.

"Listen, you spoiled little brat! I get enough bullshit without having some lost puppy following me around! You better learn quick, and then leave me the hell alone, got it? Don't expect me to be your fucking mother!"

"Okay! Okay, I get it! I'll learn quick!"

Inez shoves Blake away from her, and he struggles to keep his balance.

"Look," says Blake, fixing his shirt, "I don't know what everyone's problem is, but can you tell me *yours*? You don't even know me, and you're acting like I'm here to undermine you somehow. Do you even know my name?"

The fire on Inez's face cools as she looks away. "I know your name; it just doesn't matter. We all know you're here because you got on Hartman's good side. You're just a pampered pup who ran away from home. You aren't family."

33

Blake's heart drops in his chest. He expected to be an outcast until he earned everyone's respect, but why would they despise him this much already?

Inez groans, rolling her eyes as if she knows what he's thinking. "Don't take it personal, okay? It's just…weird. Usually when people come here, it isn't because they're lucky. And," Inez shuffles in her spot, growling as her cheeks turn pink and turning her head to hide it. "It's not like we hate you or anything. So don't get all weepy and shit, okay, Pup?"

Blake bites his tongue to force back a smile as bodies hurry past them from their bedrooms.

"Dinnertime," says Inez, leading the way back downstairs, still hiding her face in her hair. "Come on."

"Wait, me too?" Blake asks, keeping close behind.

"Yeah, stupid. You live here now."

"So, everyone here eats together?"

"Mostly. Some eat in their rooms, and sometimes people go out. The point is, we have the option. I usually sit at the table with Mishkin and a few others."

Blake pauses, taking a second to reflect on the one person who had shown him any kindness since arriving— albeit unsettling kindness. "He's an interesting character. I thought the cat stuff was just for the stage."

"Nope, he made himself catlike on purpose. That's why his title is Stray Cat."

A warm smell fills Blake's nose as they reach the bottom of the staircase, making his stomach growl.

Two people walk by, and Blake catches his breath. A tall man with dark skin and dreadlocks that hang over muscled arms walks beside a woman with skin as pale as porcelain. Her head barely reaches his shoulder, and their fingers are intertwined. A powder blue dress falls just over her knees in lacy frills, and long white waves hang

34

to the center of her back. She smiles at Blake with lavender eyes and black framed glasses. They're both attractive, and that almost makes him shocked they didn't play the leads in the last show. Or any show, for that matter.

A weight fills Blake's chest. He'd seen this woman on stage as a child and didn't notice when she disappeared. The man is a tightrope walker who played one of the prince's soldiers in the last show. *What was his title?* It's been years since Rex has announced anyone at the show.

The thought slips away as Blake tosses his gaze around, and a giddy smile creeps onto his face. He shifts his weight from one foot to the other, doing his best to keep his smile from getting too wide.

All around him, he's recognizing their faces from their roles in *Cinderella*, remembering the talents they had as kids and the magic they create now.

He hasn't learned their names yet, since Rex gave them all titles, but seeing the faces makes him feel like he landed in the center of Hollywood.

"Hey, Pup," Inez sighs, "do us both a favor, try not to gush over everyone you meet here, okay? You're one of us now, and you'll be joining us on stage next season."

"Right, sorry."

The two grab their plates, and the buffet table is making Blake's mouth water. So many options for proteins and sides. Inez grabs a steak for herself and hands him the tongs. He pulls a thick steak under the label "medium rare" and plops it onto his plate, surprised by its size. He looks at Inez to make sure this is okay. She signals him to hurry, and he rushes to grab mashed potatoes, mixed vegetables, and a roll.

They're making their way to the table when Mishkin finds them. "Hey guys! I already put my plate down.

Blake, come sit next to me! Did you meet my husband Vladik yet? He's been right behind you the whole time!"

"No, I didn't realize." Blake turns with a smile to where Mishkin is gesturing. "Hi, it's nice to...meet... you."

Mishkin and Inez stifle their laughter while Blake takes a minute to process what he's seeing. A rock wall trying to break through navy fabric? No, this is a person. He looks up to see a pale man with a golden beard and bald head smiling down at him.

"Vladik here is our strong man," Mishkin says.

"You don't say," Blake responds with a tremble in his voice. He recognizes the man's face, but the stage doesn't do his size justice.

"*Dobroe vecher*," says Vladik. His voice is soft and friendly, but it carries so much strength that it startles Blake.

"Ah! I'm sorry, I don't understand!"

"Good evening," Vladik says in a thick Russian accent. "Do forgive. My English is no good."

Blake smiles with a sigh of relief. "That's alright. I'm glad to meet you!"

The group sets their plates down and settles into their seats. Blake watches the others dig into their food before he musters up the courage to cut a piece of his own. *Is this really okay?* He takes the first bite of his steak and chews slowly, his eyes closing to appreciate the flavor—real flavor. A smoky roasted garlic with a black pepper undertone and a hint of vinegar. The taste lingers on his tongue even after he finishes the bite. *Delicious!*

He watches Inez interact with Mishkin from across the table, and she doesn't seem as scary anymore. Vladik isn't saying much, but when Mishkin makes a vulgar joke, his face turns bright red, and Inez stifles her laughter to avoid choking on her food. Vladik's eyes beg Mishkin to take things down a notch, and Blake laughs along as Mishkin loops him into the conversation. Inez's mood has lightened, and she speaks to Blake as if they'd known each other for years.

Good food, warm laughter, and not a single roach in sight. Blake hasn't felt this at home since his birth mother was alive. Maybe the thought should make him sad, but he's enjoying it too much.

Can you see this, Mom? I'm one of them now.

Chapter 5

The audience seems thrilled to have Blake on stage. The applause is deafening as he and the others whip and throw their bodies into beautiful dance poses, tossing clubs back and forth between each other while the acrobats whoosh through the air above them.

Inez and Mishkin whirl around the floor, twirling staffs with flames on either end. Blake has never juggled so vigorously in his life, and his clubs seem to float through the air until he catches them. The patterns and shapes are like nothing he's ever practiced, surprising even himself.

As their routine ends and the clubs stop moving, the audience booms into a standing ovation. Triumphant music blasts through the speakers in the background as

Inez grabs his hand and lifts it to take a bow with him. *This is all too good to be true!*

Blake's eyes blink open, and he gasps as he sits up, darting his gaze around the cream-colored walls and unfamiliar furniture, in a room much larger than his at home. *What is this place?*

His eyes land on his unpacked suitcase, and he lets out a heavy sigh of relief as the events of the day before return to his memory.

★ ★ ★

THE HALLS ARE EMPTY AND QUIET as Blake approaches the stairs. The sun is still too low to send direct light into the hall, but the mansion is well illuminated, nonetheless. The doors are all closed, and the air is so still, similar to when Blake arrived for his interview. They don't wake up as early as he anticipated. It makes sense, considering their tour had just finished, but for some reason, he expected a more strict schedule from such an incredible troupe.

Would exploring be okay? It's not like they gave him anything else to do. He takes a quick glance at his jeans and T-shirt to make sure he looks presentable, in case he bumps into someone. He freezes a few steps down when a voice echoes from downstairs.

"I thought you loved me."

"I never said it like that," responds a familiar voice. "You should know what I mean by now."

Blake crouches down to peek between the stairs and the second floor and sees a blond man in black pants and a lavender button-up standing face to face with a cross-armed Inez. His black vest has lavender embroidery on the front, and his short, golden hair is combed back. His

39

blue eyes are pleading with her. Blake catches his breath. *That guy is the Prince of Illusion; he's played the lead in every show!*

The Prince huffs, and his face goes firm. "You know, I didn't have a choice in this either. This is my father's circus. I was forced to be here too."

Blake holds his place, trembling but ready to charge in if he needs to. But should he? He doesn't want Inez to think he'd eavesdrop on purpose, but what should he do if it escalates? She might kill him if she knew he was listening.

"I'm done talking about this," says Inez. "I have somewhere else to be."

She hurries off, ignoring his pleas for her not to leave. The front door of the mansion closes, and he runs his fingers through his hair. Blake stands and takes a few slow steps down the stairs.

"Hey, man," he says. "Everything alright?"

"Hey." The Prince smiles. "You're the new guy. I'm Allistair, nice to meet you."

He extends his hand, and Blake shakes it before he gestures between Allistair and the door. "So uh…you and Inez…?"

"Oh that," Allistair says, forcing a chuckle. "Yeah, I really had myself fooled. I always thought her turning me down was just a result of how guarded she is, but I guess it's not so simple."

"Are you okay?"

"I will be, thanks for asking. Anyway, Victor wants to see you in his office. Your application process isn't over yet."

"YOU HAVE TO TAKE A TEST," says Victor from his desk chair. "Have a performance ready for us by this Friday. If you do well, we'll keep you. If not, your contract will be terminated."

"What? Why are you springing this on me now? Why couldn't I audition before I moved in?"

"It was a last-minute decision." Rex shrugs from his spot next to Victor. "My children are quite daunted that an outsider has joined, and as an adult, no less. I like you, and I've seen your talent. They, however, need convincing."

"Why don't I just do it tonight, then?"

"That won't do," says Rex, waving the idea off like a fly. "Anyone can juggle. You must create a performance worthy of our stage. I'm sure Inez will help you since she's already your mentor."

"But Inez is—"

"She's gone again, we know," Victor grumbles. "We meant when she gets back."

"That's all. Off you go now." Rex shoos Blake away with his hand.

Despite the racing of his heart, and his dream now hanging by a thread, Blake stands and heads for the door. *They're not testing my skills; they're testing my will. They're going to put me through hell until I've earned their respect.* He takes a deep breath, doing his best to calm his heart. This is exactly what he was expecting. *The fool must always suffer before he can rise.* Rex was warning him.

"One more thing," Rex calls, and Blake stops. "I'd like you to ask Inez where she's been going lately. You can tell me the next time we chat."

Blake hesitates, but he won't risk losing Rex's favor, and he's curious too. "Sure."

41

★★★

IN THE BACKYARD AFTER LUNCH, Inez opens a drawstring bag and pulls out three short ropes, each holding a ball of thick, black fabric on one end and a small, bright green knob on the other. Other members of the circus are filling sets of aerial rigs behind him, while others are sitting on the lawn or wandering the yard. Inez holds up the flopping props in her hand.

"This is the closest I have to juggling clubs, but I've seen how they work, and it should be fine."

"Wait, so no one else here juggles?"

"A lot of us can juggle, I just use my props. Ian uses knives, Vladik uses kettlebells, and Maya uses hoops. We never really needed them."

Blake shrugs with a tiny grin. "Call me basic, I guess."

Inez chuckles as she holds up her prop. "These are called poi. I'll show you some juggling patterns with these, and you can try it with your clubs. We'll see what you know, what you learn and what you can teach me."

Blake nods as Inez tosses the bag toward a nearby tree.

"Thanks again for helping me prepare. I really appreciate it."

Inez smiles before she juggles the poi in a basic cascade. The ropes that flop so easily are staying straight in the air as they rotate over their assigned arches. Blake's energy pulses through his veins as he follows Inez's lead, recreating the same pattern with his clubs. She switches up the pattern, and he follows without hesitation.

He changes the pattern for Inez to follow, and she does so without flinching. She narrows her eyes at him with a cocky grin, grabbing two poi with one hand and the third with the other. She turns a few times so that the poi create perfect circles around her body in a spellbinding display, similar to what he'd seen her do so many times on stage.

Blake follows her lead until two clubs fumble in his hand, and the last one lands with a clunk on his skull. "Ow!"

Inez breaks into laughter, holding her arms against her stomach. Despite the sharp pain pulsing through his skull, her laugh spreads to him and some performers in the distance.

"Maybe we should keep it simple," says Inez as her laughter subsides.

"Let's keep it juggling. I can't learn the magic stuff that you do."

"Fair," Inez chuckles.

Practice continues with less fumbling, and Blake is excited that Inez seems to enjoy his company. His excitement grows when he finds a pattern she hasn't seen yet. With a little direction, she nails the pattern in a few quick minutes.

Awhile later, they put down their props and sit by the tree for a drink. The water turns his throat to ice and chills him from the inside out.

The two sit in silence as Blake's gaze wanders over the other performers, whose names he's still learning. His eyes glue themselves to Axel, who bends and twists herself around a hanging loop. His gaze shifts to Maya, the Lost Empress from China, and Xavier, the Fallen Angel.

They're practicing some sort of fight routine on a high wire with swords. On the ground, three other members are climbing each other to create striking poses.

Everywhere he looks, members of the circus are oozing talent. Even the ones who sit and chat seem to shine with a light of their own, despite not doing anything. *How is that possible?*

"Stage presence," Inez's voice pierces through Blake's thoughts and turns his attention back to her. "Your test isn't about talent, it's about stage presence. Anyone can learn to do the things we do, but all of that is useless if you can't hold the audience's attention. Even breathing fire can be boring if you don't put on a good show."

"I see," says Blake, taking a moment to process her words as he looks around again. "What can you teach me about it?"

"It isn't something I can teach; it's something you have to learn as you go, with your own flair, to own the stage and demand attention. You need to lay the bait for the audience, lure them in, and capture their hearts. It isn't always easy, but the applause from a truly mesmerized audience…"

Inez's voice trails off as a smile creeps onto her face. She wraps her arms around her knees, pulling them into her chest as her eyes gaze into an unseen memory. "That kind of applause has a special sound."

Blake smiles along with her as she blinks herself back to the present and clears her throat, returning her legs to their previous outstretched position. She turns her gaze to the other circus members around the yard, trying to pretend that moment didn't happen. Somehow, this makes Blake more intrigued.

"Can I ask you something?" says Blake. Inez flicks up her brows in response. "Where have you been going lately?"

Inez's gaze shoots to a fiery glare, and Blake shrinks in his spot.

"What do you mean by that? You've only been here one night, and in that time, I've gone out once."

"Well, uh…you see—"

"Did *Rex* tell you to ask me that?" The King's name leaves her mouth as if she were spitting out an awful taste.

Blake swallows hard, trembling as her glare burns into his skin. "Y-yeah…"

Inez growls as she shoots to her feet. "It's none of your business! Or his! Don't let yourself be that *fucking* King's little spy!"

"That's not what I meant by it! I swear!"

"Whatever." Inez harrumphs and storms off back into the mansion. Blake holds out a hand to stop her but quickly retreats.

"Bro." A dark hand lands on Blake's shoulder. "I really thought you were going to burst into flame there for a second."

Blake relaxes as Ronan sits at his side. "You and I both."

"She's got a hot temper." Ronan chuckles. "But she's a big softie once you get on her good side."

"How do I do that? It feels like no matter what I say, I fuck it up."

"Just respect her." Ronan shrugs. "And don't let Rex tell you what to say. He didn't adopt her, Victor did, so Rex ignores her until he wants something. She makes her own rules, too. Doesn't really answer to anyone."

"*Victor* adopted her?"

"He's her uncle. When she lost her parents, he took her in, and I guess Rex never liked her very much. The tension between them is palpable; it makes everyone uncomfortable. That's why Rex doesn't invite her to the meetings. She listens from a distance."

"She hardly seems to like *me*. What makes Rex think I would have a better chance of finding things out?"

"I think he's just trying out every option he has." Ronan pauses and glances at the performers over his shoulder before he leans in closer, his voice lowering to a whisper. "Listen, Inez might not like you, but she doesn't hate you. You're only doing what you're told so you can stay here. Rex, however…"

Blake furrows his brow as Ronan seems to choke, taking one more scan of the area for peering eyes or curious ears. As he turns his head, Blake notices a thin scar in front of his ear, leading to his cheekbone. Ronan turns back to him before Blake can see it more closely.

"I can't say much right now, but Rex…isn't as nice as he lets on."

His voice trembles at the last few words, and it sends chills over Blake's skin. "What do you mean?"

Ronan shakes his head. "Now's not the time. Just promise you won't tell Rex anything Inez trusts you with. He'll take whatever you tell him and use it against her. If he asks about her, you keep your mouth shut, understood?"

Blake's mouth is wide open, taking his own glance at the others before he turns his attention back to the grass. He forces his mouth closed and nods to establish his promise, and Ronan breathes a sigh of relief. He offers to switch the subject to juggling, but Blake is more interested to hear about Ronan's work backstage. As the conversation clears his mind, the last few drops of anxiety linger, making him tremble. Inez's glare continues to pop into his vision.

Eventually, Ronan waves him off to resume his own work. Blake sits alone, Inez's words ringing in his mind. *Stage presence.*

How can he perform in a way that impresses other performers? What does Inez do that captivates him? It isn't just the fire. Blake has seen numerous fire dancers and breathers at other circuses, carnivals, and celebrations. Inez does things the audience doesn't expect. Everyone here does.

While they were practicing, Inez stopped juggling to dance around with the poi in perfect unison with her movements. It was captivating.

Everyone here knows Blake can juggle. He needs to find a way to surprise the audience. A thought crosses his mind, but he tries to brush it away. Inez would kill him if he mentioned it.

A fool gets nowhere by sitting comfortably.
Maybe he can try.

Chapter 6

"I'd like Inez to teach me to use fire."

"What?" Inez screams, making Blake and Victor cringe. Rex puts a finger to his chin, unfazed by the sudden rise in volume. Her reaction makes Blake grateful he chose to say this with Rex and Victor present.

"It's just a thought," he says. "But juggling won't be enough. Mishkin and Inez have made it clear that at least a handful of the other members have seen me juggle before. It won't be any different from what I've done countless times. Adding fire to the mix would throw in an element of surprise. And since I'd have to learn it quickly, it would be a demonstration of how fast I can learn."

"But why fire?" Inez asks.

"It's in the contract, rule number one: The fool gets nowhere by sitting comfortably. I don't have the core strength to learn aerials that fast, nor am I sneaky enough to learn magic like Allistair does. Besides, the poi looks...kind of cool."

Blake shifts in his seat, his cheeks turning a light pink. Inez crosses her arms as Victor shrugs, turning his gaze over to Rex.

"It's your call, King. Using fire isn't what you had in mind, but he is following the rules."

Rex's pensive stare doesn't change for several slow-passing seconds. They're glued to Blake, unblinking and icy enough to send a chill up his spine.

Finally, he lowers his hand and smiles at Blake. "I like this idea. You have my support. Inez, you will teach him to use fire safely. You have extra props to lend, I'm sure."

"You can't be serious," Inez grumbles.

"I have nothing more to say on the matter, so I'll be leaving. Best of luck to you both."

Rex strolls out of the room with his head high, ignoring Inez's burning glare as it follows him out. After he closes the door, Inez slams her hands onto Victor's desk. "You know why Rex approved this! Tell him to fuck off and leave me alone!"

"I-I can't do that," says Victor, doing his best not to appear startled, but his frown and shuddering voice betray him. Without Rex at his side, his commanding demeanor has completely vanished. "He's concerned about you! And I am too. You won't even tell *me* what you're doing!"

"I'm twenty-two! It's none of your business! You and the damned King need to back off and stop pestering me! I'm fucking sick of you both!"

49

She pushes herself from Victor's desk and rages past Blake, who sits in his seat with his eyes wide. The office door slams behind them, making him and Victor flinch. Blake peeks over his shoulder, surprised the glass didn't shatter from her force.

"Sir," Blake mutters after a moment of silence, "is there another motive for Rex going along with this?"

Victor lets out a heavy breath and takes his glasses off to rub the bridge of his nose. "Sort of. She's been sneaking around to get out of the mansion, and if she's here teaching you, Rex can keep a better eye on her. He thinks she and Allistair are having relationship troubles, which would be a problem, considering they're expected to marry."

Blake remembers when he overheard Inez and Allistair that first morning. "Maybe it's better if he doesn't get involved? I don't know the details, but I'm pretty sure that's not his decision to make."

"All decisions in this mansion are his to make. Everyone signed the contract, to live under his command at the mercy of the stage."

"This is the twenty-first century. Aren't arranged marriages illegal?"

"*Forced* marriages are illegal, but arranged ones are still common in wealthy families and those of status."

"If Rex isn't giving her a choice, that's forced marriage."

Victor slams his desk. "That's enough! You have no idea how anything runs around here. Or what I have to do to keep her safe. She's my niece, and I'll do what I must to make sure she's taken care of. Don't get involved in what you don't understand."

Blake shifts in his seat, biting his lip. He takes in a breath through his nose and huffs out his remaining protests. *Don't lose Rex's favor.*

"So this thing with her and Allistair, is it really okay for you to tell me? It's not like it's any of my business."

"It's common knowledge; you would've found out eventually. Believe me, whatever happens in this mansion, everyone will hear about it before morning. It takes a special kind of sneaky to keep secrets in this place, and Inez has made it her duty to master that level of stealth. But she's been here for years, and you're still learning. So, as I said before, be mindful of what you say and do."

Blake's heart sinks as he remembers when she stormed off yesterday. She has no control. No privacy. Of course it pissed her off when he asked where she went. And with his request to use fire, he handed Rex a golden opportunity to add another restraint. Twice now, he's played right into Rex's hand. Inez probably hates him now, and he can't blame her.

"In any case," Victor continues, snapping Blake out of his frustration and trying to cool his own, "give Inez a few minutes to calm down, and she'll be ready to work."

Knowing a dismissal when he hears one, Blake trudges out of the office. As soon as the door is closed behind him, he hurries out to the yard, where Inez stands with fists balled at her side and a concerned Allistair in front of her. He approaches cautiously, so Inez knows he's there, but so he doesn't stir up more tension.

"I get what you mean," says Allistair, "but it's not something my father would do."

"Whatever, I didn't expect you to listen anyway." Inez storms to the nearest tree and plops herself onto the grass next to its roots. "Just get out of here. Pup, sit."

Blake and Allistair exchange glances before Allistair opens his mouth to argue. Inez shoots her glare into his eyes, forcing him to shut his mouth and walk away. Blake hurries to sit by Inez's side before she can strike that red-hot stare at him as well.

They sit in silence for what seems like an hour, and Blake has resorted to staring at the changing leaves as they shiver in the breeze.

His mind travels to when they first met and how eagerly she wanted him to learn so she wouldn't have to deal with him anymore. And now she has to teach him her craft. He searches through his brain for proper apologies, assurances that he never intended to make her feel more trapped than she already does. But no words come to mind that don't sound like lame excuses.

He shuffles his feet, keeping his gaze glued to the grass. "Look, you don't have to teach me to use fire if you don't want to. I was just trying to step out of my comfort zone in a way that—"

"That's not the problem," she grumbles. "I'll teach you whatever you want."

Blake sighs, trying to think of any way to ease the tension. "Allistair didn't believe you?"

"He believes his father agreed to the suggestion, but not that he's doing it to spy on me."

"That wasn't my intention, I swear."

"I know. Actually, I'm kind of proud of you."

Blake blinks hard, staring at her with wide eyes.

"It's true that to put on a great show, an element of surprise can only help you. I don't mind teaching you what I know. I think you'll do great. That said, with Rex breathing down my neck, don't expect us to become friends for it. You still trapped me here, and I still don't trust you as far as I can throw you."

52

"Right." Blake focuses his attention back on the grass. "For what it's worth, I am sorry. I should've asked you in private first."

"Why didn't you?"

"Because you'd throw me farther than you trust me. You already don't like me, I'm not going to hand you a blade for my murder."

Inez snickers. "I wouldn't have killed you, per se."

"Thanks, you're *so* sweet." Blake rolls his eyes.

"Be honest, though," she says, throwing him a smirk. "Are you scared? Of the fire, I mean."

"A little," Blake mutters. "It's beautiful when you do it, but I'm sure it's harder than it looks."

"Not really. Dangerous, for sure, but the tricks are easy to learn. The most important part is following safety protocol and knowing the risks."

Blake's eyes grow wide as Inez lists burns, health complications like fire-breather's pneumonia and cancers from the fuel. She mentions hyperthermia, and a chance of burning the throat and lungs.

His mind drifts back to the times he's watched her, knowing that fire is risky, but never realizing the extent of it himself. She risks life with each burning breath and limb with every flaming dance. He shudders to think of these things happening to her now.

"That's terrifying."

"It's not for the faint of heart," Inez says. "Even my father tried to scare me out of it, but I guess at the time I just felt so immortal. But hey, I started at nine and I'm here now, so don't freak out too much. Though I didn't breathe or eat fire until I was fifteen. I found out Victor used to do it with my father, and I begged him to teach me."

Blake purses his lips to the side, wondering if her father was really a careless parent, or if his own parents' perfectionism is making him feel that way. Would his late mother have allowed him to learn that skill if he had the opportunity? He never considered being a dad before, but if that ever became his life, would he let his own child do something so dangerous?

"I won't hold you to it," Inez continues, her voice gentler and her eyes softer. "If you change your mind, you should let Rex know as soon as possible. I can't promise he'll be happy, but your safety comes first."

"You don't think I should do it, do you?"

"I think you should give it more thought. The idea popped into your head because your dream job is on the line. Performing with fire isn't something you should be doing purely on impulse. Think about it. If you're absolutely certain, I'll teach you."

Blake nods, and his eyes drift to the performers on the rigs, trying to imagine himself using fire, but the image of the flames erupting over his skin ends every scenario.

Maybe that's a hint in itself.

"One more thing," says Inez. "Don't go around spitting out the rules like that. They're different for everyone based on what they've been through and what their habits are, so it doesn't make sense to hold someone else to rules made for you. Besides, if you justify all of your decisions based on that, you'll look like one of the King's little pets. You're expected to follow them, but there's no reason for anyone to announce them like that."

"So, it's like shouting 'parkour' when you're doing parkour?"

Inez laughs. "Pretty much."

"Can I ask what your three rules are?"

Inez closes her eyes and looks away with a tiny smirk on her face.

"Right," Blake scoffs. *You still don't trust me.*

Chapter 7

Blake sits in bed, reading through an article on the dreaded fire-breather's pneumonia, and his stomach churns. He closes his laptop with a cringe and focuses on the black sky outside his window, where a few stars shine around the glare on the glass.

He always told himself he would do anything to join The Fools' Circus, and he meant it. But damn if it isn't nerve wracking. He takes in a deep breath, forcing the whirlwind of anxieties to slow down. He's still willing to do whatever it takes to secure a place on stage. He'll just have to power through his worries until it becomes second nature, just like he did with juggling.

If he never breathes the fire, the pneumonia will be harder to catch, right? Maybe he can just dance with it. There's no reason the stage would need two breathers. Though it would be interesting to explore the possibilities of having two.

The option can wait in his back pocket for now. Manipulating a fire prop is the first step. That's how Inez learned, after all. That's how everyone learns. Step by step. As long as he continues to learn and improve, his spot is secure.

But thoughts of dangers and risks aren't going to help him sleep. A quick walk should clear his mind. Heading for the door, he pats his leg to make sure his pants are still on.

The hall is dark with silver beams of moonlight shining through the windows, making everything in its path some shade of blue. It isn't very late, but everyone has already retreated to their bedrooms, and the stillness is unsettling.

Thud.

Blake freezes in his spot as the sound fills the air. Footsteps echo through the dark halls as the pounding in his chest fills his ears. He holds his breath as the footsteps get closer, eyes darting around, but seeing no one in the hall.

No. This mansion can't be...haunted?

The footsteps center in on the stairs as Blake's blood runs cold. He locks his eyes on the staircase, waiting. A shadowed face springs from the darkness, making Blake yelp and fall back, hitting his head on the door behind him. He clutches the sore spot, groaning as the features of the face come into his memory.

"Pup?" Inez calls. "What's going on?"

"I thought you were a ghost," Blake pants with a hand clutching his heart.

Inez laughs, leaning at the top of the handrail. "Sorry. I went out again and just got back. Where are you going?"

"I couldn't sleep. Thought I'd wander the halls a bit, but now I think I'm scared of the dark for the night. Thanks for that."

Inez snickers and drops herself against the rail next to the staircase, patting the floor beside her. "Come sit. I need to talk to you, anyway."

Blake rubs his head again as he walks over, peering into the abyss that swallows the bottom of the staircase. He sits against the rail with Inez, hoping there isn't some creature waiting to yank him down from behind. He does his best to appear calm, but he can't help taking a quick peek at the darkness over his shoulder. Just in case.

"I know I was rude before," says Inez. "A few times. Rex gets under my skin, but everyone loves him *so* much, so it's not like I can even rant about it. Honestly, I wanted to hate you for idolizing him too, but I can see you aren't stupid. You don't know anything about us yet. You're bound to make a few mistakes, and I could probably stand to be more patient. I'm trying to work on my temper, too. So, I'm sorry."

"That's okay," says Blake. "Victor explained a little of the situation after you left. He said Rex wants you to be with Allistair."

"He's right."

"Why can't you tell him no?"

"I want to, but Mishkin and Vladik keep warning me against it. Apparently, something bad happened. But it's not like he's violent or anything. Hell, I'm pretty sure he'd avoid fights just to keep his hair flowing perfectly. I'm not afraid of him. Besides, if I have to take a little torture to earn my freedom, so be it. I need my normal life back. I miss it."

"I understand. It must be tough being so closed off from everything."

"Don't you think you'll miss your old life?"

"Not one bit," Blake scoffs. "The process of being adopted seemed great, but when it became official and I was there for good, my parents set some ground rules. They seemed simple at the time. Chores, homework, curfew, and the like. My grades were their biggest concern. They made me take online classes after school. Things like business, Spanish, anything they believed would give me some kind of advantage.

"They even gave me a strict bedtime while I was in high school. I started staying out after curfew to get a break, and the reins got even tighter. But after every lecture, after every time they grounded me, and every time they added more classes and more restraints, they always insisted they loved me. It's not that I don't believe them. I just...don't think they know how to express parental love...the way my real mom did."

"That's almost how it is here. Rex expects everyone to do what he tells them. Mostly, his commands are roles in the show or household tasks, so it's hardly a problem. But I can't marry Allistair. I'm not even sure if I ever want to get married. I've never even been in love before. And my uncle is a lot like your parents are. He expects me to do everything Rex says, and it's not that he doesn't care, but he isn't great at the whole parenting thing."

"You're right, though. Marriage should be with someone you care about."

"Do your parents expect you to marry someone?"

"Nah, I think they'd be happier if I never did. Especially my mom. She had a rough divorce before she met my dad, and they decided they were too old to handle a baby, so they adopted me. They must've thought

59

thirteen-year-olds were easier. You know, the angsty ones who are just *dying* to rebel."

Inez smirks as she pulls her knees into her chest and rests her head on them, eyes fixed on the marble floor. "So, you've felt it too. A cage. I'm sorry to say this, but our stage isn't exactly a path to freedom."

"Well, right now, my options are a fancy mansion with new friends or a roach-infested apartment with a horny roommate and a girlfriend who never leaves. God, they're so obnoxious, too. The walls shake and everything."

Inez snickers. "Okay, I see your point. So, what was your birth mom like?"

"She was terrific, the best mom." Blake darts his eyes around the painted animals across the ceiling. "She's the one who brought me to the first performance of The Fools' Circus. I think I remember you too. You had brown hair, and Rex called you 'The Fire Goddess, Defender of the Earth!'"

"Oh God, don't remind me!" Inez hides her face in one hand. "I believed it too. I really felt like my nine-year-old self would be chosen to save an entire planet."

"That's adorable!" Blake laughs. "Can I ask what your parents were like?"

Inez hesitates, and she leans against the rail with her legs sprawled out. "My dad taught me to use fire, but I was close to my mom too. Just like you were. We loved to read, and we'd tell each other about our stories all the time. Every couple of weeks, we'd go to the library and pick out a cookbook. We usually adjusted the recipes based on what we liked. Most of them were delicious, but every once in a while, we'd mess up the whole dish and have to order pizza. Once the whole house filled up with smoke, and when we threw away the food, it melted through the garbage bag. Dad came home to the smell of burnt plastic, and I was so embarrassed my mom blamed the neighbor."

Blake chuckles at the image of the tiny, brown-haired Inez with huge oven mitts that reached tiny elbows, blushing because she messed up.

"I'm sure you could've taught my adoptive mom a thing or two. She refuses to use seasonings because she thinks it's all salt. Blandest dinners every night, and when I finally moved out, she'd bring me extras. Honestly though, I still consider myself lucky. A pampered pup, if you will." He nudges Inez with his elbow, and she chuckles.

"That's good. They're overbearing, but they aren't evil."

"No, they're evil. Killing every bit of fun the second it enters the door," he says with a smirk.

Evil. The word rings in his mind as Ronan's terrified face flashes into his vision. No one has said it yet, but could Rex really be evil? Sneaky and self-centered for sure, but evil? Now would be the time to ask Inez, but she's already standing and giggling at his last remark. Besides, another thought has flittered its way into his mind.

"I should get to bed," she smiles. "I'll see you at breakfast tomorrow?"

Blake follows her lead, his leg tingling as he rises. He wiggles his foot to regain circulation. "Sure, but I need to ask you something."

Inez tilts her head to listen as Blake searches for a way to word his nagging question without making it sound like an accusation. "I don't know if you heard, but there are rumors floating around about this circus. Stuff about pedophiles and missing children. That's not true, is it?"

Inez tightens her lips and drops her eyes to the floor. After a moment of silence, she shakes her head.

"We weren't kidnapped," she says. "This isn't one of those pedophile rings, or anything like that. Rex adopted everyone legally. Well, except me. Some people here *do* come from dangerous backgrounds that include pedophiles and murderers and stuff like that. I bet that's where the rumors came from. But they were saved from all of that, not led into it."

Her eyes flick to the darkness down the hall before she steps closer and lowers her voice.

"I probably shouldn't tell you this, but Mishkin's father almost killed him when he was younger. If he ever found him, Mishkin would have to run away and change his name all over again. Imagine what would happen if we opened our doors and let strangers in."

Blake shudders and his eyes follow her previous glance down the hall, as if Mishkin would suddenly appear. When he doesn't, he turns his attention back to Inez. "That must terrify him. So, how do you think it got so mixed up? I'd expect Rex to hold a higher image of himself than that."

Inez shrugs. "The truth has always been a long game of telephone. I think it's natural that people would mix up their facts and draw their own conclusions. Rex can only fix so much. It doesn't help that we don't have any information about ourselves available to the public. But what matters is that those rumors aren't true. That said, our King isn't the heavenly saint he thinks he is. And Hartman…"

Blake raises a brow when Inez hesitates. "Hartman?"

Inez shakes her head. "I've said enough. You still have some thinking to do on the fire stuff, so get your rest. Good night, Pup."

Inez moseys to her room with her head hung low and looks back at him over her shoulder, mouth open, before forcing it closed and giving him one last brief smile before retreating for the night. His mind is whirling with questions, but he returns the smile and trudges back to his own room.

Closing the door behind him, he shuts off his light and takes off his pants and shirt. With a heavy yawn, he wobbles to his bed and crawls under the covers. The cold fabric chills his skin, but it's his spinning thoughts that are making him shudder. The people he's admired for so long, in such terrible situations. The things that must haunt them at night. Even Mishkin, who lights up any room he walks into.

He shakes his head to push out those thoughts and focus on Inez. What happened to lead her here? How did her parents die? Despite their chat tonight, he's still in no position to ask. Then again, she knows he isn't messing up on purpose. Her apology echoes in his ears. His heart is slowly calming itself as images of their practice sessions take over his mind.

Is this what her good side feels like? Her smile is soothing, bright, and beautiful. Now he just has to avoid invoking her wrath again.

★★★

HE'S WEIGHED THE PROS and cons all day, but after another warm and delicious dinner, Blake's mind is made up, and he has to let Inez know now.

He's heading upstairs when he sees Inez at the top with the bald man he recognizes as the Blades Master, the one who couldn't be bothered to waste his time on a lost pup. *Ian.*

Inez's back is to the wall as Ian leans in with his arm over her head. She's giving him an even worse glare than she's ever given Blake, but Ian seems unfazed as he slides a hand up her thigh. She grabs the hand before it reaches up her skirt, and slaps Ian with her free hand. He winces in response but ends up chuckling.

"You're so cute when you're feisty," he grins.

"Hey!" Blake calls, finally reaching the two. "She's not interested! Fuck off!"

"Or what?" Ian raises a brow at him, and Inez uses the distraction to lift her leg and kick him in the chest, making him fall onto his back.

Blake blinks hard with raised eyebrows and gestures toward Ian's fall. "Or...that."

"Thanks for that, Pup," Inez grabs Blake's wrist and leads him back downstairs. "I was hoping he'd let his guard down. You were a great distraction."

Blake peeks over his shoulder to see Ian struggling to stand, glaring at the two as they walk away. A smirk forms on Blake's face as Inez's kick replays in his mind. Even if she doesn't like him much, at least he isn't on her drop-kick list.

"So what's going on?" Inez asks once they find a spot outside. "Were you looking for me when you came up the stairs?"

"Yeah, I was," says Blake, shifting in his space and glancing around as if he was hiding a dark secret. "Listen, I've been thinking about it, and I know this might sound stupid, but I want to do it. I want to spin fire."

Chapter 8

The morning sky is clear, and the dew on the grass sparkles in the sunlight that eases the bite of the autumn chill. Inez hands Blake a set of three poi, similar to the ones she used the other day.

"I'm a little scared," he says, holding them out at arm's length. "They won't burst into flame, will they?"

"No," Inez chuckles. "I'll show you how to light them later, but for now you need to focus on the basics. We'll start with two and throw in the third later."

Blake readies himself, but instruction goes quicker than expected. He learns a few simple circles in various sizes and directions. Inez teaches him about the various planes around his body and how to create limitless patterns, shapes, and visuals.

"Good," Inez says after almost half an hour. "It looks like you've got that stuff figured out. Let's work on some three-poi patterns, and then we'll take a break. You already know how to juggle, so just follow my lead like you did before."

Blake agrees, and Inez juggles her poi in a basic cascade, each one rotating while the rope holds a straight line until it lands back in her grip.

Blake grins and throws a poi up. The rope wobbles, the poi doesn't fully rotate, and Blake grumbles when the next few tosses have the same result, and one poi plops on the ground.

Inez snickers and holds on to her stomach as she lets out her laughter. Blake stops to enjoy it as she spurts out fragments of how bad he is.

"These things just flop around!" Blake shouts in playful defense, holding the poi out to wiggle them in his hands. "Help! How?"

He tries again, letting out playful growls with each fumble until he finally gets used to the difference. Inez's smile is lifting his spirits the whole time until he can finally get a decent cascade started.

He attempts a few other patterns, and the poi are still flopping and curving, but he's catching them and mirroring Inez's tricks.

She takes a step back and makes a familiar gesture, swinging one poi in his direction.

A smile plasters his face as he nods and readies himself. They each toss a poi and catch the one coming to them. They flip in the air between them, some straight as poles, and some curving.

His gaze drops to Inez as they continue, and the light in her eyes hypnotizes him, and the sun makes her skin glow. A hard *thunk* sounds from his head.

Inez covers her mouth to hide her snicker. "I'm sorry."

"No worries," Blake chuckles as he rubs the sore spot. "How is fabric that solid?"

"It's kevlar. If it's going to hold against fire, it can't be flimsy. Want to take a break?"

"Please."

The two of them plop down by the same tree as yesterday, watching the other performers continue their practice and taking sips from the water bottles they brought with them. If hurting his head is going to be a regular thing around here, he may need to invest in a helmet.

A soft breeze caresses his arm, cold as ice, cooling the sweat on his body. He takes in a deep breath as it cruises past them, filling his body with refreshed energy.

"Inez! There you are!" Allistair rushes over to them with an excited grin. "I just talked to my father, and preparations for the Blasphemer's Ball are going to start soon!"

"That's great!"

"Yeah! So, listen, I was hoping we could go together. I mean, as friends of course."

"Hmm, maybe. I'll think about it."

"Hey, take your time, it's okay!" says Allistair, turning his attention over to Blake. "I'm sure you'll get a date too. Though, even if you go alone, you're in for a treat!"

"Uh, sure," Blake mutters. "But I have no idea what any of that means."

"The Blasphemer's Ball is our Halloween celebration," Allistair explains with a smile.

"It's just a dance," Inez chimes in. "But Rex goes all out for food and decorations, and we get dressed up all fancy. It might sound corny, but it's always a lot of fun."

"No, it sounds great!"

"Sorry to split so quickly, but I've got to spread the word. I won't make it to lunch today, but I'll see you both at dinner."

"Hold on, *you're* spreading the word?" Blake furrows his brow. "Why doesn't Rex make an announcement?"

"He will," says Allistair. "But with me being the link between those in charge and the performers, leaking bits of news ahead of time is a fun way of making sure I hear what everyone has to say. It's all with my father's approval, of course, but they don't need to know that."

Blake isn't sure he understands, but he nods anyway as Allistair waves them off. He turns back to Inez when he's out of earshot.

"So, are you going with him? Dancing as friends might be fun."

"Yeah, but there's this superstition most of the members have. They call it the Midnight Dance. They say if two people dance in the center of the ballroom at midnight, they'll be together forever. I'm pretty sure Allistair might try to rope me into it. I don't believe in it, but attending the ball with him is how the rumors of us started, and they spread like wildfire. I'm not letting that mess happen again."

"Understandable," says Blake, his mind filling with classical music, images of fancy gowns, and— "Shit, I don't have a suit."

"Victor will make one for you, don't worry."

"No good, I can't pay him."

"Whatever money they spend on you before you perform is put on a tab, and part of it will come out of your paycheck until it's paid off. They'll explain it all once you start stage rehearsal."

"Wow, it's really that easy?"

"Assuming you don't fail your test and get kicked out of here, yes."

"Thanks for that," Blake grumbles. "So, is there any basis behind that Midnight Dance superstition?"

"Mishkin and Vladik. Apparently that dance is how they started dating. But that was long ago. They were already an official couple by the time I got here. Later on, Knox and Melody had that dance and became an item."

"Knox and Melody?"

"The tall guy with the dreads and his girlfriend. You were gushing over them on your first night, remember?"

"That's right," Blake smiles and the image of the couple floods his mind. "Did you ever have that dance with anyone?"

"No, I usually slip away before it happens."

Blake chuckles. "Pretty smart." *Leave it to a Fire Goddess to turn any amount of restraint into a burning pile of nope.*

"All right," says Inez as she stands up. "Back to work. Want to try some partner stuff?"

"Sure, why not." Blake follows her lead in grabbing two poi.

Inez steps closer to him, looking him in the eye. His heart leaps in his chest, paralyzing him. The sun glows against Inez's face, and her brown eyes look almost red enough to match her hair. Her skin is like porcelain, and her smile makes his breath catch in his throat.

"Partner work means we have to get close," she says. "But if that's not comfortable for you, we can skip it."

"N-no, it's fine," Blake stammers, praying that she can't hear his heart pounding. He's seen partner work

69

with fire spinning, acrobatics, and dancing. Of course the partners have to get close, that's how a good routine is created! He shouldn't be this flustered.

Practice begins with coordinating patterns while Inez has her back to him. She's giving him commands and directing his motions, and his autopilot is following along while the front of his mind tries to ease his breathing.

Her hair wisps into his face, her scent caressing his nose with notes of flowers, argan oil, and a hint of sweat. Such a warm fragrance—invigorating and inviting. She makes a swift motion of turning to face him, and the two use tricks that interlock their arms, pulling them close and pushing them apart.

The poi whoosh behind his back before his arms move around her. Her body is touching his, sending warm chills across his skin. It would be so easy to take her into his arms—so wonderful to pull her close. He shouldn't, but he keeps his eyes focused on her plump, pink lips, parted to keep her breath. His eyes fall to her chest, almost brushing against his as she whips her poi around him.

Don't get hard, dear God, please don't get hard.

Her eyes focus on their poi, barely noticing him. He's fighting the urge to lean in, to give in to his craving, until one of his poi hits Inez on the head, prompting her to laugh, and Blake's jaw drops in shock.

"I'm sorry, I'm so sorry! Are you okay?"

"It's fine." Inez laughs, rubbing the sore spot. "Let's just call that payback. I got you twice, so you still owe me one."

"Nope, I'm done." Blake drops his poi and shakes his head. He takes a step back and tries to recenter his thoughts.

"Don't worry so much," says Inez. "That happens a lot with partner work."

"Sure, but I still feel bad. Besides, it's not like I need partner work for my test, right?"

Inez's eyes drop to the ground as she purses her lips, and Blake regrets his words. It isn't the bump on her head that's making him nervous. *You don't understand, Inez, I almost...*

"Yeah, I guess you're right." Inez smiles. "You've managed to learn a lot pretty quick. Let's relax for a bit, and we'll meet up again at lunch, 'kay? I'm starting to get a little cold out here."

Blake agrees, and they gather their poi before heading inside.

"You can bring those to your room to practice in private," says Inez.

Blake thanks her, but he can't bring himself to say much else. The thoughts he had earlier, the urges. Where did those come from? He bites his lip. He shouldn't have lost his head so easily. He tries to shake the already distant memory of her body close to his, her scent dancing in his nose, her eyes glistening in the sun.

"By the way," Inez continues, "what did you tell your parents when you left?"

"Nothing too bizarre. I told them I was going on a road trip with some friends of mine. They weren't too happy about it, so no doubt they'll have an earful waiting for me when I get back."

"*If* you go back."

A smile creeps onto Blake's face. That's right, they could renew his contract at the end of the year! If he passes this test, he may never have to go back to retail work again. The words echo in his mind, filling him with new energy.

If you go back.

★ ★ ★

BLAKE AND INEZ STAND with Mishkin and Vladik, in the food line. Dinner has a tangy, citrus smell to it, and Blake's stomach is getting impatient. At home, it wasn't uncommon for him to skip a meal, and his body wouldn't miss it, but all the practice and new information at the mansion has been building his appetite.

"Look at those two." Mishkin smiles toward Knox, seated with his plate and playfully taunting Melody with a look of pure love in his eyes. "I'm so glad they're finally tying the knot."

"What?" Blake gapes. "They're getting married? When?"

Mishkin, Vladik, and Inez all exchange looks, shifting in their spots as if deciding who forgot to fill him in.

"Tomorrow," says Mishkin. "Sorry, I guess we all dropped the ball there. We meant to tell you."

"So now I need a suit for tomorrow?"

"Nah," Mishkin waves his hand. "There are a ton of extra clothes to choose from. You can find something to wear while we're all getting dressed."

"Is only to borrow," Vladik adds. "For ceremony. We change before reception."

Inez nods. "Yeah, you'll need some kind of nice clothes for that, but a suit won't be necessary. Mishkin, do you have anything he can borrow?"

"Yeah." Mishkin smiles. "Tonight, we'll head to my room and get you set up."

Blake thanks him, and the group continues to coordinate ideas of clothing and wedding preparations as they fill their plates and settle themselves around the table.

The food is delicious as always, and the talk of weddings shifts to nonsense, making Blake laugh harder than he ever thought possible. Inez's words still echo in his mind as the conversations and laughter continue.

If you go back. If you go. If.

Chapter 9

B lake stiffens when he finds everyone in one large dressing room, many of them already half naked. Mirrors line the walls, and some members compare one outfit to another and check their forms in the outfits they're wearing. He glues his eyes to the floor as Mishkin leads him through the chaos. Blake's cheeks heat up, and his jaw clenches.

Mishkin stops at a clothing rack and shoves the hangers around, pulling a few of them to drape their contents over his arm. Blake quietly rushes him, but he takes a deep breath.

If he stares straight ahead, he can hide his discomfort without having to be obvious about it. He lifts his eyes, hoping to lock them on the wall ahead of him.

As his head lifts, his eyes land on a pair of bare breasts as Maya breezes past him without a single glance, and he drops his eyes back down, wondering if he should apologize, but he's too afraid to look at anything but the floor.

He's relieved when it's time to keep moving, but the thought of turning around to change in his own room is tempting.

"Get used to it," says Mishkin as he settles the clothes onto a small rack near an unused mirror. "We all share a dressing room like this when we go on tour. Except Rex, Allistair, and Axel."

"Rex won't even buy curtains? I can't imagine it'd be that much of a splurge."

"Why bother?" Mishkin shrugs. "It's not like nudity is a secret. Billions of people have dicks, tits, and slits. What's the scandal?"

Blake's muscles relax; he hadn't thought of it that way before. His mother always taught him about respect, but maybe in this case, pushing his discomfort to the side might be more respectful than averting his eyes. It isn't like they expect him to stare.

"Anyway, try some of these on." Mishkin drops a pile of clothes onto a nearby chair. "I'll get us some makeup."

Mishkin rushes off, and Blake tilts his head. He was prepared to wear makeup when the members went on stage, but would he really need it for a wedding? He shrugs, figuring it'll just be a touch-up for photos. If there's a wedding video, of course everyone would try to look their best.

He takes off his shirt and shuffles through the pile of clothes Mishkin grabbed from the rack. He furrows his brows at the color options as he lifts each one to see the next. Gray, light gray, lighter gray, dark gray, almost black but not quite there yet, gray patterns, gray stripes, gray, gray, gray.

Blake scans his eyes around the room. Most of the members are dressed now, all of them in various shades and tones of gray. His eyes land on Ronan, all dressed in light gray, and applying dark gray makeup to his face.

A compact circle pops into his line of sight, a small black container with a light-gray pigment inside.

"I don't think Ronan's shade will quite match yours. This one will suit you better."

Blake grabs the makeup from Mishkin's hand. "I'm confused. Are we performing or something?"

"The wedding ceremony is a performance of dreams," Mishkin says as he takes off his own shirt and plucks the almost black one from its hanger.

"A performance of what?"

"A long time ago, human beings used to dream in black and white. At least, that's what Rex told us. So, at every ceremony, the wedding couple are the only ones permitted to be in color. It's supposed to make the whole thing feel like a dream, so when they wake up to their lover in the morning, their dreams have come true."

Blake can't help but smile as he pulls a light-gray shirt from the rack and puts it on. He still has no idea why Melody left the stage, but she looks happy with Knox at her side. Their interactions at each meal make their love clear, and it almost makes him jealous to be single.

He's undoing his zipper when his eyes fall onto Inez, who is in black lace underwear and a matching bra. He darts his gaze back to his mirror, but her reflection is there too. He tries to keep his gaze low again, but he catches Ian's reflection as he steps into view, a disgusting grin on his face as he walks by. He gives Inez's behind a light tap, and it seems Inez is the only one who noticed.

Blake whips around to say something, but Inez has already kicked the back of Ian's knee as he tries to walk off. Ian falls to the ground with a groan and some choice words that don't seem to faze her.

Blake holds out a finger at Ian. "Ha!"

Swish.

Blake's face heats up as he realizes his pants are now at his ankles. He scrambles to pull them back up, though it's already too late.

Inez snickers before turning back to her own mirror, and Ian rolls his eyes before he slumps off. Mishkin bursts into laughter at his side.

He catches Inez's reflection giggling at him from her mirror as she buttons the top of her dress. His cheeks are hot, but he turns back to the clothing rack to find a pair of pants.

"That was a thing of beauty, Pup!" says Mishkin, his laughter settling down. "You're not as intimidating with your pants down, but you've got a pretty cute ass!"

"Yeah, yeah. Can we drop it, please?"

"Sorry. It was just too good!"

Blake rolls his eyes, his cheeks still red.

Mishkin puts a hand on his shoulder. "Hey, relax. It's over now. Finish getting ready, and we'll all sit together."

Despite no longer wanting to see anyone else for the day, Blake tests a dark gray pair of slacks against his waist.

He changes quickly, trying to stop the incident from replaying in his head. His eyes float back to Inez, who is rubbing gray wax through her hair. Her face is still its pale

77

color, and her loose, gray dress falls just above her knees. Tiny, charcoal hearts cover the fabric, and the way it hugs her curves makes her look sweet, as if she couldn't hurt a fly.

He pats himself down when he realizes what's missing. His eyes scan the floor until they land on that makeup Mishkin brought for him. He snatches it back up and opens it to pull a tiny amount onto his fingers. The mix feels creamy, but sturdy.

"What you said earlier," he says to Mishkin. "About people dreaming in black and white. Is that what this makeup is for? We have to make ourselves entirely gray?"

"Yep," says Mishkin, pulling a slightly darker shade from his pocket. "And each with distinct tones to match our skin. We have to look like we're in one of those old-timey films."

Mishkin pulls some makeup brushes from a cup on the floor. He hands one to Blake, and the two cover every inch of skin that's showing. Blake is grateful he grabbed a long-sleeved shirt; painting his right hand with his left is harder than he expected.

Mishkin grabs a few tubs of gray hair wax and holds out the lighter shade to Blake before scooping a glob from his own.

"Isn't your hair already black?" Blake asks, following Mishkin's lead and hoping he's doing it correctly. "Why bother?"

"Against this kind of background, there is a more brownish undertone that sticks out. Besides, black and white are colors reserved for the married couple. Everything else needs to be some shade of gray."

"Which color did you wear when you and Vladik got married?"

"Black, of course," Mishkin smirks. "My suit was black and Vladik's was white. We each had a pink rose to throw in some color. Neither of us is huge on flowers, so we didn't have a bouquet to do that for us."

"Did you feel like you were in a dream?"

"Being with Vladik every day feels like a dream. My parents weren't exactly on loving terms, so I never really thought relationships were a good thing. Sometimes I'm worried he'll change, and it scares me. But then he never does, and I just feel like the luckiest man alive."

Inez's words about Mishkin's father ring through his mind. If he tried to kill him, then where is Mishkin's mother?

He shakes his head. Mishkin will tell him when and if he feels comfortable enough. "Where is Vladik, by the way?"

"Inez knows Ian is going to try something, so Vladik is playing bodyguard."

"Really? But Inez can clearly knock him out with one kick."

"Not when Rex is around."

Mishkin leads Blake into the room called the temple, and Blake goes slack jawed. Every wall is a deep gray, with lighter-gray pillars and borders. The windows are stained in greys and silvers, featuring various tarot cards, with The Fool on the biggest display at the front. On the ceiling are black-and-white paintings of other cards: characters with swords and chalices, and a Death figure who is facing away from those below him. A night sky full of constellations fills the gaps in between. The shades of gray are so distinct, so vivid, that Blake can almost see what color everything is supposed to be.

The sunlight filtering through the stained glass covers everything in a silver glow, and Blake's head spins. *This really is like a dream. It doesn't feel real.*

Vladik's hand waves the two over, pulling Blake from his thoughts. Inez smirks as Blake settles himself next to her. Mishkin slips past them to sit next to his husband.

"I saw your undies," Inez taunts.

"I saw yours, too." Blake shuts his mouth too late, hoping that doesn't make her angry. He's surprised when she laughs.

"I'm not the one who put on a goofy pose."

"That's fair," Blake sighs, praying that the gray makeup can hide his reddening cheeks.

"What were you so happy about?"

"You knocked Ian to the floor for the second time since I've been here. And you did it half naked."

"So?"

"So, it makes me kind of proud to know you. And a little afraid to piss you off again."

Inez nudges him with a scoff. "You aren't *that* bad, Pup. Just don't turn into a creep."

That's a simple enough request.

An organ plays from a platform above the front area. Allistair has been standing at one of the pews, chatting with a few members in the front row, but he hurries to the front with a book in his hand. He takes a firm, authoritative stance as Knox struts down the aisle with Axel at his side.

His dark skin has a warm glow to it, and he holds his head high with a confidence that Blake can only dream of. They reach the front and exchange a small peck on each other's cheeks.

Axel steps behind Allistair, off to the side while Knox solidifies his stance in the center.

Moments later, Melody enters with Rex on her arm. Her skin is as white as her dress, but her cheeks are flushed with soft pink, and her lips are painted in a similar color. A veil hangs over her curled, white hair, and pink roses line the band. Her empty hands are folded neatly in front of her, with white lace from her elbows to a band around her middle fingers. She and Rex put on the same display as the others, then Melody and Knox face either, hands entwined, eyes enamored. The music fades as Allistair opens his book.

He, Rex, and Axel are as grey as the rest, but Allistair has a lavender rose on his chest. Axel's rose matches his, pinned to the brim of her low-cut dress. Rex's rose is royal purple, and Blake is surprised that a flashy leader like Rex would blend in with the others.

"Dreamers, adventurers, and challengers," Allistair begins, "we're gathered here today to celebrate an undying love between Knox Herald and Melody Valentine. Two fools, each drowning in their own tar pit, reaching for help to no avail. But at the last minute, your hands found each other, unseeing, unknowing.

"You each pulled and fought, until you finally reached the surface, able to breathe for the first time. When you gazed into each other's eyes, you found that you were both dripping with the tar that nearly consumed you. In your darkest, most perilous moments, you unknowingly saved each other.

"With this in mind, it seems only natural that your love would bloom from a garden of pure trust, understanding, and support. After everything the two of you have been through, it is the highest honor that I'm able to marry you today.

"So, Melody, do you take Knox as your husband, to weather every storm, climb every mountain, and claw your way out of every tar pit, hand in hand?"

"I do." Melody smiles.

"And Knox, do you take Melody as your wife, to weather every storm, climb every mountain, and claw your way out of every tar pit, hand in hand?"

"I do." Knox returns the smile, and Melody beams.

"You brave fools are headed for a wonderful future together. With my blessing, my father's, and the love of those around us, the way forward is brighter than the sun. With your next kiss, I pronounce you married."

Their kiss comes on slowly, gently, and Allistair closes his book as he smiles at the two. Everyone applauds and stands as Knox and Melody stroll back up the aisle, arm in arm.

Allistair follows with Axel and Rex close behind him. The applause dies down as they pass by, and the organ is still playing. The procession leaves, the organ finishes on a low note, and there's a moment of silence before everyone makes their way back to the dressing rooms.

Mishkin appears at his side. "So, what do you think? Our weddings don't exactly match the movies, but it's not too shabby, right?"

"It was beautiful," Blake says. "Quick though. Are we really changing back already?"

"Of course," Mishkin responds as he and Blake find their mirror. "Why drag on such an uneventful performance? They've said their I-do's, now we get to shower and wear things we actually like!"

Blake chuckles as he and Mishkin change back into their previous clothes. Face wipes are being passed around to remove the majority of their makeup and hair wax.

"That speech Allistair gave was incredible!" Blake exclaims.

"Wasn't it? I'm so proud of him." Mishkin beams. "I was a little worried, this being his first time ministering and all, but he really killed it!"

"You mean he's never done it before?"

"Nope! Usually, it's Rex who ministers. But everyone knows Allistair will be taking over the circus once he retires, so he occasionally takes on some of the leadership roles to prepare."

"Really? What about Axel?"

"Axel wouldn't be caught dead doing paperwork and writing speeches. Her love belongs to the limelight."

"I see. So Rex ministered your wedding?"

"Yep! And each wedding is given a different speech based on each couples' story. I think Allistair really hit the nail on the head for this one."

"Wow, it's different for each couple? What was your speech like?"

Mishkin shrugs before pulling his shirt over his chest. "I don't remember it word for word, but it was something about having to fight and persevere and doing it together. I was too wrapped up in what was happening to pay much attention. Anyway, you can shower and change in our room. Let's go"

Blake nods, straightening his outfit before following him out. Vladik joins them on the way, and Blake's smile refuses to fade. He'd only been to one wedding before, and it wasn't bad, but it couldn't hold a candle to the passion of Allistair's speech. If he ever gets married, that's the kind of passion he'd want in a ceremony. One that can make everyone swoon.

Chapter 10

"Cheers!" The cast and crew toast with their champagne in the air.

Knox and Melody make their way through the warmly lit ballroom to the dance floor. Round tables in white fabric dot the floor, and each centerpiece features a white vase with a pink bow and three red roses. Veils of white and pink hang from the ballroom ceiling, and matching decor lines the walls with spots of red to accent the hanging points.

Blake squirms in Mishkin's shirt. The seams are a bit tight, but he didn't think to bring any fancy clothes. It'll suffice for now.

Inez sits next to him, eyes lovingly glued to the couple as she takes another sip of champagne. Her gown is pink with black lace on the torso and a black ribbon around the waist that ties into a perfect bow on the back. Another bow sits on a headband, pulling the red hair back, though her side bangs are still cupping her face. Blake pushes back his own hair, worried it isn't neat enough.

"Hey, darlin'!" A woman in a yellow dress rushes over and throws her dark arms around Inez's shoulders. "You look beautiful!"

"Hey, so do you!" Inez smiles, hugging the woman back.

The woman gasps when he sees Blake and leans over with a smile.

"You're that new kid, ain'tcha?" She says in some kind of Southern accent. Baton Rouge maybe? She holds out a gloved hand. "My name is Celia, it's very nice to meet you! I know we all seemed a little rude before, but it's not every day a newcomer finds their way in here."

Blake takes her hand. "That's alright. Inez mentioned that it's kind of strange. It's nice to meet you too. And I loved your stepsister routine in Cinderella."

"Aww, you really are like a sweet little puppy dog! How do you like it here so far?"

"I'm having fun. I've been watching you all since I was— well, since *we* were all kids. I'm enjoying getting to know everyone."

"I'm so glad! Has Inez been treating you well? I know she's a little rough around the edges, but I swear she's really a big softie!"

Inez's jaw drops. "I'm not rough around the edges!"

"Oh honey, your temper is all over the place. I keep telling you to work on it. Tell me, Pup, did she threaten you when you first met?"

"Don't ask him that!" Inez slams her hand on the table.

"She did, though, didn't she?"

"Um, you can just call me Blake," he chuckles.

"Shall we dance then, Blake?" Celia holds out her hand.

"Don't ignore me!"

"Nezzie, you can join us when you cool off. Now let's go." Celia pulls Blake onto the dance floor, where many other members have already joined Knox and Melody.

"Sorry," says Blake as Celia settles her arms around his neck. "I'm not the best dancer."

"That's all right, I just had to pull you away for a second. Nezzie hasn't been too hard on you, has she?"

"Not at all. She's teaching me how to use fire poi. As far as I can tell, it's been fun for both of us."

Blake twirls Celia, who smiles as they step side to side, rotating with the music.

"I'm so glad. She's been a little closed off for the past few months, but I'm hoping a new face will help her open up a bit. You're like a breath of fresh air. A friend she didn't know she needed."

"I don't think I'm all that," Blake chuckles, glancing at Inez, who is giggling through cheese and crackers with Vladik and Mishkin. "I don't even think she likes me very much."

"She likes you just fine. What she's most concerned about is Hartman's plan in all of this."

"Hartman's plan?" Blake's mind flashes back to what Inez almost said when they were talking in the hall.

"We all know Hartman is using you, but we don't know why. You're not here because you're talented, you're here because of some weird scheme of his."

A pang shoots into Blake's chest. *No, there's no way.* "If I'm here for a scheme, why would they bother testing me?"

"Well, we're not sure if Rex has anything to gain from it, but even if he plans to keep you anyway, you still have to prove you can perform. You *do* want to be in the show, right? If there is a plot, they probably won't *need* you on stage for it."

"Good point. So why didn't Inez want to tell me?"

Celia's eyes soften. "You wanted to come here because of a dream, right? You shouldn't give up your passions. Besides, none of us want you to get hurt. But I think you're better off knowing that something is up. You might catch a clue somewhere if you pay attention."

"How do you know so much?"

"There are no secrets in a home that never changes. Everyone here knows everything about everybody. Since we don't know very much about you, of course we're all going to gossip just a teeny bit."

Blake chuckles. "That's fair, I guess. Thank you for telling me."

"Don't hold it against them, okay? Everyone means well; we just tend to be a little protective. They'll come around. Just relax and try to enjoy yourself. And don't you *dare* hold out on your test just because you can't be kicked out."

"I wouldn't dream of it."

"Good. I can't wait to see what you come up with. Especially if you're going to use fire."

"Thanks. It should be fun, provided I can learn quickly."

"I think you'll do just fine."

The music picks up, and the main lights go out to let colored beams flash through the air. Inez, Mishkin, and Vladik swarm the two, all bouncing and wiggling to the beat.

So many questions are still running through his mind, but he smiles along with the rest of them; forces the whirlwind of thoughts to dissipate and allows himself to get lost in the music.

Tomorrow he can ask more questions, dig deeper. For now, he can let everything go. For the first time in his life, nothing else has to matter.

Chapter 11

The next morning, Blake practices some two-poi tricks he learned from previous practice sessions. The constant movement makes the brisk October air feel refreshing on his bare arms, and he enjoys watching the other performers use the surrounding rigs. Mishkin, however, is content sitting on the grass at Blake's side.

"So that guy Hartman," says Blake. "What did he mean when he said having me here would 'get things moving'?"

"Hard to say," Mishkin says with a shrug. "Rex doesn't like him much, but it's thanks to him we can afford a place like this."

"C'mon, you know something, sneaky Cat. Talk to me."

Mishkin chuckles. "Sorry, but I really don't know either. Hartman always talks about having a plan, but he hasn't told me anything in detail."

Blake rolls his eyes as he turns his attention to the sky, and his control over the poi shifts to autopilot as his mind races.

His chat with Celia at the wedding has been replaying in his head since it happened. If he can find a way to get more clues to his motives, he might be able to put the pieces together and find out the real reason he's here.

Inez's face pops into his mind, and their last practice session makes his cheeks warm. He prays it isn't noticeable.

"What I *can* say," Mishkin continues, "is that having someone like you around is good for her."

Blake scoffs. "What can I do? Ian seems like a douchebag for sure, but she's perfectly capable of dealing with him."

"It's not about Ian. She's been sneaking out because she wants to leave, and honestly, I don't blame her. She's the only one who regrets coming here. Having you around gives her a purpose in the mansion. She can focus on something besides herself."

"Yo!" Inez calls out as she steps outside and makes her way toward them. "Mishkin, are you distracting him? Let him practice in peace!"

"How rude!" Mishkin stands. "Shooing the Cat away like a pest. Or are you just jealous cause I got to spend time with the cute little Pup?"

"Ex*cuse* me?" Inez shouts.

Blake lets out a snicker, and Inez shoots a glare at him. Blake looks away, continuing his poi circles.

"You are such a fucking child, damn Cat! Get outta here!"

"Fine, no one likes to be a third wheel anyway." Mishkin wanders off with his hands on his hips and his nose high. "See ya, Blake."

"Bye," Blake laughs.

Inez growls to herself as she readies her poi for practice. Blake is getting used to their friendly bickering, but something about her tone seems different this time.

"You're using fire tonight," she snaps. "You need to get used to the flames before you perform in front of an audience."

"Wait, tonight?"

"You only have two days. Make sure your pants and shirt are 100 percent cotton, don't use any gel or sprays in your hair, and don't wear anything loose or dangly."

"Okay, sure, but Inez, are you okay?"

"Mind your business and practice!"

Blake is about to protest, but Inez's voice is flat, and her face is blank. She's focused on her own routine now, moving her poi too quickly, too intricately for him to follow.

He tightens his lips, grateful that her fiery gaze isn't scorching into him this time. Even as he channels his anxiety into his poi, his hands are trembling.

He knew this was coming; he should've prepared for it. It never occurred to him just how little time he has to prepare.

I'm going to light the poi tonight.

I'm going to dance with fire.

I'm going to die.

DINNER GOES BY FASTER than Blake hoped, and Inez isn't giving him any chances to stall. She and Mishkin lead the way toward the yard in silence.

She revealed to him at dinner that her uncle somehow knew where she was while she was out, and the lack of privacy was wearing her thin. Guilt still riddles his gut for trying to pry before. He's still curious himself, but there's no way she trusts him enough for him to ask without her believing that he's doing it to win Rex's favor.

When they get outside, Inez turns away from the aerial rigs ahead, where they'd been practicing all this time, and toward an open space. A large fire pit sits a short way away under a clear night sky with pinprick stars and a quarter moon overhead. The night air threatens to freeze him from the inside out, and he curses the circumstances that require his first burn to occur tonight.

The yard is empty except for the three of them. Mishkin holds a fire blanket at the ready. Inez grabs a set of poi from a spot next to a bucket of fuel, and hands it to Blake. He isn't sure if she's unaware of his trembling or ignoring it, but she doesn't look like she's about to give him any wiggle room.

"All right. Safety review. Mishkin is right there," Inez points. "If you need to stop, say 'red.' Never, *ever* shout 'fire,' understood?"

Blake nods, lips tight, eyes focused on his poi.

"If you have to stop before the poi goes out, let us know, and you'll put the poi on the blanket, okay?"

Another nod.

"All right, here we go!" Inez flicks her lighter, and two pillars of flame shoot up from the wicks. They trail up the rope, threatening Blake's hands, and the heat tempts him to drop the poi.

"Get 'em moving," Inez commands, taking a few steps back.

Of course she warned him that the flames would be loud when the poi moved, but he didn't expect them to be *this* loud. Even a gentle swinging motion causes the fire to growl like an angry dragon, making him hesitate to do anything else. The flames are much larger than he expected, and the heat coming off them is much more intense.

"Use what you've learned!" Inez calls out.

Blake swallows hard, takes in a deep breath, and in a quick motion, whirls his poi into the air, pulling the flames around him in perfect, roaring circles. The sound rings in his ears, and the light stains his vision, plastering a little smirk on his face.

I'm doing it. I'm really doing it!

One poi head taps his thigh, but he continues, recovering those perfect circles once again.

"Right leg! Put it out!" calls Mishkin.

Blake holds both poi in one hand and looks at his leg to see a bit of flame on his pants. He pats the spot with his free hand until it's out before he separates the poi and continues with the flower patterns he's recently mastered.

Blake loses himself in the light and roar of the flames, drowning in the excitement pulsing through his veins, every moment making his grin grow wider and wider. He watches the fire dance around his vision, leaving trails of light on the back of his eyelids. He watches the light blaze across the grass, the night sky, even the distant aerial ground catches tiny glimmers of orange.

Minutes fly by like seconds when everything goes dark all at once. He stops short and realizes the fire has gone out. Mishkin and Inez applaud, and Blake takes a small bow before stepping over to rejoin them.

"That was pretty good, Pup!" says Inez. "Tomorrow night, we'll try it with juggling patterns, and then the next night is your test."

"That felt incredible!" Blake exclaims. "I never thought I could do something like that!"

"Very nice," Mishkin says. "You could use a little work on your form, but you're a natural."

The three make their way inside, exchanging memories of the early days of The Fools' Circus.

The trails from the flames still stain Blake's vision, and though his heart has stopped racing, his smile hasn't faded.

I did it. I'm a fire spinner!

Chapter 12

The next two days of practice fly by, and Friday's dinner is here before Blake can realize it.

The table is loud and vibrant with friendly chats and light mockery. Inez is hiding her face in embarrassment as Blake gushes over Allistair's magic in previous shows.

Allistair, basking in the attention, uses a napkin to make a rose appear upright in his hand. Blake grabs the rose with excitement and shows it to Inez, who can no longer hold in her laughter as he brags about Allistair's gift.

"My beloved fools!" Rex's booming voice quiets the room as he stands from his seat. This is the first time Blake has seen him sit with everyone for dinner.

"This year has been another outstanding success. I'm happy to announce that the event guest book, the profits, and the audience responses have never been better!"

The table erupts into a roar of cheers, whistles, and applause.

"Yes, well done." Rex pats the air beside him, and everyone follows the prompt to quiet down. "And I want to congratulate and thank you all for being such an amazing cast and crew. Seeing how you've all grown from your dark origins and become an inspiring beacon of light for the world warms my heart. I am immensely proud of each of you! Furthermore, I'm delighted to announce that preparations for the Blasphemer's Ball will begin next week!"

More cheering erupts from the table, and Blake joins in the applause.

"More great news: I am officially training my son, Allistair, to be the next King of Fools."

Excited words turn concerned, and faces dart around, throwing whispers back and forth.

"Allistair has seen the work I do, learned it from childhood, and knows how things should be."

"Are you retiring?" someone asks.

"Not yet," Rex responds, pulling a wisp of his hair, and a few glints of white peek through the blond. "However, I cannot deny that my age is catching up to me. It may be a few years, but alas, I am not immortal. Therefore, Allistair will be working with me to prepare for his role as the King of Fools."

Everyone applauds, including Blake, and Allistair nods his thanks to everyone around him.

"Inexcusable!" calls a voice. Everyone turns to watch a familiar bald head rise from the table, bare chested as always.

"Ian," Rex frowns. "You're speaking against me?"

"In favor of your children, I assure you." Ian grins. The sudden shift from his usual tone sends a thick air of tension across the room.

"My King, my adoptive father, shining beacon of truth in a dark world of lies. I feel as though you've taken away our voice. Each of us, when we arrived, was given choices for our acts, freedom to branch out, and encouraged to speak our minds.

"Well, I'm speaking now, and I find it rather unfair that you would elect your own son as the future King, the heir to the circus you built from the ground up, without even considering that there might be another more qualified for the job."

"And I suppose you're speaking of yourself?" Rex raises a brow.

Ian grins and shrugs. "I'm the oldest here. Allistair is a fine illusionist, and he may even make a fine King. I, however, would do better."

"A challenge then," Rex says. The tension in his face has lifted, as if the idea is suddenly entertaining somehow, but it hasn't left the air. "I propose a challenge to see which of you is more qualified, both as a ringleader and our new King."

"Accepted." Ian nods with a sly grin.

"Is there anyone else who would like to take on this challenge? Now is your only chance to fight for this opportunity. Who else believes they will make a better leader than my son?"

The cast and crew toss glances around the table. Some of them push their plates away, as if the very thought

97

disgusts them. A few sink in their spots, and others shake their heads at each other.

"In that case, the competition is between my son, the Prince of Illusion, Allistair Brandt, and our beloved Blades Master, Ian Demir. You'll each have a small team, and I will announce them tomorrow. One will win, and the other had better not disappoint. Everyone else will vote for the winner. Then, our upcoming ball will double as a celebration of the new King-to-be."

Allistair and Ian exchange icy glares that send chills through the room. Rex sits back in his seat as the thick silence hangs in the air. He gives a quick wave of his hand, and the tension lifts almost immediately.

An uproar of chatter takes its place. Most of it involves Allistair and Ian being bombarded with questions and support and offers to help in any way possible.

Blake can't bring himself to eat as he glares at Ian. He peers over at Inez, and she looks just as disgusted, though she continues eating as if holding back some choice words.

BODIES SCRAMBLE TO FINISH CLEANING. Blake's heart races as he helps Ronan with the dishes, wishing he could slow everything down, so he doesn't have to perform. Maybe he could smash a few plates? Pretend there is some food that won't come off? But doing this right would impress Inez and secure a spot on stage for him.

Yes, but it's still terrifying!

He sneaks a peek over his shoulder at Inez as she sweeps the kitchen floor, and he freezes when he sees Ian approach her.

They talk for a bit, Inez refusing to look him in the eye. When Ian lifts a hand toward her, she flinches and shoves his arm away.

"Don't act so tough. I'm trying to help you."

"You're being an arrogant piece of shit!"

Ian chuckles as Inez turns and continues sweeping in the other direction, her head hung low.

Ian steps over and puts his hands on her waist. "I know what you want, Fire Goddess. Play nice, and you just might get it."

Inez clenches her fists. "Get off of me."

Kick him Inez! Hit him. Don't put up with this.

Ian grins and presses his nose to her head. Inez cringes, but doesn't move. Should he do something? Even though Inez can handle herself, he feels wrong about standing around.

"Just think about it. No one else here is going to help you."

Like hell. "Ian!" Blake storms over, standing at Inez's side. "It doesn't look like Inez cares too much for your attitude. Why don't you focus on your challenge instead of harassing your coworkers?"

Ian releases Inez with a smirk, but she doesn't move from her spot.

"Harassing? I was making her a generous offer. I know what everyone wants, and when I win, I'll make sure they get it. And you, you pampered pest..." Ian makes a movement so quick that Blake can't see what he's doing. A spot of ice-cold steel stings his neck. "Watch your fucking mouth before I carve out your tongue from its roots."

A loud crash behind Blake makes everyone jump and the dishes tremble. The cold steel pulls away in Ian's hand so Blake can see it. *A switchblade.* Blake turns his head to see that Vladik and Mishkin have stepped up behind him and Inez. Everyone in the kitchen is staring in stunned silence. Ian makes one last glare at Blake before he storms off, folding the switchblade and putting it back in his pocket.

"Inez, are you okay?" Blake asks as he turns to face her.

"Why did you do that?" Inez growls. "What's your problem?"

Blake blinks hard with raised eyebrows before returning her glare with his own. "My problem is that Ian is an asshole! Sorry that I can't just sit around and watch him treat you like that!"

"Don't be stupid!" Inez crosses her arms. "You know I can handle him. You need to stop doing shit that makes things worse!"

"What did I make worse? I didn't do anything wrong!"

"Hey," Mishkin cuts in, putting a hand on each of their shoulders. "Look, we're done cleaning. Let's get outside and let our worries burn in the bonfire."

Mishkin skips away with Vladik close behind, leaving the kitchen with everyone else.

As they leave, Blake catches a glimpse of long blonde hair trailing down the hall. *Not while Rex is watching.*

That's why she wasn't doing anything. What will happen if Rex sees her attack him?

"Look," Inez says, turning his attention back to her. Her eyes are softer now. "Everything that happens here, I'm used to it. People are already skeptical about you in this place. Don't make it worse by acting so high and mighty."

"I wasn't trying to do that, I just—"

"I know, but you can't afford to lose Rex's favor. Worry about yourself. Let's go. It's almost time for your test."

Blake follows Inez to the yard, begging for the awkward air between them to stop nipping at his conscience.

They get outside and head to the fire pit, now burning with the cast and crew huddled around its warm glow. A few feet away, Axel is bending and twisting herself into odd shapes and poses that make Blake wonder if she even has bones. She pulls back her shoulders, yanking off her shirt to reveal a bright red bra with tassels draping from a band below her breasts.

The crowd whoops and whistles as Blake and Inez make their way over to catch the rest of the show. Blake's cheeks heat up a bit. This performance is nothing like her innocent and graceful Cinderella. Even her grin has switched from sweetheart to succubus.

"It's easy to see why she gets all of the lead roles, isn't it?" says Inez as they plop themselves into the crowd.

"Does anyone else ever get a chance?" Blake asks without looking away.

"No one really cares. If someone else wants a lead role, of course they can audition, but mostly we all like her as a lead. There isn't anything she can't do. She's Rex's daughter, but not the heir to the circus. She has to prove her worth somehow. At least, that's the way she sees it."

"So, Rex didn't adopt her?"

"He did, but he adopted her before the circus even started. Rex might call everyone his children, but Axel and Allistair are the only ones who call him Father."

The other members cheer as Axel unties herself into a handstand. Her feet lower over her back to rest on her head before they come back up. One foot comes down to

101

rub the opposite leg, and then the other foot copies the motion. This continues until a sliver of red peeks out from her pearlescent leggings. The crowd's yips and catcalls continue as her feet guide her pants to her ankles, still high in the air, until they hang limp from her foot. She twirls them in the air a few times before flinging them off to the side.

Her underwear is red lace, and Blake's cheeks get hot when he realizes they're see-through. He clears his throat to center himself. He'd seen burlesque before, but never with see-through fabric over the crotch. *It's just nudity, it's not a secret.*

Even Inez yips next to him and gives him a look, encouraging him to do the same. Axel's feet land in front of her face and she pulls herself to a stand. Her hips shake, and she bends and moves in ways that make it look as though her breasts might spill from her bra.

Axel turns her back to the crowd, walks a few steps away, and undoes her bra. Shouts and whistles erupt from everyone as Axel holds the bra out to the side with her finger and thumb, dropping it to the ground.

The music picks up and Axel turns back around, revealing red tassels over her nipples. A grin pops onto her face as she twirls them in circles, leaning forward for added fan service. The music ends, and Axel lands in a split with blades of grass barely covering the slit between her legs.

Blake and Inez applaud when Axel takes her bow and Maya runs up with a handful of others, all of them raving about how beautiful and talented she is.

Axel gathers her scattered clothing as everyone settles back into their toasty spots by the fire.

Inez leaps up to take her place, settling odd frames and shapes around that Blake can't see yet.

"You're going on too, right?" Mishkin asks, tapping Blake's shoulder from behind him.

"Yeah, right after Inez. I'm kinda nervous."

"You'll be fine."

Inez lights a small torch, and Blake's mind trails off. She holds the lit torch in one hand and a matching, unlit torch in the other. She drags the unlit torch down her arm, then pulls it away and taps the lit one onto it. A line of flames sparks along her skin. It only burns for about a second before Inez gently blows it out. She repeats the process on the other arm as cheers and yips rise from the audience.

She sits on the grass and takes off her shoes, keeping her bare feet just off the ground. She drags the unlit torch along her shin, causing the other members to howl and whistle. She lights the trail along her leg like before and blows it out before doing the same on the other. When that goes out, she rises to her knees and sticks out her tongue. She dabs the unlit torch on its surface, then the lit one, then the unlit one again, and pulls her flaming tongue back into her mouth and holds up the two lit torches. The other members continue cheering while Blake stares, slack-jawed and wide-eyed.

Inez turns her head to the side and places one torch onto her tongue, carefully guiding it inside her mouth and closing her lips around it. When she parts her lips again, the fire is extinguished, and Inez grins at the audience as a bit of smoke sneaks out of her lips and caresses her cheeks as she grins. Her eyes land on Blake's, making his heart skip a beat, and she reaches to a spot behind her to pull an oddly shaped wire contraption. It looks like a triangle, but with a curved base.

Inez lights a wick at the corner of the curve, then stands and blows out the torch before tossing it aside. She twirls the contraption on her fingers, and the flame grows to cover the entire curve with multiple wicks. She tosses it, and it splits into two parts.

Fire fans!

She catches one in each hand and spins her body, twirling claw marks of flames around her.

Lines of orange and yellow cut through the night air, lighting up Inez's face in a warm glow that leaves Blake breathless. The roar of the flames sends chills across Blake's arms, and with each blink, there are trails of light etched onto his eyelids.

Inez moves with the music as the fire traces and frames her body. She tosses one fan, then both, then juggles the two with one hand, making everyone scream and cheer, including Blake.

She catches them both in one hand with the wicks forming an O shape and dances with them for a minute before separating them again. The flames have gotten much smaller now, and Inez puts them out with one quick motion, and the audience erupts into applause and cheers. Blake follows suit as Inez kneels beside him.

Don't say it.

"Your turn."

Shit, you said it.

Blake nods and grabs the poi, taking his place in front of everyone.

At the back of the audience, Rex stands with crossed arms while Victor sits at his side with a hand on his chin. In front of the audience, Mishkin holds a safety blanket while Inez approaches him and lights the poi the way she'd done before. Blake swallows hard and swings the poi into all the shapes and patterns he can think of.

There aren't many.

As the music shifts, he spins both poi in one hand; meanwhile, he wiggles his foot under the third poi that lies on the ground, kicks it up, and catches it by the rope in his free hand. He meshes the circles of the third poi with the other two, lighting it with the trails they leave behind. The rest of the cast cheers, and a smirk grows on his face.

Blake takes a deep breath and lets it out quickly as he tosses all three poi above his head, creating a ladder pattern in the air. As they fall, Blake's hands move in the patterns and routines he'd practiced with Inez.

Shit. He's trying to use too many club patterns he hadn't practiced yet. He tosses one poi too high, another too far, and almost drops the third. He tosses one as high as he can while maintaining control and swings the other two around his body until the third poi passes his face. He catches it on his ankle and kicks it back up to go into a more familiar juggling pattern.

His fumble must have been obvious, and it sends a pang into his chest. He goes back into the new patterns, attempting some turns he hadn't rehearsed yet. A risky move, but it works, and the others don't seem to care about his previous mistake. Perfect, they're in the palm of his hand now.

Just like he rehearsed with Inez, he kicks up a fourth poi, lighting it with the others, and goes into juggling two in each hand.

Everyone roars as he continues spinning in the only patterns he was able to master with four. He snuffs out the first three and rolls the fourth up and down his bare arm, making quick work of putting out the flame that trails his arm, and blows out the poi in one huff.

Applause echoes into the night air as Blake holds the poi out at his sides and gives the members a quick bow.

The applause and cheering are like music to his ears, and they cover his arms with goosebumps.

He lifts his head to look at Rex, whose grin has disappeared into a pensive glare.

I messed up. Of course he'd notice.

Blake's heart sinks in his chest as he takes his place next to Inez, who is still applauding with a smirk. Other members are giving him friendly punches and words of praise.

"Not bad, Pup," says Inez. "Looks like you've got a place here after all."

Blake opens his mouth to thank her, but Rex's figure looms over the two.

"You weren't perfect," he says, "but your showmanship makes up for your fumbles. I look forward to seeing what you bring to the stage." He makes his way back inside the mansion, leaving Blake at a loss for words until a hand pats his shoulder.

"You did it," says Mishkin with a smile. "You passed!"

"I passed?" says Blake, and he's bombarded with compliments and congratulations by the others, including Ronan, who holds out his hand with a grin.

"And to think I tried to keep you away. Brothers?"

Blake shakes Ronan's hand with a smile and a firm grip. "Brothers."

The night goes on with marshmallows and more freelance performances.

MOONLIGHT SHINES THROUGH the empty halls of the mansion as Blake approaches one of the doors, double checking the plaque.

INEZ MARQUIS

He takes a deep breath and knocks on the door—hard enough to hear but quiet enough not to wake her if she's asleep. It's well past one in the morning, but everyone only retreated to their rooms a short while ago.

When a few seconds pass with no answer, he turns to leave, but then the doorknob shifts, startling him back into place as Inez peeks through a crack in the door.

"Pup?" she whispers. "What are you doing here?"

"I wanted to check on you. The way Ian's been acting is pretty fucked up, even if you can handle it. I just wanted to see if you were okay."

"You wanted to check on me?" Inez asks, a slight pink forming on her cheeks.

"Of course. And you were right. I have no idea how this place works, and I shouldn't be jumping into situations I don't understand. I'm sorry for butting in earlier."

"It's okay," Inez says, eyes lowering while she shifts her feet. "Your heart was in the right place. I shouldn't have yelled. It is nice knowing that you would stand up for me like that."

Blake smiles and shifts in place. "I also, um…I wanted to thank you. I would never have passed this test without your help. And uh…listen, if I can ever return the favor, if you ever need my help, I'll be right there. Not that you *need* it, but…you know."

A tiny smile creeps onto Inez's face, and Blake's heart flutters.

"Thanks, Blake. That means a lot."

Silence fills the air between them, and Blake can't take his eyes off of her. The blue hue of the night caresses her face, and her brown eyes sparkle through the darkness. A tiny smile forms on his lips as Inez narrows her eyes at him.

"What?"

"You said my name."

"Oh, please," she scoffs, rolling her eyes and hiding red cheeks behind her hair. "That's what friends do, isn't it? Good night, Blake."

"Wait, what did you say?"

"I said good night!" Inez barks just before closing the door, and Blake lets out a quiet laugh as he heads back to his own room, ignoring every instinct to barge into hers and pull her into his arms.

Inez is too adorable.

He stops in his tracks and looks back over his shoulder at her door.

Yeah, she is adorable, isn't she?

He shakes his head, rushes into his room and closes the door behind him, leaning on it and tilting his head to the ceiling.

Inez is adorable. Beautiful. Magical.

He drags his back down the door and plops down behind it. Seeing Inez has been making his heart race. He shuffles his fingers around to check, and yep, his palms have been sweating the entire time.

Is this a bad thing? Maybe not. Inez said she doesn't care for Allistair that way, and never mentioned having feelings for anyone else. He can ask her to breakfast tomorrow, then to the ball.

He leaps to his feet and throws his arms around his pillow as he drops himself onto his bed. His heart flutters again as images of Inez in his arms flash through his mind.

He stares out the window at the star-speckled sky and begs to whatever or whoever might be watching.

Please, please let this work.

Chapter 13

It's warmer today than Blake had anticipated, but none of the other members are out enjoying it. He and Inez practice more partner work, and they're much closer this time than last time. He tries to pretend he doesn't notice, but it seems like Inez is doing it deliberately. Her breasts rub against him as she steps closer, and she looks up at him with her eyes glossed over; her lips parted, cheeks red, and she's leaning up.

"Please," she breathes.

Without hesitation, he presses his lips to hers; heat surges through his veins when she pulls him close, confirming her desires. He drops his poi and wraps his arms around her waist, guiding her onto the grass while his tongue parts her satin lips to taunt hers.

Delicious.

Her body is warm against his, and her fingers grip at his hair. He licks and nibbles the smooth skin on her neck while a hand traces her sides. She's as beautiful to touch as she is to look at. He considers asking her if she wants to go inside, but he can't wait anymore. He wants her, needs her, right the fuck now. And she doesn't seem too patient either.

Her moans are like music, filling his blood with joy and his body with hunger. His cock grinds against the warm slit through their clothes, and their mouths fall open, panting.

He kisses her again as he lifts her shirt, revealing pink nipples, begging to be tasted. He teases one with his tongue and grabs the other, while his free hand slips down her pants, spreading over the soft skin just below her stomach, waiting for her prompt or rejection. She raises her hips toward his hand, and his fingers slip further down.

The blaring alarm yanks him from his sleep, and a heavy groan escapes his throat. *Whyyy?*

He slams the clock to stop the nagging and sits up, glaring at the pole in his lap that confirms how good the dream was.

Every image replays in his mind: her scent, her taste, her warmth. Desire pulses through his body, begging for release. He double checks the clock and shrugs.

I still have time before breakfast.

BLAKE STEPS OUT OF HIS ROOM, his hair still damp from his shower. The cloudy sky creates a soft light through the mansion. Cast and crew members crowding the halls must be a sign that breakfast is coming. His eyes flick to Inez's door as she's leaving.

His heart skips a beat and he takes a deep breath, forcing the images of his dream back down.

"Hey," he calls as he approaches her, "is there any way we can get out of here today? I'm going a little stir crazy, and I'd love to buy you breakfast."

Inez looks surprised by the question. "That sounds fine, but the restaurants around here aren't cheap, and you haven't been working. I can pay if you want."

"That's alright. I had a job before I came here, and it's not like I spend much when I'm served three hot meals a day."

Inez purses her lips to one side and shrugs. "Sure, I know a place nearby. We can walk there."

Blake agrees, doing his best to hide the leaping in his chest. When they get downstairs, everyone gathers around a bulletin board in the lobby.

Inez nudges her way through the crowd, and he struggles to follow, being much more apologetic to everyone they're passing. He reaches the front and spots a large white sign pinned to the board.

CHALLENGE FOR THE NEXT KING OF FOOLS

EACH CHALLENGER WILL HAVE A TEAM AND WITH ONLY THAT TEAM, THEY WILL PUT ON A PERFORMANCE. THE WINNER WILL BE DECIDED BY VOTES FROM EVERY

MEMBER OF THE CIRCUS, INCLUDING THOSE PARTAKING IN THE CHALLENGE.

PERFORMANCES MUST BE 7–10 MINUTES LONG AND SHOWCASE THE TALENTS OF EACH PERFORMER.

THE SHOW WILL TAKE PLACE AT THE END OF THE WEEK. EACH TEAM HAS TWO HOURS ON STAGE PER DAY TO REHEARSE, STARTING AFTER LUNCH. FAILURE TO COOPERATE WITH THESE TERMS WILL RESULT IN DISQUALIFICATION.

IAN'S TEAM: CELIA, MISHKIN, AND XAVIER

ALLISTAIR'S TEAM: MAYA, AXEL, AND KNOX

LET THIS BE AN HONORABLE COMPETITION WORTHY OF MY STAGE

"This is insane," says Inez. "I can't believe Rex is letting it go this far."

"Does he generally shut these things down immediately?" Blake asks as they walk away from the bulletin board.

"I don't know. I've never seen anyone go up against Rex's demands before. I always assumed it wasn't allowed. It would be fair to let the others have a say in who the next King will be, but I have a bad feeling about this challenge."

Against the far lobby wall, Allistair is sitting with his head hung low. Inez rushes over to sit next to him as Blake stands close by.

112

"So, you get to put on a performance," Inez chirps. "Are you nervous?"

"I'm terrified," Allistair mumbles. "I don't know why Ian is doing this. My father doesn't even know. It's not just friendly competition, and it never would be with Ian. If it were anyone else, I could at least try to have fun with it. I'd even know the circus would be in good hands if I lost."

"It'll be fine," says Inez. "Just don't lose. Make that asswipe cry like a little bitch!"

Allistair chuckles, and Blake gives his shoulder a supportive pat. Before anyone can say anything else, a trio surrounds them.

"Allistair's cast and crew reporting for duty, sir!" Maya raises her hand to her head in salute.

Axel rolls her eyes, and Knox chuckles as he does the same. He gives Axel a tiny nudge, and she begrudgingly mimics the movement. Maya's brown eyes sparkle under her black bangs, and her petite frame is shifting in excitement.

"At ease, team," Allistair chuckles, standing as they lower their hands. "Thank you all. I won't lie, I'm really nervous, and I have no idea what's going to happen. But we can gather on the stage after lunch, get some ideas together, and put on a show we all love."

The team agrees, and as they chatter on about their excitement, it seems they're all rooting for Allistair to win.

Behind the crowd, Blake sees Mishkin sitting on the floor against the wall with his arms around his legs and his knees hiding his face. Vladik is crouched next to him with an arm on his back. Blake taps Inez, who follows his sightline, and she's just as intrigued. She signals him to follow, and they sneak over while Allistair is busy.

113

"Mishkin," Inez calls, "what's wrong?"

Mishkin lifts his head from his knees, eyes raging. "I'm on Ian's team."

Blake freezes as he remembers the blade on his throat last night. He touches the spot, trying to push the memory out of his mind. "He won't hurt you, will he?"

"That's not the only problem," says Mishkin. "I have a heart defect. Too much strenuous activity can be dangerous. It's why I'm only a side character in the shows. Nothing I perform can be too physically demanding."

Blake glances at Inez, whose color had drained from her face. She quickly replaces her wide eyes with calm ones and crosses her arms. "You're overthinking it. Ian can't put you in danger. He'd lose his chance of ever being on stage again. Get your ass up and quit scaring yourself."

Mishkin shoots a glare at her, lifting himself and taking a step forward. He towers over Inez, whose gaze flicks down for a split second, but she stands her ground.

Blake's heart pounds against his chest, and Vladik holds an open hand behind Mishkin, ready to grab at him if need be.

"Yeah right," Mishkin scoffs as he walks past her. His demeanor remains threatening, but he keeps his eyes ahead. "Thanks, Inez."

Vladik stands from his spot, stepping over to give Inez's head a light pat before following his husband upstairs.

Inez keeps her gaze on the floor, her bottom lip pinched in her teeth.

"You *are* nervous," says Blake.

"Don't tell him that. Just go get a sweater."

Chapter 14

"**Y**our performance last night was beautiful," says Blake as he and Inez stroll down the sidewalk. Scattered leaves crunch under their feet as the breeze carries a few toward the blue sky. "I can see your love of fire when you use it."

"Actually, I hate fire."

"You hate it?"

"When I was nine, my home burned down. My last memory with him is when the upstairs floor collapsed on us. I got free, and he urged me to keep going, get outside. It sort of felt like the fire betrayed him. The detective who investigated said it was just a case of faulty wiring and that the issue was common in older homes, so it wasn't anyone's fault.

"But I'm here because my grandmother died of cancer a few months later, and my mom's mind came undone. I had nowhere else to go but the mansion. Fire spinning was the only tool at my disposal, and part of me still wanted to perform. I thought it would be temporary. Mom was supposed to bring me back home when she got better. But she never did. She succumbed to her grief and left me on Earth alone. So, I never left the mansion."

"That's horrible."

"When I was little, Grandma told me that kids should only see happy tears from their parents. Getting bad news was okay, but kids didn't need the entire weight of the situation. That meant my grandmother was the last person my mother could lean on.

"As a kid, I hated her for abandoning me, but I understand now. She couldn't turn her nine-year-old child into a therapist, and I can't honestly say I wouldn't do the same. My whole family was stolen from me by forces outside of my control. So why do I feel like I should've done something different?"

"I think that's normal," says Blake. "It's easy to look back and wish you'd said this or done that. Especially since you know better now. But there are some things you just can't control. If you can learn to make peace with that, your heart can heal, and you can move forward."

"Move forward," Inez echoes. "I've always tried to do that, but it never felt like I was going anywhere. I'm still part of the circus. I still have to embrace this art I hate just to survive, since I can't make it outside of the mansion."

"So you *do* want to leave?" Blake asks.

"Not yet. I can't just abandon Allistair with the challenge coming up. And I have to make sure Mishkin gets out of it in one piece. If I leave now, there's no guarantee I'll be able to get in touch again. Rex keeps everyone pretty closed off."

She lifts her gaze to the sky as a breeze pushes the hair from her face. Blake's heart skips a beat. *Beautiful.*

She pulls her hood up and drops her arms by her side. Blake watches her hand from the corner of his eye, swinging at her hip. He pulls his hand from his own pocket, but Inez is already putting both hands back into hers, shivering in the breeze.

He unzips his hoodie and places it over her shoulders. Inez pauses as her cheeks get pink. Blake worries she'll refuse it, but she grabs it from either side and closes it around herself, holding it over her mouth and nose.

"Thank you," she says, voice muffled by the fabric.

Blake lets out a small laugh. "You're so cute."

Inez's blush grows brighter, and she lifts her hands further up her face with a tiny whimper, making Blake laugh again.

"Stop it!" she says.

"Stop what?"

"Stop...doing what you're doing!"

"What am I doing?"

"You know what you're doing! Stop it!"

A heavy gust of wind hits them, and the clouds in the sky get darker. One flash of light and a roaring boom later, a wave of rain crashes over them, slamming onto the ground and soaking everything in its path.

Inez points to a bus stop with a roof a few feet ahead, and they quickly scramble over and into the plexiglass shelter.

"Yeesh! Where the hell did that come from?" Blake exclaims.

Inez laughs. "I think you might need this back."

She pulls his hoodie from her shoulders, but Blake moves to stop her. Her eyes lock onto his as he guides her hands back, draping the hoodie back over her arms. He wipes a small stream of rain from her forehead before his hand slides down her cheek, and Inez's face flushes again, her chilled skin warming to his touch.

His hand settles on her chin so his thumb can rub her bottom lip, softer than he dreamed. His heart pounds in his ears as he leans down, his eyes flit from her eyes to her mouth, then back again, clarifying his intention. Inez closes her eyes and lifts her face toward his, a quiet welcome to the sweet invitation. Blake leans closer.

Angry buzzing pierces through the rainstorm. Inez jumps back, and Blake stiffens in his spot, heart sinking at the sudden distance between them. There's a moment of stillness before the buzzing sound comes back, this time from Inez's pocket. She pulls out her phone as the thundering rain continues on the clear roof above them.

"What is it?" Blake asks.

"It's a flash flood warning. We can't go anywhere in this. We have to get back to the mansion."

He nods, and they prepare by having him hold his hoodie over both of them. On the count of three, they dash out from under the shelter, laughing at themselves as they try to keep an even pace. Their feet splash on the sidewalk, socks soaked by the rain.

Lightning flashes, thunder crashes, and after a few exhausting minutes, they plunge through the front door of the mansion, hands on their knees while laughing through heavy breaths.

A few cast and crew members watch them with raised and furrowed brows as they quiet down and head upstairs, hair and clothes dripping behind them.

They get to his room, and Blake shuts the door before Inez scoffs to herself, her cheeks turning a light pink.

"Sorry, I ran in here without thinking. I'll go to my room so you can change. We'll have the leftovers for breakfast."

She turns around and barely has her hand on the doorknob when Blake's figure whips itself directly behind her, one hand stopping hers.

"Do you have to go?" he whispers into her ear as his other hand caresses her hip, resisting the urge to tease the smooth skin on her neck.

"Yes. I don't know who saw us come in here."

To hell with them, he wants to say, but he doesn't know how the rules of the mansion works. He has to trust her. He takes a reluctant step back, pulling her hand off the knob and pressing his lips onto her knuckles.

"Until later then."

"Right," she says, red-faced. "I'll see you downstairs."

He grins as she closes the door behind her. All those years of growing up so close, and yet so far. Him in the audience, her on stage. Never in all that time did he realize the emotional strength in her heart. Never would he have guessed that she would be so beautiful up close, inside and out. Never in his wildest dreams of joining his favorite circus did he expect to be falling for a part of it too.

There's no denying it anymore—no hiding it. Thoughts of what might've happened if she stayed cross his mind as he yanks off his dripping shirt and sopping pants. How do her lips taste? How soft is her skin? How beautiful would it be if she returned these desires?

He puts on a set of fresh, dry clothes and leaves the others in a soggy heap in the corner. He grabs a towel from his suitcase and ruffles it through his hair.

Before anything happens, he needs to know what she's hiding from and why. Before all that, he should find out if she even feels the same.

Chapter 15

Blake and Inez practice outside the next morning, and the autumn chill assures him that he isn't dreaming again. He passed his test, but he's eager to learn as much as he can. Most of the aerial rigs are empty today, likely due to the cold or practice for the challenge. Moving with the poi is keeping him warm as his lessons become trickier, and Inez doesn't seem to shiver either. The door to the mansion opens, turning Blake's attention to the emerging figure.

Mishkin wobbles down the steps and onto the grass, and Inez turns in time to see their friend flop onto the cold grass beneath him. The two rush over, dropping their poi behind them.

"Mishkin, are you okay?" Blake asks.

"I think so. For now," he pants, and wisps of his hair stick to his face as beads of sweat drip down. "But Ian is terrible. I can't keep doing this."

"This can't be good for you," says Inez. "I'm going to find Allistair right now and have him fix all of this. Blake, watch him for me."

"Yeah, of course."

Blake watches Inez leave, taking a quick glance at the sway of her hips before turning his attention back over to Mishkin. "Hey, are your eyes closed?"

Mishkin doesn't answer, and his chest isn't moving.

"Hey," Blake leans in, gently shaking him. "Mishkin, wake up!"

Mishkin yelps in Blake's face, making Blake scream and jump back. Mishkin bursts into laughter between coughs and lies back on the grass with his hands behind his head, sweat still dripping from his temples.

"Not cool, man!" Blake yells. "I was seriously worried!"

"I know, sorry. I really needed that laugh."

Blake lets out a frustrated breath, refusing to admit that Mishkin's ability to prank is comforting. His breathing is still heavy, but it seems to be slowing down.

"So, have you two kissed yet?" Mishkin asks with a smirk.

"What?"

"I see how you look at her, those little glances. I can't say I blame you. Inez has a killer body."

"I don't care about that," Blake grumbles.

"But you care about *her*. So have you?"

"No," he says, staring into the grass. "It's weird. As a kid, watching from the audience, I thought you were all magic. Then, after growing up and learning how juggling and practice work, I lost that notion. Not that it mattered, I still wanted to perform with you guys anyway. But upon getting to know her, and seeing her perform up close, I feel like Inez really *is* magic. And I'm just a naïve, spoiled dreamer who couldn't even finish college. I could never be good enough for someone like her.

"She was willing to share her art with me, even though it sacrificed part of her freedom. I want to thank her. I want to be her rock on the days she feels weakest. I know she *can* get by on her own, but I don't want her to *have* to. When we got caught in the rain yesterday, I really thought she'd give me that chance. But even after everything, even after calling us friends, she isn't letting me in."

Mishkin nods with his lips in a thin line. "It's true, she's a fortress. Actually, I've never even seen her cry. But I wouldn't worry too much. She told me about your visit to her room, and how you checked on her because of Ian. And how sweet it was."

"She thought it was sweet?"

Mishkin nods, and Blake smiles at the scenery ahead of them, the blackened fire pit with all those benches and a distant wall of trees that line the edge of the property. Inez has been talking to Mishkin about him. His heart flutters at the thought of it.

"By the way," he says, mind recentering, "why don't you quit Ian's team? I'm sure someone else could take your place, right?"

"Maybe, but no one goes against our King. That's the one rule we all have in common. Ronan tried it once, and it took a while before he was back to his normal self. And he still had to do what he was told anyway."

"What happened?"

"Can't say. It's not my story to tell."

123

"What about Allistair? Doesn't he have any control?"

"Not over his father."

"But isn't Ian going against Rex by challenging Allistair?"

"Yep. He might be all high and mighty now, but all things considered, I'm not so sure this will end well for him either. Rex never mentioned what would happen to the loser."

Blake opens his mouth to ask the next of many questions, but the back door slams open, startling the two. Inez storms over with a stumbling Allistair in hand. She yanks him forward, and he wobbles toward Mishkin. "Go ahead, Cat. Tell him what you told me."

"Allistair." Mishkin stands tall, surprising Blake with the sudden shift in tone. "I left Ian's practice unable to breathe. I was stumbling, and he threw a knife at my face. His rehearsals are a nightmare. He wouldn't let us grab water until we mastered the routine he set up. Then Celia threatened to leave, and he threw a knife at her too."

"No," Allistair shakes his head with wide eyes. "That's horrible!"

As if on cue, a familiar voice shakes Blake to the core.

"Hey, Stray! You got a lot of nerve leaving rehearsals early, especially after my warning." Ian approaches them with a cup of hot tea in hand, wearing his usual gray sweatpants with no shirt.

"Ian!" Allistair yells. "What's this I hear about you throwing knives at your teammates?"

"Celia has no respect for authority. I'm the leader of the team, and I expect to be treated as such. And Mishkin," Ian glares at the Cat. "Tch, what a deadbeat."

"You asshole!" Allistair smacks the mug onto the ground, the tea pouring over the grass, steam rising from its trails. "You're not a leader, you're just trying out for the part. I'm going to make sure my father sees this as a failure. I'm telling him to cancel the challenge!"

"Great idea," Ian says with a smile. "Run away and tell Daddy, like a good little lapdog. Take away everyone's chance to decide who their leader is going to be. Inherit the circus Daddy bought for you. Take away my chance because I'm not Rex's precious baby boy. I'm sure the others will be thrilled to hear that."

"That's not what I'm doing!" Allistair argues.

"Yes, it is. Rex underestimates us—casts us aside while you and Axel take the spotlight. I'm done with it. I won't let his son continue that injustice."

"My father's not like that. No one has ever complained about who the leads are."

"Why do you think that is? You're not suited to be the King of Fools. All you do is follow Daddy's orders. If you take over, you'll be just as corrupt."

"None of that is true!"

"Prove it, *Prince*." Ian spits the title as if it leaves a bad taste in his mouth. "Accept the challenge. Show me how much you deserve to be in charge."

Allistair clenches his fists, jaw grinding. "If you swear to treat your team fairly, I'll accept. Give them water breaks. Keep your knives in your room!"

"I'm not making that promise." Ian walks away, gesturing toward the fallen mug. "And I'm not picking that up."

Allistair lets out a heavy breath, turning back to his friends. He looks at Inez, then to Mishkin. "Listen, I—"

"I get it," says Mishkin. "Your hands are tied. I'll give it my all."

"Please be careful," says Allistair. "I'll talk to my father right now. I'm sure he'll talk some sense into him. It'll be fine, you'll see."

Allistair hurries off as Mishkin and Inez exchange doubtful glances. Blake darts his gaze between them, heart racing.

What's going to happen to Mishkin?

Chapter 16

Blake wanders the mansion while Inez is away, still having no idea of where she is or what she's doing. Exploring the halls is the next best option to practicing, and he could use the break. He tries to focus on taking in the art and décor, but the thought of Inez wanting to leave is weighing on his mind.

He'd like to take her out at least once before she does. He needs a chance to talk to her, let her know how he feels. She doesn't have to stay or return his feelings, but he'd like to have a solid answer.

A chime rings from his pocket, and he pulls out his phone. *Mom?* He hesitates before sending her to voicemail. *No doubt she's just going to nag me and insist I come back home.* He continues strolling and shoves the phone back into his pocket, ignoring the twinge of guilt poking at his gut.

A blur of colors fills his vision, and he's forced against the wall by his throat. The face glares at him from a few inches away. Blake tries to breathe his name, but the hand is pressing on his windpipe.

"I see the way you look at the Fire Goddess," Ian sneers, pulling out his switchblade. "I know you're not stupid enough to think you have a chance."

Blake struggles to take in a breath, clawing at the hand squeezing his throat.

Ian releases his neck, leaving red spots from his fingernails. He chuckles as Blake hunches over, coughing, gasping for air.

"When I'm king," Ian continues, fiddling with the switchblade between his fingers. "Inez will come back to me, and you will run out of this mansion with your tail between your legs. Mishkin is a deadbeat who barely does anything. He and Allistair will be fired, and the circus will live on as it should. No favorites. No rules."

"Inez," Blake gasps, holding a hand on his throat as he straightens. "She was…?"

"My girlfriend. She belonged to me. Then that *fucking* King demanded that she marry Allistair. But she doesn't love him, I can tell. I'll free her from the fire, and she'll come running right back."

"I doubt it. Inez probably dumped you for a reason. Otherwise, she wouldn't have to kick your ass every time you get near her."

Ian swings a fist into Blake's gut, forcing the air from his lungs and making him collapse as the pain shoots through his torso. His body twitches, fighting for a breath. Ian grips Blake's dark curls and lifts his face with a grin.

"She's just putting on an act. I remember, she loved when I had her just like this," Ian grins, a bulge forming in the crotch of his pants. "You want to get close to her? Why not bond over how my cock tastes?"

Blake manages a breath and slams his fist into the gray bulge. Ian drops his blade and clutches his crotch, falling to his knees. He growls low in his throat, a vein throbbing in his forehead. Blake forces himself to stand, the pain still gripping his abdomen.

"I don't care what kind of history you two have. Inez doesn't *belong* to anyone. I'm sure she wouldn't go back to you if her life depended on it."

Ian flicks his arm toward Blake, and a blur of silver whips past his face and into the wall behind him, leaving him frozen on the spot. Ian wobbles to a stand, chuckling.

"I could kill you any second, you worthless dog. I'm trying to be nice here, since we're housemates. But if I find out you put hands on her, if I see her come out of your room again, I'll slice your fucking throat."

"You do that, and you're out of a job," a familiar voice calls from the side. A woman with a black bun on her head stands tall, her dark, thin figure storming over. Blake smiles, remembering their dance at the wedding.

"You keep up this crap, Rex will dump your sorry ass," she continues. "And no one is going to bat an eye."

Ian snorts, holding out his hands with a soft grin. "We're just having a friendly talk, doll face. No need to get huffy."

"Do *not* call me that. My name is Celia. Now, you have two choices, *doll face*. You can walk away on two feet, or you can crawl away on four." She holds up a fist to emphasize her point.

Ian frowns, stepping over to Blake, who holds his ground as he saw Inez do before. Ian glares at him, pulling

129

his switchblade from the wall. He storms off with a huff. "Practice is in twenty, Doll Face. Don't be late."

Celia's eyes soften at Blake. "Are you okay?"

"I should ask you the same thing," says Blake, trying to mask the pain lingering in his torso. "I heard about what happened at practice yesterday."

Celia lowers her head and the two trudge off to sit in the lobby. Her perky energy has been replaced with an invisible chain that weighs her down, her eyes are lifeless, and seeing her like this breaks his heart. If she hadn't emphasized her name when she confronted Ian, he might believe she was a different person entirely.

Her dark skin glows in the beam of sunlight shining through the window, her black eyes glued to the floor.

Tell no one where you are. Maybe that's a rule he should've broken, at least to Judy, in case Ian's threats come to fruition. But he shakes the thought away and asks about Ian's history. Even with her somber tones, her Baton Rouge accent has an adorable charm that lifts his spirits.

"Rex saved Ian from a street gang when he was fourteen," Celia explains. "Most of us are pretty sure he's killed in the past, but Rex refuses to talk about it. With Ian's temper being how it is, I think that speaks for itself."

"What would he see in a kid like that?" Blake asks.

"Oh honey, Rex wasn't looking for no good, well-spoken little brainiacs. Those kids have a bright future on their own. He wanted the rule benders, mold breakers, the ones society was ready to give up on. He had a vision, and those were the kids who would make it happen."

"What about you? How did Rex get to adopt you?"

He's grateful to see the chains lift from Celia's heart as an unseen memory paints a tiny smile on her face.

"I've always loved climbing trees and walking along fences. Being high up made me feel free as a bird. Hence my stage title, 'Eagle Eye.' My daddy was the only family I had, till he was killed one day, and the police came looking for me. I was just ten at the time, I didn't know what to do. So I ran away. And where do you think I was hiding the whole time?"

"Up in a tree?" He grins.

Celia laughs, a small sparkle returning to her eyes. "They ran right below me and everything! Never looking up! I came down when the coast was clear. Slept on the ground that night and went back to school in the morning. Teacher said she was calling someone to say she found me, and I ran away again, back up a tree. Everyone thought it was the strangest thing. Rex saw an article about it in the paper and came to find me. He said I could learn to climb as high as I want, fly across the stage, and even get paid to do it. What little kid would refuse that kind of offer?"

Blake chuckles through his nose as images of baby Celia climbing trees flood his mind. "Do you ever regret coming here?"

"Hell no! Rex gave me a chance I never would've had otherwise. I owe everything to him, and I know my daddy is proud of me."

Celia's eyes tear up, and Blake puts a gentle hand on her shoulder with a smile. "He absolutely is."

Inez steps through the front door, her attention immediately going to the two of them.

"Celia!" She rushes to sit by her side. "Are you doing okay? I heard about yesterday's practice."

Celia wipes her eyes with a smile. "I'm fine, darling. Just need to find my happy place before I go back to meet Mister Scissorhands."

"I'm worried, Celia," says Inez. "This challenge is giving me a bad feeling. We have to stop the whole thing before it gets worse. We can tell everyone what Ian is doing to you and Mishkin, then convince Allistair's team to refuse. Rex can't punish that many people, and I highly doubt he'd punish his own son."

"That crossed my mind," says Celia. "But if that happens, Allistair wins by default, and rumors of unfairness spread. The entire troupe could fall apart. I hate this as much as everyone else, but it's the only way Rex can prove he's being fair."

Inez pouts and lays her head on Celia's shoulder. "You're amazing, I hope you know that. You're my sister, and I love you. I'd rather be homeless than let you get hurt."

Celia runs her fingers through Inez's hair. "I'll be fine, sweetie. The challenge will be over before we know it, and we can celebrate with champagne and cupcakes."

Inez chuckles. "You could always hold back so Ian loses."

Celia shakes her head. "Rex would notice and call foul. Besides, *me* hold back? I don't think so! I plan on earning a lead role one of these days."

Blake smiles. "You really are incredible, Celia."

Celia's face grows stern. "But listen, I'm not the one in the most danger here. We all know Mishkin can't handle these intense rehearsals. I'll take care of him during, but I need you to be on your toes. Both of you."

Blake isn't sure what Celia expects him to do, but he nods in agreement. He takes in a shaky breath as flashes of Ian and his threats flood through his mind. Should he tell Inez about all of it? She could beat his ass to the curb. Blake would stand proudly behind her. But what would happen after? What would the King do? What would the rest of the mansion think?

"We'll do everything we can. Right, Blake?"

He nods again.

"Thank you, guys. If you don't mind, I could use some alone time to breathe and recenter."

Inez agrees, planting a small kiss on her cheek. Celia hugs her in response, and they exchange one last smile before Inez walks off with Blake. She takes a quick glance over her shoulder before yanking him a little closer.

"I know you were comforting her. Tell me, is Celia really okay?"

"Your guess is as good as mine. When you came in, she was telling me about her father."

"Did she tell you how he died?"

"She said he was killed, but that's it."

Inez purses her lips, lost in thought, but not uttering another word. The question pops into his mind, and he swallows hard.

"If you don't mind," he says as they step into the backyard, "can I ask where you went, today? I'm asking out of my own curiosity this time. If you don't want to tell me, you don't have to."

Inez's eyes narrow toward the ground. "If I don't have to answer, why would you ask?"

"Because we're friends, and I want to understand you."

The two plop onto the ground, and Inez's gaze lifts to the clear sky. "I had a job interview this morning. I applied the day after you arrived. Most of my time away has been filled with applications, interviews, and phone calls. They called me in to say I got the job."

Blake's mouth falls open, eyes wide.

"Relax, I turned it down. But once I know how the challenge turns out, I'm done. I still plan on leaving this mansion."

"Why?"

"Fire betrayed my father. It's only a matter of time before it betrays me, but I can't seem to stop. I learned to juggle and use the aerial rigs so I can find a new love to embrace on stage. I try, but I can't put the fire down, no matter how much I want to or how sad it makes me. It's not just because of Rex either. Something else keeps pulling me back to it. I think if I leave, I'll be able to put it down for good."

"Will that make you happy?"

Inez purses her lips to the side for a moment before she shrugs. "I guess I'll find out."

Chapter 17

The day of the challenge, Blake and Inez take their seats in one of the center rows. The theater is small, with roughly sixty or seventy seats. Even so, it's much bigger than anything Blake could imagine in a home. Red fabric lines the walls between gold-painted columns. Cushioned chairs with red linen line the viewing area, so comfortable Blake could fall asleep.

A familiar chime goes off as he slouches in his seat, and he huffs as he pulls his phone from his pocket. *Mom again.* He sends her to voicemail and glances at Inez, who tilts her head at what just happened.

"Is Vladik coming?" he asks, avoiding eye contact, praying that she takes the subject change.

"He's watching from backstage," says Inez. "He's even more worried about Mishkin than we are."

"Well, he made it through the week, right? Maybe we're worried for nothing?"

"We can only hope," Inez sighs, staring blankly at the stage. "Celia hasn't looked so good either. I just want them both to make it out of this in one piece."

"They will." Blake places his hand over hers, but Inez yanks it back before he can grab it.

"Don't," she whispers, forcing her eyes to stay glued to the stage. Something in her eyes is hurting from this, almost apologetic.

A pang shoots into his chest, and he falls back into his chair with a sigh. That's how she feels. That moment in the rain might have been coincidence, but this was deliberate. She's not interested. He forces himself to applaud with the rest as Rex takes the stage to explain the purpose for this challenge, as if everyone didn't already know.

Blake's heart is tearing in his chest, begging him to run away, hide. He barely applauds when Allistair takes his father's place on the stage with a long, silk cape. The main lights dim, and warm colors light up the stage.

Allistair weaves a familiar tale about a doll so realistic that her maker falls in love with her. He believes she's coming to life at night. Allistair swirls his cape around his body, and it falls, revealing Axel in his place. Knox walks onto the stage with a toolbox and an apron.

Axel is beautiful, her face made up like porcelain, twisting her body in ways only a doll could. Knox stands behind, moving his arms to make it look like he is the one moving her. Every move matches the music perfectly, and the synchronization between the performers is flawless.

The yellow light fades into blue as Knox makes the move of a man falling asleep.

Axel moves on her own, and Knox's surprise sends a light chuckle through the audience. His expression turns from shock to wonder, and the two begin a beautiful dance, with Axel continuing to bend in unnatural ways. The deliberate fumbling is stunning, and their chemistry is incredible. She climbs onto his limbs, and he holds her up in beautiful poses.

The tone of the music shifts from dreamy to threatening, and the light turns red as a giant metal ring lowers from the ceiling. Maya storms onto the stage, eagerly dancing over until she stands face to face with Knox in sheer jealousy as Axel becomes still again. He tries to explain to her with exaggerated arm motions and awkward dance movements.

Unconvinced, Maya moves Axel into odd poses like Knox had done before. Just a doll. Knox and Maya burst into a scene of fast-paced acrobatics. They climb and hang on each other in moves and poses that resemble fighting. They flail about in chaotic poetry until their arms form a grid. Axel leaps back, using their locked arms as a boost to reach the bottom of the aerial hoop, pulling herself up to balance on her stomach. The audience cheers as she twists, twirls, and maneuvers her way to the top of the hoop, spinning as it lowers a bit more.

Maya and Knox grasp at the spinning hoop, slowing it down and struggling to reach Axel, who hangs from the rope rig at the top. Knox reaches with lust, Maya reaches with envy, and Axel's resulting wrath causes her to jump off the hoop. The lights go out. The audience screams until the lights come back on a second later. They scream again to find life-size doll parts scattered on the stage floor.

137

Allistair appears in a puff of smoke to finish with a speech about being blinded by lust and jealousy, and how one's actions can invoke another's emotions.

The audience erupts into applause as Allistair's team lines up to take a bow. His performers and crew members are all holding hands, enjoying the applause together. The aerial hoop rises as Rex steps on stage to praise Allistair. They leave the stage with waves and air kisses.

Rex's introduction of Ian is quick and simple, almost careless, but it carries a tone of importance. Blake blinks hard and furrows his brow at the apathy, darting his eyes to Inez, to the other members, and finally back toward the stage. He can't be the only one to have noticed.

Ian takes the stage and begins telling a story of how a person's soul is in a constant battle between light and dark. Good versus evil. The worst of it isn't the battle, but the inability to tell one from the other.

A long rope lowers from one side of the stage, and smooth, pink fabric fall from the other.

"The line is blurred into a landscape of gray areas," Ian announces as ominous music plays.

Xavier and Celia each step onto the stage, mirroring each other in a dazzling floor routine. They flip themselves into the air. Xavier grabs onto the rope, and Celia grabs the cloth. They twist and turn themselves into their rigs. Xavier's movements are lively, bold, like a violent storm. Celia's movements are elegant, smooth, like a river drifting under fallen petals. Two different styles to complement the same song.

Ian steps to the front of the stage, reaching a hand down, grabbing onto a familiar shape by the hand. "We all find ourselves in those vast, gray areas far too often!"

The music turns violent, and in one swift motion, Ian throws Mishkin onto the stage with one hand. Mishkin somersaults in the air, reaching out to the side, and he's caught by Celia, who pulls him gracefully into her silk. The two perform a stunning romantic routine. Their performance sends fiery crackles through the air, with a chemistry that sends chills across Blake's skin.

"We can never be sure whether our actions are good," Ian continues as Mishkin pushes himself from Celia's arms to fly across the stage.

Xavier catches him, holding the rope while Mishkin performs off his body, only grabbing the rope on occasion. Mishkin drops so that Xavier is holding him up by the waist. Their faces come heart-throbbingly close before Mishkin kicks himself off Xavier's legs, and Celia catches him again.

"Why is Mishkin the one switching?" Inez whispers as the audience cheers. "This can't be good for him. Someone else should be doing that part."

Blake hears her but isn't sure what to say. Mishkin looks so lively, so in control as he bounds back and forth, creating beautiful poses and stories with each performer. Even in their stage shows, Mishkin has never shone this brightly. He doesn't look as exhausted as he must be feeling. Has The Fools' Circus always hidden these kinds of secrets?

"In the end," Ian exclaims as Mishkin stops in the middle, a performer grasping at each arm, the aerial rigs slanted to reach him. "We all live and die in the cold, gray areas of right and wrong."

Mishkin's chest is heaving, his eyelids drooping, sweat dripping, and color draining from his face. The lights go out just as Mishkin's body goes limp. The audience lifts into a standing ovation, except Inez and Blake, who stand in silence.

It takes a while for the lights to come back on. Rex stands with Ian and Allistair on either side of him, encouraging the audience to vote for the best performance.

"Ian!" Vladik storms onto the stage at a surprising pace.

Ian lets out a high-pitched yelp and scrambles to climb the rope that hasn't been raised yet. Vladik grabs it from below to whip it in violent circles, shouting angrily in Russian. Ian is gripping for dear life, screaming for help as his body becomes a whirling blur.

Allistair throws himself onto Vladik's beefy arm, calming him just enough to let the rope go, but not enough to stop him from shouting in Allistair's face.

Ian climbs a few feet down, letting himself fall once he's close enough to the ground. Everyone stands in stunned silence, watching as Vladik yanks Allistair and Rex backstage, leaving Ian to pull himself away from the commotion, arms trembling, legs dragging behind him. He drops at the front of the stage, losing his lunch over the edge. The audience groans.

Inez and Blake shoot an understanding glance at each other, as if reading each other's minds, and rush to get backstage.

Behind the curtain, Allistair is performing CPR on an unconscious Mishkin, while Vladik continues to stomp and curse in red-faced fury. Ronan is putting on his jacket when he notices Blake and Inez.

"We're taking him to the hospital," he tells them. "Allistair, keep that CPR going in the car. Vladik. *Vladik*! There's no time; get Mishkin into my car!"

Vladik grunts in obedience and lifts his husband into his trembling arms, allowing the tears to pour down his cheeks. Allistair follows close behind, rushing out with Ronan.

Blake's eyes fall to Mishkin's arm, hanging from Vladik's grip. Dangling, lifeless, not even a twitch in response to the surrounding commotion. His fists clench, and he grits his teeth, each heavy breath making his blood boil hotter and hotter. He runs to Rex and grabs him by the shirt.

"You let this happen!" Blake screams, shaking Rex with every sentence. "You let Ian do this to him! And for what? What did anyone gain from this? You fucking pompous bastard!"

Blake raises a fist. Inez grabs his arm. Her mouth is moving, but he hears nothing beyond his own voice, continuing to spit curse words and threats to Rex's unwavering indifference. Celia pries his fingers open to free the apathetic Rex from his grasp. Xavier and Knox each grab an arm to drag him out of the theater. Inez follows, her mouth continuing to move, forming soundless words.

Outside the theater, Blake breaks free and runs back. He grabs the door handle when something collides with his face, stars filling his vision until everything disappears.

★★★

RINGING FILLS BLAKE'S EARS, splitting his skull. It fades as his sight comes back into focus. The sky outside his window is dark, and the ceiling light sends another jolt of pain through his head. At his side is a beautiful girl with short, strawberry-red hair.

"Blake," says Inez, "are you okay?"

"I'm great," Blake growls. "I love being punched in the face after seeing my friend unconscious." He turns on his side facing away from Inez, resisting the urge to add rejection to his list of grievances.

"Believe me, we're all pissed off at Ian. But you can't go after Rex like that."

Blake's body shoots to sit upright, lips pulled back like an angry dog. "Ian! Where is he?"

"Rex locked him in his room for the rest of the day. His form of punishment, I guess. He won't even let him eat until tomorrow."

"Good, fuck him," Blake hisses. "Let him starve to death."

"Blake, I know you're pissed. Believe me, so am I, but you really need to be more careful. I don't need you getting hurt, too."

"Too late for that." He bites his tongue, but the words left his mouth too quickly.

Inez tenses on the spot and drops an empty gaze to the floor. Blake lets out a long sigh, guilt wrenching in his chest. That was horrible of him; uncalled for. How long did she wait by his side under no obligation? She cares enough to be here; shouldn't that count for anything?

He scoots down to sit on the floor beside her and drops his head on her shoulder. "I'm sorry, Inez. For everything. I'm sorry you had to see me like that. I'm sorry for my attitude, too. I'm just...not thrilled about the bruise on my jaw. And I'm worried about Mishkin."

"I know, it's okay. No one is arguing, though. This shouldn't have happened."

"Did he wake up?"

"We don't know yet."

142

Chapter 18

The air hangs heavy in the mansion. Breakfast lines the table, but only a handful of people can eat. Those who have grabbed plates are taking their time, eyes glossed over as their minds travel elsewhere, and only a few of them manage to clean their plates. Throughout the halls, cast and crew members mumble among themselves about how terrible it all is. Echoes of "poor Mishkin" or "poor Vladik" or "Ian is a goner."

Word of Ian's cruelty had spread before, but the few who refused to believe it can no longer ignore his actions. Ian remains locked in his room. Given some of the whispers among the crowd, it's likely for his own safety. Blake and Inez sit in the lobby on a cushioned bench.

"I hate them both," Blake mumbles. "Ian and Rex. They both had their part in this."

"I know," says Inez. "But going up against Rex is a death wish. He's our king, and most of the people here love him. Unless you want to be in the same position as Mishkin, you need to be more careful."

"How can you say that?" Blake exclaims. "How does everyone just allow this?"

"No one is allowing this. They're all blaming Ian. Mishkin never had this problem before. The heart condition was always there, but it was Ian's terrible coaching that triggered this."

"And what do *you* think? Do you think I'm wrong to blame him? Rex put Mishkin on Ian's team for a reason, right? Even Allistair went along with it."

"Allistair puts his father on an untouchable pedestal. He won't believe that Rex would do something like this. I think you're right to be angry, but I don't think it's a good idea to point fingers so loudly."

Blake clenches his jaw and focuses his burning gaze on the floor. Flashes of Mishkin's limp body in Vladik's arms have been racing through his mind all night. The lack of sleep isn't making Blake feel any better now.

Allistair comes in through the front door, holding it open for Knox, Melody, and a crew member that Blake hasn't met yet. Knox has an arm around Melody's shoulder, his head hung low. Melody is wiping her eyes with her dress sleeve.

Allistair looks to them with a blank expression. "Inez and Blake, let's go."

INEZ SITS UP FRONT, and Blake slouches in the back, brooding at the circumstances. The weight of the silence in the car is making his chest ache. "Are there any updates?"

"Not yet," Allistair responds. "It could still go either way. His heart stopped, which means no oxygen was getting into his body. Even if he lives, there's a chance of brain damage."

Inez covers her mouth and Blake growls. "Mishkin is our friend!" he yells. "And hell, you've known him longer than I have! How could you let Ian do this?"

Allistair swerves into the breakdown lane, so fast that Blake's head hits the window. A car blares its horn behind him, and Allistair slams hard on the brakes, yanking all of them forward. He turns in his chair to glare at Blake.

"Don't you *dare* say that again!" he yells. "I didn't let Ian do anything. I tried to stop him, and he ignored me. I tried to get my father to cancel the challenge. And we couldn't because I had to fucking prove myself. I couldn't just take over. I had to prove I deserve it."

Blake glares back, body trembling, the bump on his head throbbing. Silence paralyzes them until Allistair turns to sit upright in his seat and covers his face with his hand. Inez lifts her crying eyes from where they were hiding in her hands.

"It's not that proving myself is bad or unfair. I get it, and I want the others to have a voice in the mansion. But Ian has always been this way. Always fighting back things that weren't against him to begin with. It's all his fault. He didn't obey the rules." Allistair's voice wavers. "When I'm in charge, people like him won't have a chance at my circus. I won't let people challenge each other out of pettiness. If it was anyone else, it would have

145

been out of integrity. I would've welcomed it. But it had to be *fucking* Ian."

Allistair leans his head on the steering wheel, his body quivering. "He challenged me out of spite. For no reason other than to stroke his own ego! And now Mishkin might…"

His voice trails off into a sob as Inez rubs Allistair's back. Blake's head is hanging low from his shoulders, and his own eyes are stinging. "I'm sorry."

Allistair lifts his head from the steering wheel, drying his face and forcing the tears back with a deep breath. "We have to get a grip. Vladik was there all night and can't stand any more water works."

"Can we stop to get flowers?" Inez asks, following his lead and fixing her own posture. Allistair nods as he pulls the car back to the street.

Silence drowns the rest of the car ride and nags at Blake's gut.

✯ ✯ ✯

THE THREE CREEP INTO THE ROOM where Mishkin lies on his back, an oxygen mask covering his mouth and nose. Vladik is lying next to him, pressing his lips to Mishkin's forehead. He stands as if the weight of the world is on his shoulders; the light in his eyes has dimmed. He trudges over to grab the bouquet from Inez and hugs her. "Thank you, Kroshka."

Blake steps over to look down at Mishkin, who may as well be naked without cat ears.

"Wow, you look almost human," he mutters, glancing at the others to make sure they don't hear him. "Got to wake up if you want to see what happens with me and Inez. You'd like that, right? Nosey cat."

Flashes of Inez's rejection flood his mind and his heart sinks. "Then again, I'm not sure there's much to tell."

Vladik squeezes Blake's shoulder, and Blake turns to hug him in response. "I'm so sorry."

"My husband is stronger than this," Vladik responds. "Since I met him, he's always made me jealous of his optimism."

"Do you mind if I ask how you met?"

Vladik sits on the bed next to Mishkin, gazing at his unconscious face with gentle eyes.

"In Russia, I had friend in neighborhood. I loved him. When I told my father, he beat me, saying how filthy I was to have such thoughts for other boy. I was boney, skinny child. How I survived is mystery. I told friend how I felt, and many friends with him beat me down, spit on me. At night, I snuck onto train. Traveled for days, back and forth, anywhere but home.

"They found me, threw me off in Italy. There I find frail boy doing handstands and flips on bridge. People threw coins into hat and cheered. It was amazing. I never saw so much energy from such a bruised, dirty child. His name was Alesandre. He lost his mother to abusive father and lived on street, but he was still so cheerful. I had to protect him. I worked out to build muscle, and soon I could lift him, and we worked together, his agility and my strength. My love grew every day, but I was afraid to say. So afraid his smile for me would turn to disgust.

"Then, Rex found us. Offered us food and shelter for performing in circus. I wasn't so sure, but Alesandre decided, optimistic as always. I couldn't let him go alone. When we arrived, they greeted us with warmth. Gave me courage to confess my feelings to Alesandre. Instead of being disgusted, we shared first kiss during Midnight Dance. He changed name to Mishkin, and we married

147

with Rex's blessing. I can't imagine life without him now."

"By the time I got there," Inez chimes in, "Mishkin was already wearing the cat ears. Vladik called me Kroshka because of a headband I was wearing."

"She had knot on top," Vladik chuckles. "Like rabbit ears. But she was also skittish, like bunny."

"These two helped me open up. Vladik was fifteen and Mishkin was thirteen. He was so excited to get the dermal piercings and fangs. I remember your wedding too. You guys had Black Forest cake, Mishkin's favorite."

"It was happiest day of my life," Vladik says with a smile.

A smile finds its way onto Blake's face, and he's doing his best to picture a tiny, skinny Vladik and a Mishkin who wasn't wearing cat ears. It warms his heart to know this kind of love exists in the world. He asks Vladik about some of his favorite memories with Mishkin, and he tells them with a new spark of life in his eyes.

As they chat away, Blake can feel his heart lifting again. While Allistair is throwing in a few memories of his own, Blake turns his attention back to the unconscious Mishkin.

You can hear all of this, right? We're all here for you, Mishkin. We're all waiting for you.

Wake up.

Chapter 19

"We've delayed preparations for the Blasphemer's Ball," says Victor. "We won't start until we know more about Mishkin's condition."

Blake nods from his seat in the office, heart pounding as he waits to hear his punishment for lashing out at Rex, who is—of course—standing right next to Victor. The tranquil demeanor about him somehow isn't comforting.

"On a lighter note," Rex says, smiling, "Victor will make you a suit as soon as he is able. He also likes to match suits for the couples. I must say, the set for Mishkin and Vladik is absolutely stunning. So, is there anyone you plan to attend the ball with, so you can match?"

Blake wants to say Inez's name, but her rejection flashes into his mind again, and his heart sinks. "No. No, I guess I don't."

"You see?" says Victor. "I told you, nothing to worry about."

Blake shoots a look at each of them.

"Inez and Allistair are childhood sweethearts," Rex explains. "I was concerned that Inez didn't like him anymore, but that can't be true. People don't just fall out of love so easily."

"So that's it?" says Blake. "You brought me here about a suit and Inez's relationship problems?"

"Not quite," says Rex. "I did ask you to find out where Inez has been going, but unfortunately we haven't had time to talk. So, what did you find out?"

Blake's heart leaps in his chest, but he clears his throat to hide it, trying to keep his voice steady. "Sorry. She hasn't told me anything."

"Is that so?"

Blake nods.

"I find that quite hard to believe, considering I saw her leave your room the other day."

"We were out," Blake pauses to consider his words, choosing them carefully. "Practicing. The rain got us. We could hardly see from all the water dripping down our faces. She left almost instantly."

"That must have been quite disappointing." Rex smirks.

Blake shrugs. "Not really."

"You can drop the apathy," says Rex. "I've seen the two of you practice."

"We get along," says Blake. "Practice is fun. That's about it."

"See?" Victor butts in. "The practice! Blake is a talented man learning a new skill. That's fun for those showy types. My brother was the same way—"

"Silence," Rex snarls at Victor, who shrinks in his seat. Rex turns his attention back to Blake with a softer smile. "So, your love belongs to your new skill, is that it? Your eyes trace Inez's body because you're in love with the poi?"

"I don't know what you're talking about."

"Do not confuse foolishness with stupidity," Rex's voice thunders through the office, sending a jolt of fear through Blake. Even Victor tenses at the shift in tone. "You're as transparent as a teenage virgin. Do you truly believe you have a chance with someone like her?"

A pang shoots through Blake's chest as the memory of her rejection pops up again. His eyes fall to the carpet beneath him.

"No. Of course I don't. But I also don't expect her to marry someone she doesn't even love. She isn't exactly the submissive, obedient type. But I'm sure you figured that out, already."

Rex's lip twitches, as if holding back a snarl. "You hardly know the woman. And based on your somber tones, I'm guessing you already confessed your feelings, and she turned you down, didn't she?"

Blake's shoulders slump as if they held weighted chains.

"That's what I thought. Don't fret, Pup. When you return home next year, you'll meet plenty of girls that are more in your league. After all, I can't deny that you are quite the handsome young man. It's just a shame your talents can't keep up."

Blake shrugs with gritting teeth, doing his best to pretend his blood isn't boiling.

"Rex, please," Victor mumbles, but Rex holds out a hand to quiet him. Victor shoots Blake an apologetic look before dropping his eyes back to his papers.

Thanks anyway.

"Say it," says Rex, his voice quiet, but stern. "Tell me you've given up your hopes of seducing our Fire Goddess."

Blake's head lowers as the chains get heavier. Rex's glare burns into his skin.

"No. I didn't tell her how I feel yet, but I will."

"Beg pardon?" Rex sneers.

Victor's wide eyes dart at Blake, and he shakes his head, making a slashing motion with his hand.

It doesn't matter. Rex has made it clear he won't renew Blake's contract at the end of the year, so it's not like he needs to kiss up anymore.

"You're right, I can't measure up to someone like Allistair. I can't compete with anyone around here. All logic points Inez in Allistair's direction. But emotions aren't always logical. I care about Inez. I want to be with her. I'll find out how she feels. If she turns me down, then so be it, but at least I'll know for sure." He stands from his seat and nods to Victor. "Thank you for the suit in advance. And Rex, I'm sorry for my outburst when Mishkin passed out. I know it isn't your fault. I just got carried away. Mishkin is my friend and I was worried."

"I understand," Rex says with a small smile. "It comforts me that you would look after my children as if they were family."

Blake turns and heads toward the door.

"One last thing," Rex calls. Blake stops, but he doesn't turn around, in case the hurt is showing on his face.

"If you insist on telling Inez how you feel, you have my blessing."

Yeah, right.

"But please understand—for as tough as she is, she is fragile at heart. I'm concerned for her. I need your word that whatever she decides, you won't force your feelings onto her."

His jaw clenches at the hypocrisy; at Ian's harassment and how long he let it happen. And how she couldn't do anything to protect herself if he's watching.

Choice words pile up at the back of his throat, begging for release, but he swallows them down. *Going against Rex is a death wish.*

"You have my word. I would never force Inez to do anything."

Blake hears Victor groan to himself but takes Rex's silence as a cue to leave, shutting the office door behind him. He heads toward the lobby and sees Inez sitting in stone-faced silence. He sits next to her, amazed at how, even in doubt, just being near Inez can lift his heart.

His conversation with Rex is replaying in his mind. He doesn't care what Rex thinks—he knows he has to ask Inez to the ball. He has to tell her how he feels as soon as he can. But he'll have to be more careful. Trying to kiss her or flirt won't get him anywhere.

"What did they say?" Inez asks.

Blake blinks hard to bring his brain back to the present. "Eh, most of it was about the ball. It's being delayed. Victor's going to make me a suit, though."

"Is that all?"

"That's all that matters," he says. "Listen, I know there isn't much I can do, but if you ever need a shoulder to lean on or someone to talk to, I'm right here. I know it's hard to reach out, but if ever you find the power to do so—"

"Thank you, Blake," says Inez as she lays her head on his shoulder, closing her eyes. "That's exactly what I need."

Blake sits in wide-eyed silence, heart racing as he slowly, gently puts an arm around her shoulders. She scoots herself closer, and a smile grows on his face.

So what if she turns him down later? He's still important to her, and that alone makes his heart soar.

The front door crashes open, making everyone around leap in response. Allistair darts in, standing in the middle of the lobby, looking around at the few scattered faces with an ear-to-ear grin.

"Mishkin's awake!" he shouts. "He's going to recover!"

Inez puts her hands over her mouth, and Blake catches his breath. The other scattered members approach him with new light on their faces. Allistair puts his hands up in defense. "He has a lot of tests and stuff today, so we can't visit until tomorrow. But he'll be okay!"

Allistair rushes down the hall, up the stairs, and takes a long lap around the second floor, shouting the joyous news at the top of his lungs. Everyone cheers, and the entire mansion seems to light up. Even the chains from Blake's office visit feel lighter.

Blake and Inez have smiles plastered to their faces. Blake looks over at Inez and becomes hypnotized by the glimmer of hope shining through her eyes. His eyes flick down to her lips, but she throws her arms around him, burying her face in his chest, staining his shirt with her tears. He pulls her in as close as he can. Whether she feels anything romantic or not, this is one of the happiest moments of his life.

Everything is finally okay.

Chapter 20

"**Y**ou played me like a fucking pawn!" Ian shouts with a finger pointed at Rex.

The entire mansion has gathered in the lobby to watch Ian leave. A small truck waits outside, already packed, and the black suitcase at his side is the last of his belongings.

He stands a few feet from the door, moments away from leaving the mansion for good. Rex stands in the center of the hall, arms crossed, and eyes narrowed.

"No, Ian," he says. "You have been harassing several of my fools for a while now. With lust, envy, pride, and wrath. I tried to keep my faith in you, but you've hurt fools who have done you no wrong. One has barely escaped with his life."

"You wanted me to put him in danger so you could look like a hero when you kick me out! And then your precious little son can take over, just like you wanted! It's that easy for you, isn't it?"

"The challenge was to play to each performer's talents. That was the rule. You, however, worked against your performer's weakness. That isn't a leader. You aren't a leader. If you had power, you'd be nothing more than a petty tyrant."

Ian pulls his lips back as he growls, clenching his fists and gritting his teeth.

Blake and Inez watch with Allistair and Vladik, who only came home an hour ago to gather fresh clothes for Mishkin. Blake is trembling in his spot, expecting Ian to lose his mind and throw another knife. Instead, he points his finger again.

"You're nothing but a schemer!" Ian shouts. "A selfish, pathetic excuse for a King!"

"Yes, of course," Rex chuckles. "I love you all and we've found a common ground for us to make a living doing what we love. I protect you and encourage you to inspire others. Of course, it's all because I'm selfish."

Rex gives a soft laugh, and a few others follow suit, while others scoff and shake their heads at Ian's accusations.

"You'll see!" Ian continues, gaze shooting around the others. "You're all disposable pawns to him! Just ask Ronan!"

Ronan steps back, shooting a wide-eyed look at Rex, who doesn't even glance his way. Vladik huffs, eyes blazing as he steps out from the sidelines to face Ian, who shrinks in his place. Ian braves up to give Vladik one last hiss, then whirls around and storms from the mansion, slamming the front door behind him. Blake's ears ring from the boom.

There's a moment of silence before the mansion erupts into cheers. Inez throws her arms around Blake with happy giggles, and Blake squeezes her. Allistair throws his arms around them from one side, and Vladik does the same from the other, lifting them all up with raucous laughter. Blake's ribs are being crushed, and he worries his spine might snap, but they're back on the ground after a second. They all laugh until Rex approaches them. His frown kills the mood in an instant.

He steps over to face Allistair, towering over him, and Blake is just now realizing how much Allistair looks like his father.

"He may be gone," says Rex, looking Allistair in the eye, "but you should know, I had two questions on each ballot. The first was who had the best performance, and the second was who they believed should be King. You won the popularity vote, but Ian won the challenge."

Blake's breath clutches in his throat, and Allistair goes pale. His eyes are wide, and he can't seem to get words out.

"You failed. If you intend to replace me, I expect much better from you. As it stands, I'm quite disappointed. I almost wish there were a third challenger."

Rex turns away without a single glance toward the others. He holds out his hands in a welcoming pose to the rest of the mansion. "Let the preparations for the ball begin!"

Cheers rise from the other members of the mansion, while Allistair's chin flops to his chest. His eyes haven't blinked the entire time Blake has been watching, and the color has left his face. Blake puts a hand on his shoulder, and Inez grabs his hands as Rex walks off without looking behind him. The other members rush around, getting their plans and materials, while others cook lunch as quickly as possible.

"Are you okay?" says Inez.

He doesn't respond.

"Allistair, snap out of it! Talk to me."

Allistair blinks back to life and forces a smile for Inez. "I'll be alright. I just have to work harder. Vladik, we can head back to the hospital as soon as you're ready. Did you grab clean clothes for Mishkin?"

Vladik nods and holds up a drawstring bag.

"Good," says Allistair, turning his attention back to Inez. "You and Blake have fun setting up. Thanks for being there."

He lifts Inez's chin and places a gentle kiss on her forehead before he turns to Blake with a smile. "Don't let her worry too much. We've all got a lot of work ahead."

Inez opens her mouth to speak, but Allistair is already leading the way out with his head high and Vladik close behind.

She crosses her arms with a light scowl. "I don't worry too much."

Blake chuckles. "Is it okay that he kissed you like that?"

"It didn't have the same intention as before, so it's fine. I'm more worried about what Rex said. He must be devastated."

"Should we stop him so you can talk?"

"No, I'll check in later. Right now, Mishkin needs him more."

PREPARATIONS FOR THE BALL continue the next day. Gold and purple fill the halls, and the mansion echoes with chattering, laughing, and orders being barked around. Some hurry by with boxes and rolls in their arms, while others settle themselves on ladders and stepstools to spread the colors around.

The Cat is returning, Ian is gone, and the ball is a week away. Inez and Blake help with decorations, sharing an enormous ladder to hang fabric across the ballroom ceiling. Blake isn't sure he's ever been so high up, but he's finally getting the hang of it with Inez's direction and reassurance.

The ladder shifts under them a few times, and Blake's heart almost gives way, but Inez's laugh makes him feel a little better.

A few others are helping along the ballroom floor, sweeping and setting up tables, wall decorations, and a DJ booth.

He helps Inez with the fastener before they descend the ladder and climb for the umpteenth time, Blake's legs quivering on the way up. He quietly hopes he won't have to practice today; His legs can barely hold him up anymore. How can Inez look so unfazed?

His phone chimes in his pocket, and he grunts in response. Inez asks if he wants to answer, but he shakes his head, already knowing who it is. He keeps the fabric in place while Inez fastens it, and it takes far too long for the ringing to stop.

He glances down to see a member leaving the ballroom and realizes the entire space is devoid of life. The decorations, as beautiful as they are, can't keep his heart from quickening its pace.

"I gotta be honest," he says, trying to sound as nonchalant as possible. "Mishkin and Vladik are the perfect couple."

"They are," Inez says with a smile. "Those two are like brothers to me. I don't know what I would've done if Mishkin didn't make it."

Inez puts the last fastener in place, and they're done. They climb down the ladder and wheel it to its closet, then marvel at the colors set across the ceiling like a big top circus tent. Gold and purple are the widest, with narrow black fabric in between. Blake's gaze lowers back to Inez. The awe in her eyes is nothing short of alluring.

"So Mishkin and Vladik are like brothers to you," he mutters, trying to hide the pounding in his chest. "And Allistair is a close friend of yours."

"Yeah."

"Where does that put me? What am I to you?"

Inez tenses, and she averts her eyes, darting her gaze around the floor. "Um, well. I don't know how to put it into words."

"Then let's make it easier. I'll ask a few questions. All I'd like is a yes or no. Simple enough?"

Inez's face is turning red, but she meets his gaze head on. "Yes."

"Good." Blake grabs both of her hands and laces his fingers between hers. "Is it okay for me to hold your hands like this?"

"Ye-yes."

"Are you sure?"

"Mm-hm." Inez nods, gripping his hands in return. "I like it."

Blake smiles and steps closer, his body barely touching hers. "Is it okay that I'm this close to you?"

"Yes," Inez breathes, her knees quivering against Blake's, making his own insides stir.

"Do you enjoy it?"

"Yes, I do."

Blake leans his forehead onto hers, locking their gaze together. "Last one. If I wanted to kiss you, would that be okay?"

Inez lets out a small gasp and tightens her grip on his hands. "Yes."

Blake's heart leaps in his chest. He's leaning in when the door opens. Allistair rushes through, looking the other way. Inez pushes Blake back before Allistair sees them.

"There you guys are! If you're done, we can go see Mishkin." He pauses, furrowing his brow at the red faces in front of him. "Are you two okay?"

"Yeah," Inez answers without hesitation. "We had some trouble getting the ladder back into the closet, and when you came in, we thought the ladder was about to fall or something. I guess we both got kinda startled."

"Oh," Allistair shoots a furrowed brow at Blake, who nods along with Inez. Allistair throws an unconvinced look at the two. "Sorry. Anyway, I promised Mishkin I'd bring you guys over. Shall we?"

Blake and Inez follow Allistair to the car, both avoiding eye contact and trying to appear as casual as possible. Blake bites his tongue to keep from smiling. He lost his chance again, but this time he's much happier about it. He has his answer.

★ ★ ★

THE HOSPITAL SEEMS BRIGHTER this time, and Mishkin is sitting up, eyes open, smiling as if nothing had happened. He has just popped a few grapes into his mouth when they walk in, and he kicks his feet with excitement, beaming with full cheeks and holding his arms out for hugs. Blake and Inez hug him together, all three in teary-eyed relief.

"How are you feeling?" Blake asks.

Mishkin's smile fades as he finishes his mouthful of fruit. He glances at Vladik and hangs his head low.

"Do forgive," says Vladik, standing to pat Mishkin's back. "His brain had some damage. He will get better, but right now his words are … how do you say? Jumbled."

"It's only temporary," says a nurse who comes in with a tray of hot dinner. "Don't look so down, Mishkin. You need to practice your speech if you want it to get better."

The nurse smiles at the trio, pulling her sleeves up her plump, dark arms. "It's nice to meet you all. My name is Joyce. I'm one of the nurses taking care of Mishkin."

"My name is Allistair," he says as he shakes her hand. "Can you tell us how he's doing?"

"Well, Mishkin is very lucky to have gotten here when he did. The brain damage he received is the bare minimum of what comes with cardiac arrest. His speech and fine motor skills will need some work. He might be a little dizzy or off balance, but it's nothing he can't power through with a little help and practice. He's been getting physical therapy here, but it looks like he can get by with some help at home."

"But he will get better, right?" asks Inez.

"I'm not sure how long it'll take, but yes. Conditions like his often improve with significant results. Provided, of course, that nothing like this happens again." She shoots an expectant look at Allistair.

"It won't," says Allistair. "I swear it won't. I won't let him go through this a third time."

Third?

Joyce smiles at him, then turns her attention to her patient. "So how about it, Mishkin? Are you ready to try eating?"

Mishkin shakes his head, looking at his visitors with concerned eyes. Joyce smiles at them again, making it clear she understands this look all too well.

"I'm sorry about this, but I have to ask you guys to come back later today or tomorrow. His fine motor skills still need work, and I think it might be a little embarrassing for him if everyone's here to watch. I hope you understand."

Mishkin shifts in his spot, head hung low. Blake steps over and gently pats Mishkin's shoulder. "Hey, don't worry, we'll be back tomorrow. You just focus on getting better, okay?"

Inez and Allistair both agree, and a smile forms on Mishkin's face. He throws his arms around Blake's waist, head nuzzling his chest. Blake throws his arms around him, ruffling his fingers through his hair and chuckling.

"Love you too, Mishkin."

Chapter 21

I nez opens her door just far enough for her face to peer
out, hiding her body behind the door.

"Hey, stranger," says Blake. "Can I join you for a
bit?"

Inez's face turns red before she steps aside. "Uh, yeah,
come in. What are you doing here?"

"I wanted to see you," he says as he steps in.

Inez closes the door behind him as he enters. He turns
to face her, and his eyes drop to her body. Her pajama
shorts cover little of her silky thighs, and her matching top
has spaghetti straps, one of them holding the top hem over
her breasts, and the other falling off her smooth shoulder.
He steps over with a hungry grin, gently trapping her
against the door.

"I didn't get my kiss. As it turns out, I couldn't sleep without it."

"You had to come for it now?" says Inez in a sharp whisper.

Blake blinks hard at her response, then purses his lips to one side. "I guess I could've waited, but I didn't want to. Hey, no big. I'll see you tomorrow."

He steps away and puts a hand on the doorknob. A soft smile grows when Inez grabs his arm to stop him.

"No. I mean, it's okay."

Blake releases the doorknob to hold her hand. "Inez, I care about you, and your comfort is very important to me. If you want me to stay, if you want to take things slow, or even if you don't care for me that way at all, I'd like you to tell me."

"You...care about me?"

"Of course, wasn't it obvious? I haven't exactly been subtle."

Inez drops her blushing gaze to the floor with a small giggle. "I'm sorry. I got the hint, but I thought it was my imagination."

"Well, that probably means I should be more direct too. I like you, Inez. A lot. I have for a while now, but I want you to be honest. Did you mean it when you said yes to everything in the ballroom?"

"Of course I did. I...I like you a lot too."

A smile grows on Blake's face. "So, what would you like now? I can stay or go, whichever makes you most comfortable."

Inez grips the legs of her shorts, staring at the floor under her shifting bare feet. "You can stay for a little while."

"Are you sure?"

"Yeah, I um—I like when you're around."

Blake smiles and makes his way toward her bed, looking around at her bookshelves and art pieces that line the walls. A book rests on her bed with a scrap of paper stuck between the pages. Blake lifts it to inspect the cover and flips it over to read the back. "You like to read?"

"Yeah, I really like fantasy. To be honest, I kind of wish I had magical powers, too. Being stuck here made me feel so powerless, so the thought of magic is just...better, I guess."

Blake puts the book back in its place before stepping over to put his hands on her hips. Her cheeks flush at his touch, as he leans his forehead on hers. "You are magical. You're an amazing woman. And so, so beautiful."

Her wide eyes make Blake's heart race as he draws his face closer, stopping just far enough to give Inez a choice. With her face burning red, she leans in to press her lips to his, gently at first, then harder, their lips parting to make the kiss deeper. Blake wraps his arms tight around her waist, Inez wraps hers around his neck, and their breathing becomes heavier, hungrier.

Finally. Blake trails kisses down Inez's neck, reveling in her soft moan and her body's heated response. "I've craved you for so long."

"Blake," Inez whispers, "this has to be a secret, okay? What you tried in the ballroom earlier, you can't do that. Anyone could see us."

Blake runs his fingers through her hair before kissing her forehead. "I'll do whatever you need. But what exactly is the danger?"

Inez lets out a heavy breath, pulling away from him to sit on her bed. She pats the space next to her, and Blake drops by her side.

"It's Rex," she mutters. "I finally turned down Allistair for good, and Rex might blame you for it. To be honest,

I'm not sure what he might do. I mean, you saw what happened with Mishkin."

"You told me that was all Ian's fault."

"No, Allistair did. I said everyone was *blaming* Ian. But it makes sense when you put the pieces together. Rex wanted Allistair to take his place, and Ian went against him. Ian has always been terrible. If Rex really cared about us, would he have waited until Mishkin almost died to fire him?"

"But how could he have known Mishkin would go into cardiac arrest?"

"I'm guessing he didn't. In his mind, he could kick Ian out for putting someone in danger or have him lose because he held back on his performance. That's probably why he had Axel on Allistair's team too. Either way, his son wins, just like he wanted."

Blake thinks back to his time at the office. His heart races when he remembers his bold confession. *I guess that means I'm next.* He leans his head on her shoulder, closing his eyes and swallowing down his anxiety. "Thank you for telling me."

"You'll keep it a secret, then?"

"Sure, but it'll cost you."

"Cost me what?"

Blake lifts his head to smile at her and plants his lips on hers. "That. As many as I want."

Inez giggles and scoots herself closer, leaning her head on his shoulder. Blake puts a gentle hand on her knee and raises a brow when her body shifts.

"Are you okay?"

Inez nods and hides in his neck.

"You don't like being touched, huh?"

"Not always." She wraps her arms around him. "But I like when you do it."

167

Blake lets out a breath of relief. He reaches his arm under her knees and swings her legs to rest over his, caressing her thigh while the other hand runs through her hair.

Inez tenses at the movement, but her body relaxes at his gentle touches. He drops a hand to her arm and caresses her smooth skin, the resulting goosebumps combined with the scent of her hair making his heart soar.

"Inez, I want you to feel comfortable talking to me. You don't have to tell me everything all at once, but I want to know that whatever happens between us, you're okay with it."

"I'm fine with whatever you want."

"Whatever I want?" Blake blinks hard. "That's not the Inez I've gotten to know so far. Where's that power kick I saw when Ian touched you?"

"Shut up," she scoffs. "I'm still getting used to this. It never mattered what I wanted before. But I do like you, and I don't need to kick you off of me. I don't know what else I'm supposed to do."

"What you want matters now, especially to me. I'm not here for my own pleasure, I'm here for us. Tell me what you do and don't want. Your desires, your hopes, your fears, everything. Little by little, day by day, let me get to know you."

"It'll take a while. I still don't really trust anyone, so I'm sorry to say I don't entirely trust you, either."

"You trust me enough to let me kiss and hold you. That's more than enough for the time being. We can take this as slow as you like. What can I do to make you happiest right this moment?"

Inez's frown lifts, and she bites her lip with a tiny grin. "I want you to kiss me." She points to where her neck meets her shoulder. "Right here."

Blake smiles and presses his lips to her smooth skin, his body heating up as her moan floats into his ear. He pulls away, but she pulls him back to press her lips to his. She pulls away to shoot him a mischievous grin.

"Now I want a pony."

"Sure. Let me just pull out the thousands of dollars I definitely have."

Inez giggles, and Blake squeezes her, chuckling along. She hides her face in his shoulder, relaxing in his arms.

"I lied," she confesses. "I'm not okay with everything, not yet. With Allistair, whatever happened was fine in the moment. It even seemed okay to kiss him. But later, when I thought about it, all I had was regret. I shouldn't have let it happen but saying no felt dirty and ungrateful; Like I wasn't allowed to. Like I owed him something for being a friend. But then he wanted more, and I couldn't stand the thought of regretting something like that. And right now, I can't stand the thought of regretting any of this. With us."

"I'm proud of you." He places a gentle kiss on her forehead. "Don't let me do anything you're not comfortable with. Not even kissing."

Inez hugs him tighter, and Blake pushes her away to look at her with narrowed eyes. "You *are* comfortable kissing me, right?"

"Yes," Inez laughs. "I said that!"

"Good. Just checking." He gives her one more kiss before he pulls her close again. Inez breaks into a fit of giggles, and his heart lifts at the sound. He kisses her head, taking in the enticing smell of her hair, the smooth skin on her thigh, her warm breath on his neck. A yawn sneaks up on him too fast for him to block it.

"Getting tired?" Inez asks.

"A little."

"Do you want to leave, so you can get some sleep?"

"Absolutely not."

Chapter 22

Blake strolls through the backyard, enjoying the sunrise, lost in the beautiful memories of Inez that kept him awake even after he left her room. The smooth touch of her skin, the delectable taste of her lips, the melodious sound of her laugh.

He's passing through the empty aerial rigs when a black shadow flies down in front of his face, making him leap back with a yelp.

"I'm home!" says the figure with a catlike grin and a leather jacket, hanging on a branch by his knees. "Did you miss me?"

"Mishkin!" Blake stomps his foot as Mishkin pulls his legs between his arms to let himself down. "You shouldn't be climbing around after you've just had your heart stop!"

"I'll be fine. It's strenuous exercise I need to stay away from."

Blake shakes his head, but a smile quickly replaces his frustration, and he throws his arms around him. "I'm so glad you're back!"

"Aww, and here I thought you didn't like me!" Mishkin chuckles before Blake pulls away. "So, it's been a few days. What's the latest on you and Inez?"

"Actually, last night…"

Mishkin puts his hands on his face. His jaw drops, and he takes in a long gasp.

"Don't get too excited! We just kissed."

"Right, it's still early. So, is it official?"

"Sort of. She wants to keep it a secret. From Rex."

"That's smart. Probably good to keep it from Allistair too. At least for now, with the timing and all."

Blake agrees, and a shadow looms into his mind, remembering how Mishkin got to the hospital. He turns his attention to the mansion towering over them with a new air of menace.

"Do you think you'll still enjoy being here? Even after everything that's happened?"

Mishkin sighs and kicks at the grass. "I know it looks bad. Well, scratch that, it *is* bad. But I love the stage. I love what I do. I love living here with Vladik and Inez, and you, of course. Rex saved us, and takes care of us, and has everyone convinced he has their best interest at heart. I did too, until I woke up in the hospital. I want to speak up, but I can't do anything that would leave me back in the streets. No one here knows how to make it out there. Rex kept us powerless, and that gives him every advantage."

"What would happen if Inez told them she wanted to leave?"

"I don't know. So far only one person has left, and I think she's still struggling. She called me a few times, saying how rough it is to not have such a large family anymore. It was hard for her to hold down a job for a while. Eventually, she got pregnant and stopped calling. I guess she became too busy, but she'd been doing better by then. At least I hope so."

"So, it is possible? I could just ask them to let me leave with Inez?"

"Not right now. Remember, you're under contract for a year."

"But it's possible, right?"

Mishkin frowns at him. "You fought so hard to be here, and you're ready to give it all up?"

"I wanted to join because you and the others inspired me. But if this is what your ringleader is like, it's not worth it. Besides, Rex made it clear he isn't going to renew my contract. I've already lost his favor."

Mishkin purses his lips before he shrugs. "Well, you've still got a whole year. You still didn't tell me much about what happened last night."

"Oh, right." Blake lets out a heavy breath, trying not to get carried away with this new information. It would be good to talk to Inez about it later. He scratches his head and searches through his memories for details that aren't too personal. "Sorry, not sure what else to say. We just admitted we liked each other. Although she seemed really nervous about everything. Even as I held her, she was much more timid than I expected. Has she always been like that?"

Mishkin chuckles. "Not from what I've seen, but it's really not that shocking. Rex has been intimidating her since day one, so of course she's kept her guard up. My guess is she can relax around you, and it scares her."

"I see. But I want her to know that she's safe with me. I want her to be open with me. To trust me."

"She won't do that so easily. You have to prove she can trust you. I wish I had some clever advice, but I've never seen Inez make goo-goo eyes before, so I don't have much practice in that department. I always figured she was the lone wolf type."

"You've never seen her date anyone?"

"No, I've seen her date. I've just never seen her care so much."

Blake chuckles as Vladik approaches them, putting a hand on Mishkin's shoulder. "My love." He turns to Blake. "My friend. We should go inside. To be outside today is to catch death."

Mishkin nods, and the three hurry inside, where a large group is waiting to greet and hug the beloved Cat. Blake's eyes instantly land on Inez, capturing the image of her genuine smile in his mind—a smile he wants to see every day.

Leaving with you wouldn't be a loss. I don't need to be on stage. I need to be by your side.

Chapter 23

The light of the moon fills the mansion halls with a blue hue, and Inez sits outside her bedroom door, a folded blanket clutched under one arm. The usual shorts and spaghetti strap top have been replaced by purple fleece that covers her arms and legs in loose folds. Her face lights up as Blake approaches her.

"What's going on?" he asks.

"I want to show you something," says Inez as she stands. "But you have to be as quiet as possible, got it?"

Blake agrees, and Inez grabs him by the wrist with a giggle, hurrying toward the stairs that lead to the third floor. Blake freezes at the bottom, making Inez stop and tilt her head at him.

"Are we allowed up there?" he whispers, looking around for potential witnesses.

"Not at night. That's why I said to be quiet. Come on!"

One more tug at the arm, paired with that adorable smile, and Blake is putty in her hands. They scurry through the halls, the tile floor like ice on his bare feet, and both are doing their best not to stomp or say a word. Blake can't help but wonder if Inez is as nervous as he is, though he's convinced she isn't afraid of anything.

The halls on the third floor are lined with double doors and much larger plaques. One catches his eye as they hurry past it. The world around him slows as he examines the words.

ALEXANDER BRANDT
A.K.A. REX - KING OF FOOLS

This should worry him, but he wishes Rex could see him and Inez together now, on a midnight adventure, alone and intimate. He imagines himself kicking the door open with both middle fingers in the air. A grin creeps onto his face as the plaque falls further behind him, and time goes back to normal.

So much for not being good enough, my King!

Inez leads him to a lion statue against the far wall and smiles at him. "Watch this!"

She places her hand under the lion's chin, and something clicks before Inez slowly pulls it to the side. A loud screech echoes through the halls, making Blake catch his breath and look around for a response, his primary focus being Rex's door.

Inez seems startled too, but her surprise turns to giggles as she pulls the statue to the side. A gust of wind rolls around them, and in the wall is a narrow hall with a concrete staircase.

The space is a bit wider than Blake's shoulders, and the ceiling is barely high enough to stand. The edges of the stairs are jagged and chipped, with dust and spiderwebs lining the corners. The top of the staircase is shrouded in darkness until Inez flips a switch and a dim light flickers, barely making the steps visible.

"Follow me," she whispers. "And close the door behind you."

Inez crouches down under the doorway, hurrying up the steps. On the other side of the lion statue is a latch. Blake lifts it and closes the door as quietly as possible. When he turns around, Inez has disappeared behind a black frame door with twisted bars over a hammered glass surface.

Blake steps through, closing that door behind him as well, and his jaw drops at the view.

The night sky is a deep indigo, with pinprick stars spread into every corner. The changing leaves shiver in shades of blue and purple in the darkness, with black branches showing through the holes where leaves had fallen.

Inez leans on metal fencing similar to the door at the patio's edge, gazing into the night sky as if Blake didn't even exist. He steps behind her, wrapping his arms around her waist and pulling her in to lay his head on her shoulder. She rests her arms over his and leans her head onto him.

The silence that embraces the two has never felt more calm, more comfortable, and in it, Blake feels at home. He lifts his head to look her in the eyes for a second before pressing his lips onto hers. When he pulls away, Inez is smiling at him with sparkling eyes.

"This is beautiful," he whispers, kissing her again. "Thank you for bringing me."

"I thought you'd like it. I used to come here all the time. But years ago, Ronan fell and got hurt. He was hand walking along the rail, and he slipped. No one was around to see it or get help, so he was out here for hours, calling and pleading, with a broken arm. Rex decided it was too dangerous, and he wouldn't let us up here anymore."

"Why was Ronan walking the rail in the first place?"

"I don't know. He used to be an acrobat, so it's not surprising that he would try something like that for no reason. Plus, he was a daredevil. No sense of mortality in his teenage years. Besides, lots of us do stupid things in the name of performance. Hell, I fucking eat fire, remember?"

Blake chuckles. "Good point. So, no one's been up here since?"

"I think everyone forgot about it." Inez gazes up at the night sky. "But I could never forget those stars."

"They're beautiful. My mom used to tell me the stories behind the constellations, and how people use them for fortune telling."

Inez smiles. "I've never believed in that kind of thing. My uncle used to tell me that life would give me signs when I'm uncertain. But I learned as a kid that nothing good comes without effort. I wasn't *born* a fire spinner, I had to learn it, and practice. Why bother looking for a sign when you can just decide what you want and make it happen?"

"That makes sense. But you can believe and still make things happen for yourself. I like to think about the stories and horoscopes, but if fate existed, I'm sure I would've met you much sooner."

"Well, you know me now, and fate had nothing to do with it."

"What if it did?"

"Then I guess you're stuck with me for a while."

Blake smiles, taking in his own view of the night sky.

An icy wind whirls around them, and despite having chosen a warmer set of pajamas, Inez grabs her arms and shivers. Blake grabs the blanket from against the rail and spreads it over their shoulders.

The two sit against the mansion and Inez settles herself on his lap so she can spread the blanket over both of them. She rests her head on his shoulder as they gaze into the sky.

"So," he mumbles after a moment of silence, "about the ball…"

"If we go together, we have to pretend we're just friends," says Inez. "We can't kiss or anything."

"And the Midnight Dance?"

"We can sneak away and come back here. I don't believe in that dumb superstition anyway."

"Right," says Blake, pulling her close and fixing his gaze back into the sky. She'll go with him to the ball, so why is he disappointed? It's just superstition, right? It's fun to consider, just like the stars. *But imagine if that's all it took.*

A warm hand caresses his cheek, and Inez pulls him into another kiss, this one much harder than the last, sending ardent desire through his veins. Their lips part, and the kiss becomes wetter. Inez pulls away too soon, but she rests on his shoulder again, her warmth relaxing his muscles.

He presses his lips to her temple, then rests his head on hers. This all feels too good to be true. What made him hesitate to say something sooner?

A sinister grin pops into his mind with a bald head and a switchblade.

179

"I think you should know," he mumbles. "A little while ago, Ian told me you used to be his girlfriend. Sorry, I should've said that sooner."

"What?"

"I don't care if it's true," Blake continues. "I just thought you should know that that's what he was saying. I've seen how people talk in this place."

Inez sighs. "It's true. I wasn't trying to hide it or anything. I would've told you eventually."

Blake tenses in his spot, the Blade Master's arrogant grin flashing into his memory. The remarks he made while he had his crotch in Blake's face echo through his mind. *He wasn't lying.* He hoped he was.

Ian is dangerous, and the threat to Inez's safety makes his stomach churn. *What did he do to get what he wanted?*

"I was curious," Inez continues, "and I never thought of Allistair that way. I was sixteen, and Ian was twenty-five."

Blake tightens his arms around her, breath shuddering from more than the cold. "Inez, he didn't…"

"Not in the way you're thinking. I gave him consent in the moment, and I meant it, but looking back, it's obvious he just said whatever he had to. At the time, it didn't feel sinister. I had no idea he would turn out to be such a creep. It didn't even worry me that it was illegal. His words sounded caring, and I would've done anything to feel loved again. Not that I fell in love or anything. His true nature showed after a while."

A long, shaking breath escapes Blake as he rests his head on her shoulder. Inez rests a comforting hand on his arm.

"Come on now," says Inez. "I'm sure you've had your own unpleasant experiences, right?"

"A few. I had a couple girlfriends throughout high school, and one in college before I dropped out. She was the worst. She hated everything I did, and juggling pissed her off because she associated it with clowns. She was afraid of them. *Terrified.* But when it came to sex, she was more eager than I was. I didn't mind too much, until I found out that she was sneaking around behind my back, and I finally broke up with her."

"That's awful."

"I got payback. The other guy was clueless, so I got his help. We hid some clown masks in random parts of her dorm room and rigged a few of them to pop out at her. Then we used small clown toys in smaller places. We put together a life-size clown in her living room and waited in the hall for her to run out. We dumped her together, and the look on her face was priceless."

Inez bursts into laughter. "I can't believe you! That must have been a great day!"

"A great week, actually. She didn't find the clown stuff all at once, so her screaming fits went on for days. We hid them everywhere. Every single drawer, every cupboard, behind every door. They had to call campus police to find them all and make her stop. I think there were...seven? Maybe eight that she didn't find."

Inez laughs again, and Blake chuckles along as the memories flood his mind. His smile vanishes when he remembers how this conversation started.

"I won't lie, I'm still stuck on you and Ian. Even if you did give him consent, it's disgusting he'd stoop that low; to pray on you as a child."

"He never stopped trying to make me do it again, but I decided I'd rather be alone forever than stuck in some fake romance."

181

"Same here." Blake rests his head against hers. "But having you in my arms is nice too."

Inez smiles and presses her lips on his. "What else did Ian say?"

"Typical, jealous ex stuff. 'Stay away from her' and 'if you touch her I'll kill you,' and blah blah blah."

Inez scoffs and leans to her side, guiding his hand to the back of her pants. "Oops, you're touching me. Guess you're in trouble now."

A low, hungry chuckle escapes Blake's throat as he tightens his grip on her ass and kisses her neck.

Inez shifts so her back is to his chest, and he buries his face into her hair as his hand slides from her ass to her hip. He slips his hand up to her neck and gently presses one side as his lips tease the other.

Her scent is beautiful, and her skin is like silk. Her heavy breath sends chills through his body before he trails his lips back up and onto hers. He parts his lips to push his tongue into her mouth while her hand reaches up to run her fingers through his dark hair. Her other hand caresses his thigh, squeezing as their breathing gets heavier. Her touch sends sparks over his skin, the sounds of her pleasure are like wine, and damn, he's already intoxicated.

Blake runs both hands up her shirt and onto her bare sides, giving her a chance to push them back down. She nudges them up instead and moans as he cups her braless breasts, running his thumbs over her nipples. They fit perfectly in his hands, soft and warm, and he lowers his lips to her neck, nibbling her skin after a few soft kisses.

His hand slithers to her lower stomach, fingers stopping just under her pants, waiting for her prompt as he lifts his head to nibble her ear. With a lift and shift of her hip, Blake's hand moves further down. He kisses her neck again, and his fingers don't hesitate to push themselves just past the lips, enjoying the wet space in between as Inez whimpers, pushing her back against his chest and hiding her face in his neck. He wraps his free arm around her and holds her close as his fingers tease her entrance.

Yes, that sound. Keep making those sounds for me.

Her breath is right in his ear as two fingers push themselves inside her, his thumb circling her clit. He's so caught up in her body that he's only now noticing that her hand is in his pants, grabbing him, caressing his length, and pulling a low groan from deep in his throat.

The space under the blanket heats up with desire, until Inez arches her back, releasing one last moan as her hand grows tighter on his cock. Her walls twitch against his hand, and she rubs him faster, until Blake holds her tighter, groaning, trembling in her grip as the warm liquid covers her hand and soaks his pants.

A few more kisses, and their blanket is no longer enough to protect them from the autumn chill.

Chapter 24

At dinner the next evening, Blake and Inez sit near Mishkin, Vladik, and Allistair, wrapped in conversation and laughter. In the middle of his sentence, Mishkin's knife slips as he cuts his chicken parmesan, and he stares at his plate in frustration. He isn't hurt, but the others stare at him in concern as he glares at his trembling hands.

"Be patient, my love," says Vladik. "Your brain needs time to heal. I cut for you."

Mishkin mopes toward the floor with reddened cheeks as Vladik cuts Mishkin's dinner into chunks.

Blake's heart sinks before he forces a smirk and nudges Inez with his elbow. "Will you cut *my* food for me?"

"What?" Inez barks. "Fuck off! I'm not your mother!"

"Vladik is doing it for Mishkin!"

"Mishkin almost died, butt munch! You're fine!"

Blake continues to pester Inez, and a tiny smirk forms on Mishkin's face before he laughs at their banter.

Allistair slams his empty glass down that the group becomes still. A few others turn from their own conversations to stare as well.

"How cute," says Allistair. "You two argue like a couple."

"Oh, please," Inez scoffs. "You know what he's doing."

"Yeah, calm down," says Blake. "I was just trying to cheer Mishkin up, that's all."

"Of course, silly me. If you were a thing, I'm sure Inez would've told me by now. We are friends, and friends tell each other everything, right?"

"Of course," says Inez.

Allistair nods, and they continue their meal in silence. Mishkin mopes again as he continues eating, hand still trembling.

When they finish, Inez and Vladik gather everyone's plates. Blake offers to help, but Mishkin holds him back. When they're out of earshot, Mishkin leans over the table toward Allistair.

"What was that about, Prince? I gotta say, jealousy really isn't your color."

"I'm not jealous," says Allistair, standing from his seat with a grin. "Why would I be? Inez wouldn't fall for such a plain guy. Especially not one who's only real talent is juggling."

Blake bites his tongue and lowers his glare to the table. Allistair waves them off and heads back to the stairs, leaving the two friends glaring into his back.

"He knows something's up," says Mishkin. "I've never seen him so mad before."

Blake shifts his jaw. Bickering with Inez wasn't his best idea, but if Mishkin was able to notice his feelings for Inez, of course others would too. Victor's warning about having to be sneaky rings in his mind, and he makes a mental note to be more careful. He sighs, taking a moment to check for anyone who might be close enough to listen.

"Be honest with me. Do Inez and I look that bad as a couple?"

Mishkin leans an elbow on the table to rest his head on his hand. "At first glance, yeah. With the timing, and Allistair, it does look sketchy; like you stole her or something. Not everyone will believe that what you have is real. But knowing you guys personally, and what you're all about, I think you two are adorable. And so will everyone else. Eventually. Don't stress about it so much. But maybe try to keep the flirty stuff to a minimum. And thanks for that."

Blake smiles as Inez and Vladik come back. The crew members prepare for another night around the fire pits, and everyone rushes to their rooms to bundle up and gather instruments and various props to take with them.

Blake makes it outside before Inez and waits for her with Vladik and Mishkin next to a fire pit. Another phone chime rings into the air, and he's quicker than ever to send it to voicemail, scanning the audience to make sure no one notices.

Maya is first in the line of freelance performances, her black hair in pigtails and an excited grin on her face. She holds a dark-colored hoop in one hand, and with a flick of the other, it glows pink. The audience cheers as she twirls and spins the hoop around her. She carries it over her body and releases it with a flick, the slight wiggle of her hips keeping it in on her body as she spins it to the rhythm of the music. Her arms dance around her as her movements guide it over her chest and down to her knees and back up again.

Inez plops herself onto the ground next to him, handing him the same blanket from the night before. He raises a brow at her with a smirk.

"No." Inez smiles and Blake chuckles, his eyes transfixed on the fire pit's glow against her face, sparkling in her eyes.

"You're stunning."

Inez's smile vanishes, and she turns her focus to Maya, avoiding his gaze. "Blake, you know you can't."

"Right." He follows her sightline and applauds with everyone when Maya's routine finishes. Vladik takes her place with Mishkin and some kettlebells when Blake glances at the clouds looming in the sky, wondering if tonight's fire pit will be cut short.

A few minutes of tossing and leaping goes by, and Blake bites his lip, begging Mishkin not to push himself too much. Their performance finishes without Mishkin breaking a sweat, and Blake's applause is louder than everyone's.

Inez stands from her spot beside him, her poi dangling at her side as she takes her place. She fuels up and lights her poi fairly quickly, and Blake tilts his head.

Compared to her last show, this performance seems almost too quick. Last time, her props were already fueled, and she took her time tracing the flame to her skin and creating a dynamic with everyone.

187

Instead, her head is low, and her face is blank. The movement of her poi is slow, as if her arms have lost their strength. She's not lost in the flames, but she's lost somewhere else; a place that stole the color from her face, and the light from her eyes.

Blake grabs his set of poi, already fueled, and makes his way over. He swings them to light with hers and curves his arms around her before she can protest.

"What are you doing?" She asks, barely audible over the roar of the flames.

"We've been practicing together, right? We should perform together to show our progress."

"What if they think something?"

"Then we pass it off as being friends who perform well together. No big. Besides, Rex stayed inside tonight."

The crowd cheers as their arms weave and wrap around each other.

Inez lets out a smirk. "Fine, but you better keep up."

She whips herself around and swings her poi in familiar patterns, and a grin grows on his face as he follows along. His heart soars at the trails that whip themselves around, like a fiery sanctuary built just for the two of them. The applause fades behind the roar of the flames, and Inez's mood seems to lift in the glow that illuminates her skin. Her gaze lifts in awe of the lines and shapes, and the heat that embraces them.

"IS SOMETHING ON YOUR MIND?" Blake asks as he and Inez sit on her bed. A sudden downpour caused the performances to move to the indoor stage. Inez asked him to sneak away with her, and Blake wasn't about to refuse any amount of alone time with her.

"Nothing you need to worry about," Inez responds, turning her face away, fiddling her fingers in her lap. The sound of the rain pounding against her bedroom window fills the air with a silence that's no longer comfortable.

Blake puts a hand on her chin and guides her face toward him. "I've learned something about you."

"What?"

"You turn your head away when you're hiding something. You do it every time, and I don't really appreciate it. Please talk to me. What's going on?"

Inez's lips tighten, and her eyes shift to the side as Blake's hand lowers. "You know how I came outside later than everyone else?"

"Yeah."

"Well, it was because Rex asked me to see him tomorrow morning. Alone."

A shadow of dread looms over Blake's shoulders. "Did he say why?"

"No. I don't know why I'm scared. I just have a really bad feeling in the pit of my stomach. It doesn't help that he wasn't out with us tonight. Allistair wasn't there, either."

"It doesn't matter what happens. I'm here for you. Mishkin, Vladik, Celia, we're all here for you." Blake places a gentle kiss on Inez's head. "You're not alone in this, okay?"

Inez leans her face onto Blake's shoulder, her trembling hands gripping his shirt. He wraps his arms around her, flashing back to Allistair's behavior at the table. *What did you say to him, you bastard?*

Minutes creep by before Inez pulls away and yawns, rubbing her eyes.

"Want me to leave?" he asks.

"Please don't."

189

"You should get some rest."

"Only if you promise not to leave."

"You...want me to stay the night?"

Inez's face turns red, and she darts her eyes to the floor. She nods a little, and Blake plants a delighted kiss on her head. "I'd love to. But is that a good idea?"

"You can wait until breakfast, leave after everyone else, and no one will notice where you came from."

"Well then." Blake lifts her hand and presses his lips to her knuckles. "Princess, I am your loyal protector for the night."

Inez giggles as she grabs his face in her hands and plants a long, hard kiss on his lips. She pulls her pajamas from under her window and pulls off her shirt. Blake watches as she takes her bra off, admiring her smooth skin. His eyes land on long, thick lines of scar tissue on one side of her back.

"Can I ask what those scars are from?"

Inez freezes for a moment, and Blake almost tells her that she doesn't have to answer, but she continues changing.

"Remember when I told you that the ceiling fell on me and my father?"

"God, I'm so sorry." He stands and wraps an arm around her bare waist and leans his head on her shoulder. He traces his fingers along each scar as Inez puts a comforting hand over his arm, still topless. "I shouldn't have asked. That must be hard to look back on."

"No, I'm glad you did," Inez mumbles. "And I'm glad you saw them. You should know that not every part of me will be beautiful, or even likeable. But I want you to see all of it. Now that I trust you, I don't want to hide anymore."

"You don't ever have to hide from me."

190

She turns to him with a smile and plants a gentle kiss on his lips. "Thank you for staying."

"I'm not going anywhere."

"Well can you go over there so I can finish getting dressed?" She smirks.

Blake scoffs and rolls his eyes. "Fine, I guess." He plants one more kiss on her forehead before he steps away to sit on the bed.

Once her fleece pajamas are on, she drops herself onto her pillow with a huff. "This is stupid. I'm really not looking forward to seeing Rex's arrogant face first thing in the morning."

Blake laughs as he settles himself next to her. "Well you'll get to see me before you go."

"That's true," she mutters. "Thank you for being here. And for understanding."

"No need to thank me." He caresses her cheek and kisses her again. "Get some rest."

"It'll be a while. I usually read before I fall asleep."

"So read."

"No, that'd be rude."

"Then read to me."

"I'm already halfway through."

"So? Just give me a quick recap."

Inez giggles and grabs her book from the other side of the bed. Blake settles under the blankets and melts when Inez sinks into his arms.

She tells him the story that she's read so far, and Blake kisses her before she starts reading, slipping his tongue into her mouth to make it last just a little bit longer.

"Go ahead. I'm listening."

Inez shifts into a cozier spot and holds the book over them to read. Blake closes his eyes, smiling as her voice shifts the tone to fit the mood.

191

He chuckles when she tries to imitate a man's voice for one of the characters, and she taps his chest. He mimics her, and she threatens to stop reading until he apologizes, promising to be quiet from now on.

Soon the chapter is finished, and she yawns as she marks her page and sets the book aside. Before she can close her eyes, his arm is around her, pulling her close so that her face is against his chest.

"Is this okay?" he asks.

Inez nods, and Blake's finger gently glides up and down her back. A small, relaxed sigh escapes her lips, and Blake's heart lifts.

It doesn't matter if they still have to hide. It doesn't matter if he doesn't get his Midnight Dance. Nights like this are perfect. He'd trade a thousand superstitious dances if it meant every night with Inez would be like this.

His eyelids grow heavy, and Inez wraps her free arm around him. The slamming rain on the glass continues, lulling the world into black.

Chapter 25

Blake's arm pats the bed next to him, and he sits up quickly when he realizes she's gone. *She must have already left to meet with Rex.*

He gets a chill up his spine at the thought of what he might say to her. He flops onto his back and stares at the ornate designs on the ceiling, trying to focus on their happiest moments together to ease his nerves.

Instead, his mind goes back to Allistair's outburst. If Rex is as angry as he was, whatever he says will weigh on Inez's shoulders. Maybe he should take her out for breakfast to help her feel better.

He didn't get to the last time he tried, and now it can be an official date. He can't resist smiling at the thought.

With a clear blue sky outside, there's no chance of their plans getting rained out again.

The door opens, and Blake leaps to a sitting position like a puppy. "There you are! How did it go?"

Inez doesn't answer. Her face turns to the side, eyes straight ahead, glazed over. She closes the door softly.

"Damn, was he that bad?" Blake's heart sinks as he hurries to her. "I'm sorry, sweetheart. Why don't we go out for breakfast, and we'll talk about it, okay?"

"Get out," Inez mutters, keeping her eyes glued to a distant spot away from him. Her voice is quiet. Flat.

Blake freezes, lowering his arms that were about to hold her. "Inez, tell me what happened."

"Nothing happened. Leave."

"You're hiding again."

"No, I'm not."

Blake places his hand on her cheek, only for Inez to smack it away. "Don't touch me! Don't ever touch me! Not ever again!"

Blake furrows his brow. "Inez?"

"Just leave!" She shoves him aside with her elbow and hurries to the far corner of her room, crossing her arms as she focuses her attention on the morning outside her window. "Get out of my room! You never should've been here."

A moment of silence creeps between them, slowing the seconds to an hour.

"I get it," Blake sighs. "You need some alone time. I'll go, but can you explain everything before the ball?"

"Forget the ball. I'm not going with you."

"Inez," Blake rushes to her side, only for her to continue turning away. "You need to stop this, okay? Talk to me. What happened up there?"

"I told you, nothing happened. I lied."

"What?"

"I lied about everything. I never liked you, I was just stuck with you. But you're done now. You passed. And I sure as hell don't want to be seen at the ball dancing with some pampered little Pup!"

A pang shoots through Blake's heart as his breath wavers. "Inez, please—"

"Don't you get it? I had to hide because it's embarrassing! *You're* embarrassing! I could *never* be with someone like you!"

Blake takes a step back with a clenched jaw. "I don't believe you. Look me in the eye and say that again. At least tell me why!"

"I don't owe you anything, Pup! Get out!" Inez shoves him to the side to storm to her bed and hide her head under her pillow. "Get out before I kick you out!"

The weight of her words threatens to make his knees buckle. With his nails digging into his palm, he storms out of her room, slamming the door behind him.

He paces the empty hall in a daze, huffing and muttering an argument that came too late. His mind examines the memories of her kiss, her promises, how she begged him not to leave her side.

That couldn't be a lie. There's no way!

He turns his glare to the staircase and holds his hands out to strangle a Rex who isn't there.

Wait, his fingers on one hand are...*red? What did I touch that's red? Is this...blood?*

He checks himself for unseen injuries and pats himself for sore spots. Nothing. His breath catches in his throat as he remembers when Inez first came back. He touched her cheek. *No.*

Blake sneaks to Inez's door, holding his breath and hovering his ear over its edge. Whimpering and heavy breaths escape through the gap. Muffled sniffling, pillows being assaulted and wept into.

That proves she didn't mean it. She's hurt. He puts his hand on the knob, ready to storm in.

No, she won't tell him anything. Worse, she might scream, and he'll lose any chance of helping her.

He hurries down the hall, scanning the nameplates until he finds the right one and slams his fist against it.

"Mishkin! Vladik, Mishkin! Open up!"

The door cracks open, and Blake shoves Mishkin back to storm into the room. "Guys, we have a problem."

"Kinda naked here," says Mishkin, despite not bothering to cover himself as he shuts the door. Vladik pulls the blankets over his waist with a furrowed brow and a pink tint on his cheeks.

"Something happened," Blake spews, paying no mind to their naked bodies as his pacing continues. "I don't know what, but I know it was Rex. Something about Rex. He said something, did something. There was blood. And then Inez kicked me out!"

He stops to look at Mishkin, who is putting on a pair of pants and isn't wearing his cat ears yet. He looks over to Vladik, who has just finished doing the same. "Oh sorry, I didn't realize you guys were naked."

Mishkin rolls his eyes. "We aren't now! Tell us what's going on. And this time in English."

Blake takes a deep, trembling breath, struggling to gather his thoughts and the words to explain them.

"Rex asked Inez to meet him this morning. Alone. Well, she did, and..." Blake holds up his bloodstained hand, leaving Mishkin and Vladik gaping.

"What did he do?" Mishkin asks.

"I don't know. She wouldn't tell me. She must be terrified, I heard her crying from the hallway! I'll kill him," Blake growls, his body trembling. "That fucking bastard, I'll *kill* him!"

"All right," says Mishkin, holding out his hands. "Deep breath."

Blake continues grumbling his threats to Rex, cursing the corrupt King through gritted teeth. His heart is tearing apart at the thought of Inez injured, crying, alone, and afraid.

"I have to see her. I have to fix this." Blake lunges for the door, but Mishkin grabs his shoulders to hold him back. When Blake continues arguing and fighting, Mishkin throws a slap across Blake's cheek, locking Blake's surprised stare with his focused one.

"Listen to me," says Mishkin. "I know you're pissed off. Believe me, I am too. But panic and blind rage won't help her. Take a deep breath, and we'll figure this all out, okay?"

Blake is still trembling, jaw tight, fists clenched. He glances at Vladik, who looks just as concerned as he is. He forces his jaw open to take a deep breath. Mishkin is right, but his blood hasn't stopped boiling.

"Are you calm enough to listen now?"

Blake nods, lips in a tight line.

"I'm going to tell you what I think is going on, but first," Mishkin turns to Vladik. "Lovey, would you block the door for us? If he loses it, he should stay in here."

Vladik nods and crosses the room to take a prepared stance.

"What do you mean?" Blake asks.

"My hunch, Rex knows you and Inez have a thing going. He expected her to marry Allistair, and she dumped him. He hurt her for it. I think it's like what happened with Ronan."

"With Ronan? What do you mean?"

"Doesn't matter. The point is, Rex wants Inez to date Allistair, not you. She got hurt for going against the King. It's awful, but there's nothing we can do right now. We just have to be patient until we can get some answers."

Blake grips at his hair, gritting his teeth as the Illusionist's smug face taunts him from his memory.

Allistair told him, I know it! That jealous little shit! How could he do this?

Chapter 26

Blake's leg bounces under the table, his teeth gnawing at his lip. "She wasn't at breakfast. What makes you think she'll come to lunch?"

"Because she'll be starving, dumbass. Trust me," Mishkin mutters.

"Hey, guys," says Allistair, plopping himself into a chair across the table. "Blake, I'm sorry about yesterday. Mishkin was right, I got jealous, and said some horrible stuff. I was rude, and totally out of line. If you and Inez really like each other, I wish you all the best."

Allistair's words pierce through his chest. Mishkin raises his brows, reminding Blake to remain neutral.

"It's fine. There's nothing between us anyway. Thanks though," says Blake, gritting his teeth.

"Nothing? That's kind of a surprise. You do like her though, right?"

Mishkin butts in with small talk to distract Allistair, but Blake can't hear a word.

Inez came down from Rex's room bleeding, and suddenly he's all friendly again. Allistair must have gone to Daddy with his jealous bullshit. He's probably the one who prompted Rex to hurt her. Jackass. I bet Rex forced her to say those things to me this morning.

Blake takes a sip of his cola, trying to focus on the carbonation so he doesn't glare at Allistair. Mishkin was right. Blake didn't like a word of what he said earlier, but it makes sense. They can't tell Allistair that they're on to him or that Inez got hurt somehow. And Blake can't keep pestering Inez for answers.

"Isn't he the biggest mush ball?" says Mishkin, wrapping his arms around Vladik's neck, nuzzling his cheek to his. "You're hopeless without me, aren't you, lovey?"

The two share a gentle kiss, and Blake can't help but smile, despite everything.

"I envy you guys," says Allistair. "I can only dream of a love like yours."

Blake's attention flicks from Allistair to the familiar red hair behind him. She approaches in a black turtleneck and baggy gray sweatpants. She looks more pristine than yesterday, as if the slightest hair out of place would destroy her image. She looks paler, and her head hangs low, puffy eyes glued to the floor.

Mishkin puts a hand on Blake's arm, shaking his head at him, and Blake's body goes rigid. *I have to go to her. Mishkin please, just let me hold her.*

200

"Inez." Blake hesitates, choosing his words carefully. "How are you feeling?".

Inez gives Blake a passive glance before she turns her attention to the side and rests a hand on Allistair's shoulder. "Allistair, darling. I've been thinking about it, and I'd love to go to the ball with you."

A pang shoots through Blake's gut. *No. Mishkin was right. This is all a plot. Rex hurt her, scared her into going back to him. But we all know how she feels, right? She turned him down, there's no way he'd be stupid enough to accept right in front of us!*

"Really?" says Allistair, shooting a confused glance at Blake. "But I thought…"

"Come on, we haven't gone together in a while."

Don't do it. She doesn't feel that way.

"Of course. I'd love to."

You bastard!

"And like I said before," Allistair continues. "I'm totally fine going as friends. I won't let those rumors start up again. Besides, there's something else I'd like to talk to you about. The ball would be a perfect time for that."

Yes. Just as friends. That's good. Blake's fists clench underneath the table, leg bouncing a mile a minute. Mishkin squeezes his arm, reminding him to keep it together.

"Actually, I was hoping to share the Midnight Dance with you," Inez smiles. "We can talk then about whatever you like."

Allistair's eyes go wide, and Blake focuses his scowl onto his untouched plate.

Say no, you idiot! Call her out!

But how could he know? Aside from her clothes, Inez looks fine. There was blood on her face, but he can't see

201

an injury. Could it be in her hair? He bites his lip, breath shuddering. *What the hell did he do to you?*

"The Midnight Dance?" says Allistair. "Are you sure? You always sneak out before it happens."

Yes! Good man! See your way through this! Tear down her façade!

"That dance should be with someone you care about," Allistair continues, shooting another quick glance at Blake. "Someone you have romantic feelings for."

Yes! Keep going! My brother!

"That's right," Inez grins, dragging a finger up his neck to lift his chin. "And there's no one else I'd rather share that experience with."

Lies! You know she's lying. Tear it down!

One last glance at Blake, this time less confused. More apologetic.

Don't you dare.

"If you're absolutely sure, Inez, I'd love to."

Blake shoots up from the table, pausing for a moment, remembering to be calm. "Sorry guys, something at breakfast didn't really agree with my stomach. I don't have much of an appetite. I'll be upstairs if you need me."

He leaves, keeping his pace slow, avoiding Allistair's apologetic frown. Trying not to let anyone see his frustration.

"No problem, man. If there's anything you need, come find me."

Blake holds back his irritated grunt and forces a smile back at him. "Thanks, but I should be fine with some rest."

He lets out his growl when he reaches the top of the stairs and storms into his room, slamming the door before grabbing his suitcase and throwing it into the far wall, scattering the clothes he never unpacked all over the floor.

He storms across the room and drops onto his bed with his hands over his face.

Memories of Inez's beautiful smile, her addictive kisses, and her infectious giggle are racing through his mind. Those are her real feelings. Nothing has made his heart happier than seeing his feelings for her being reciprocated so purely, so strongly.

She'd just learned to open up to him, trust him, and now blood. Images of her screaming at him to leave, hiding part of her face, and finding her blood on his hands flood into his vision.

Blake's mind floods with made-up scenarios of what must have happened while Inez was alone with Rex; the fear that must have filled her eyes the whole time. With no one to help her, and no way to help herself.

How many injuries is she hiding under those clothes? The blood on her face must have been from her head, a gash hiding in her hair. She must be in so much pain. How much did it hurt to clean it? To hide it? His heart is tearing at the thought. He wasn't there to protect her. He isn't there to help.

He should've gone with her. Demanded to stay to hear Rex's words. He'd take her torment in a heartbeat, whatever that was, if it meant she wouldn't have to fake-date that damned Prince.

He isn't sure how much time has passed when a knock at his door snaps him back to reality. He doesn't answer. Unless it's Inez, they can go away. Another knock.

"Blake, it's Mishkin."

Blake groans out loud, not wanting to see him either. "Come in."

Mishkin peeks through the door and looks around. "Wow, that bad, huh?"

"What do you think?" Blake snaps as Mishkin closes the door behind him. "I'm not exactly thrilled about what's going on."

"Neither am I. You have every right to be furious."

"What did Inez say after I left? Actually, scratch that, I don't want to know. Wait, tell me. I need to know as much as I can."

Mishkin hesitates for a moment, giving him one last chance to refuse the information, but it doesn't happen. He drops by Blake's side with a sigh.

"After you left, Inez kept flirting. Then she grabbed her lunch and clung to him the entire time. It was pretty disgusting, actually. Her giggles were so fake, it hurt my soul."

"And Allistair believed it?"

"Of course not. He knows her better than that. He was confused the whole time, even looked to us for an explanation. Vladik and I just shrugged."

"Why didn't you tell him?"

"If this is his fault, telling him would sound too much like an accusation. If it wasn't him, he won't believe us. No one will. Rex is a savior in this troupe. A majority of the mansion will always take his side. It's not like we can ask Inez to strip down and look for bruises."

"The dressing room!" Blake stands. "Everyone shares a dressing room, right? Won't someone notice while we change?"

"Change for what? We're still on vacation. Our next tour doesn't start until Spring. No one else is getting married soon either."

"Shit." Blake drops back onto his bed, rubbing his temples and taking deep breaths to keep himself collected. The silence that hangs between him and Mishkin isn't comforting.

"The blood was on Inez's face," says Blake. "I only know that because that's the only place I touched when she came back down. Now she's all cleaned up, and you can't even tell she's hurt. Whatever happened, it was bad enough for blood to pour from her head. Her fucking *head*, Mishkin!"

Blake runs his fingers through his hair, begging his mind to stop replaying the images of what must've happened.

Mishkin's lips form a tight line, and his eyes drop to the floor.

"Allistair has to be in on it," Blake says. "He probably told Rex that he suspected something and asked him to fix it."

"If that were the case, he'd be rubbing it in your face right now, don't you think? Not calling you a good man and giving you his support. Besides, even when his attitude gets a little twisted, he won't let anyone get hurt. Especially not Inez."

Blake drops his hands to his lap and cranes his head back to focus on the details of his ceiling. He notes each curve and detail, anything to push out the images from his imagination.

Mishkin has a point, but he can't forgive Allistair for going along with it.

"So, what do we do then?" Blake asks. "We can't just let this happen."

"No, we can't. But it'll be more effective to pull the rug out from under Rex's feet without him knowing. If we can undo his plan without coming at him directly, it'll send a message. He'll realize he's losing control, and he'll do everything he can to make sure that doesn't happen. As he does, his savior façade will slip, and they'll all turn against him."

Blake looks at Mishkin with wide eyes. "You want to tear Rex down completely."

"That wasn't always my intention." Mishkin shrugs. "But that man almost had me killed just to have his way. And now he hurt my little sister and left her blood on her boyfriend's hands. On my friend's hands. I'm not putting up with someone like that anymore. Besides, don't you want to tear him down too?"

"Of course, but how? Allistair won't help us. He doesn't seem to mind. He got his spot as the future leader *and* the woman of his dreams, all by default."

"He doesn't mind because he has no idea. Allistair's image of his father is as pure as everyone else's. Still, he's smart enough to see through Inez's lies. He'll get the truth out of her before the ball."

"And what if he doesn't? The ball is only three days away."

"Then you go with us." Mishkin smiles, patting Blake's back. "Vladik and I will be your dates, and we'll do whatever we can to make sure the Midnight Dance belongs to you and Inez!"

Blake smiles at Mishkin's offer before he goes back to staring at the ceiling. The tearing in his heart turns to a dull ache as he drops his gaze to the floor.

"Honestly, I wouldn't be so mad if that's how she really felt. If she told me she loves Allistair, it would sting, but it would be fine. Her happiness is the most important thing to me. But that isn't what's happening. She's hurt. She's being manipulated. Threatened. She's doing this because she's terrified of whatever happened up there. I couldn't protect her; I couldn't stop it from happening. And now I can't even hold her in my arms. I can't comfort her. I'm useless and it makes me sick!"

"Stop it, Blake." Mishkin places a hand on his arm. "There's no way you could've known this would happen."

"She's going to cry tonight. She's going to cry herself to sleep, and she'll probably have nightmares about it, with no one to be there for her. She's going to be alone. Terrified and alone."

"I'll check in with her tonight and make sure she's okay. I'll try to get some details out of her while I'm at it. Don't worry so much." He pulls Blake's head onto his shoulder and scratches his head. "We'll figure it out. This will all be over before you know it, and you two can go back to being all cutesy."

Blake closes his eyes and takes a deep breath. Mishkin's hold is cooling the boiling in his blood, but his heart is still too heavy to speak.

"Hey," Mishkin coos, "you know, you still need work on your form."

"My what?"

"Your poi. You still have a lot to work on."

Blake's head shoots up to look at Mishkin, a small smile curving his lips, giving his heart a tiny glimmer of hope.

That's right. The poi!

Chapter 27

"**I**nez!" Blake calls as Inez gathers some dinner plates from the table. She looks at him with flat eyes.

"Are we on cleaning duty again?"

"Yeah," she says, holding out the plates. "You can help Ronan with these."

"Sure, of course!" Blake takes the plates from her hands. "By the way, do you want to get up early to practice poi tomorrow?"

"Tomorrow we have our fittings with Victor," Inez sneers as she continues to gather dishes and pile them onto

Blake. "He has the basis for our ball clothes ready, so he needs the final measurements."

"Great! Will I see you there?"

"It's a fitting, you creep, much more half-nude time than the dressing room. Your appointment is at ten, and his room is on the third floor. Don't be late."

"Right, got it. So when do we practice?"

"You don't need practice. You've graduated from poi school. Congratulations." She turns and saunters off toward the kitchen

"How can I have graduated?" Blake follows. "Mishkin said I need to work on my form."

"Mishkin isn't the Fire Goddess here, I am."

"But it's an art form! You're never done learning with art!"

Inez whips around and glares into his eyes. "I said you're done! Quit following me!"

"I'm on cleaning duty too, remember? I have to follow you!"

Inez jumps back a bit, blushing as a few members of the mansion stare at them with raised or furrowed brows.

"Fine," she mumbles, continuing on her way. "But we're done here. Practice in your room if you want."

Blake follows her down the hall, trying to hold back the scowl forming on his face. "We did pretty well with our partner fire routine. Maybe we should practice some more before it gets too cold out."

"You said yourself you don't need partner work. Besides, I have a date with Allistair. Now stop talking." Inez walks through the kitchen door and heads to the broom closet.

"Blake!" Ronan waves him over, and Blake focuses his eyes on Ronan's welcoming smile to avoid turning his gaze back to Inez.

209

It doesn't take long to get the chores started, and Blake is talking to Ronan more about the work backstage and his previous work as an acrobat. He's careful with his eyes, keeping them on the dishes he's washing and occasionally on Ronan.

He can hear Inez making light conversation with others in the group, listening closer when he hears Mishkin's voice.

"So, Inez, when exactly did this sudden change of heart happen?"

"What do you mean?" she asks.

"You've spent most of your life saying you and Allistair are just friends and that you don't have those feelings for him."

"I guess I was just afraid to admit it. I mean, when people talk about these things all the time, it's kind of embarrassing to admit they're right. But I don't really care anymore."

"Is that so? If I recall, you were pretty relieved when you turned him down for good. Even happier when he got the hint and stopped trying. Why would you be so happy to have a crush leave you alone?"

Inez goes silent, and it's taking every ounce of Blake's energy not to turn around.

"Nice try, Mishkin," she says, "I know what you're trying to do, *and I know the Pup is listening.*"

Blake fumbles a plate, splashing water on his shirt, and lowers his head, refusing to look back.

"But it won't work," she continues. "There's nothing to figure out. I didn't want to admit my feelings for Allistair before, but now I'm happy to. I'm madly in love with him, and you'll all see that on Friday at the Blasphemer's Ball, when we share the Midnight Dance.

Now if you'll excuse me, I have cleaning to do, and so do you."

"I think you're a great couple," calls Maya as she dries the dishes.

"Thank you, Maya. I'm glad you understand."

"Hey, Pup," she continues, "maybe you should just mind your own business. Allistair is a great guy. I get that you're new here and all, but trust me when I say that there's no one else for Inez."

"Leave the man alone," says Ronan. "Inez probably told him how she came here, and he just wants to make sure that she's safe. Isn't that right, Blake?"

"Yeah." Blake smiles. "I don't butt in just to be a nosey bastard. Inez is my friend, and what friend wouldn't worry? Like you said, I'm new here. I barely know the guy."

"Yeah, alright," Maya responds, continuing her work. "I promise you, though, Allistair is a good guy, just like his father."

"Just like his father," Blake echoes through gritted teeth, hardening his gaze at Inez. She flicks a wide-eyed glance back but quickly forces her eyes shut as she continues to sweep.

Blake glances at Ronan, who looks like he's fighting back some words of his own.

"That's right," Maya continues, eyes glued to her task. "There's no need to worry. They'll take good care of her."

"Thank you for that, Maya!" says Mishkin, throwing his arms around Blake's shoulders. "But Blake isn't so bad either, so play nice, okay? He's got his own problems to deal with."

"Whatever."

Mishkin pats Blake's back as he steps away, and cleanup continues without another word.

211

The clanking dishes and hissing of the sink ring through the air. The sounds of cleaning are relaxing, something Blake enjoyed when he first arrived. Now his mind is racing, and the lack of conversation has spread a thick layer of awkwardness across the kitchen.

"Can I ask you something?" he mumbles to Ronan, who nods his head to let him continue. "Why aren't you an acrobat anymore? What happened?"

Ronan freezes in his spot, and his eyes travel into an unseen trauma. Blake's eyes flit to the scar near his ear, and he nods in understanding and gives his arm a small nudge with his elbow. "Never mind. It's none of my business."

"We've all had it tough around here," says Ronan. "I went into state care when I was eleven. They arrested my parents for making and selling meth. A few weeks later, my mother died in prison, and last I heard, my dad is still there."

"I'm so sorry," says Blake.

"Don't be. It's because of that I got to try so many new things. There were programs and events for kids like me. One of them was a gymnastics day at a local dance studio. Met Rex there, and he loved how quickly I learned. He told me I could come back the next day. When I did, he let me play on the trampoline with the kids from the show. Xavier stood out to him too. We weren't really friends before, but this new opportunity gave us a chance to bond. He's like a brother now. We practiced together a lot. I fell in love with the trapeze. Did it for about three years before I became a techie."

"So, you just followed him home?"

"No." Ronan laughs. "The state keeps track of these kids! He went through the entire adoption process, and we got to know him before we moved in. He listened to what

I had to say. Then he figured I'd do better backstage, and the rest is history."

"That's pretty cool, to have a chance like that," Blake says with a smile.

"I owe it all to Rex." Ronan's voice is grateful. Anyone only listening would miss the twitch in his forced smile, the pain in his eyes as they revisit part of the tale yet to be told.

So many stories of lost hope and Rex bringing them here. But the adoption process is harder than an application process for a job.

He knows that because of the trouble his own parents had to go through to adopt him. That's the biggest reason they never adopted a second. They often warned Blake about it in case he planned to adopt in the future. Why would Rex put himself through that for nearly fifty people?

It would be much easier to start a circus troupe with two or three friends and hire performers who already know what they're doing.

Could Mishkin be right? Did he adopt them as children to make sure they're powerless? No, plenty of them can see what Rex is really about. They may not know how to make it out there, but it wouldn't be hard to figure out. There has to be something bigger, something more threatening that keeps them under Rex's roof.

Whatever Ronan's reasons are, the King needs to go. They can't live like this anymore. How can Blake convince everyone to stand up to him?

Ronan tries to ease the tension by talking about how tech life isn't so bad, but Blake can't hear him over the pounding of his heart in his ears. He understands Mishkin's plan now. He can't just sneak Inez out of here, as much as he wants to. With Mishkin being the one to have invited Blake here in the first place, he might end up in danger all over again, especially if Rex is directly assaulting people after all.

Blake hates this feeling of helplessness. He hates that he doesn't have any idea what to do. The familiar burst of red hair appears in his periphery. Inez is getting the mop ready. He watches her with a side eye, doing his best not to be obvious.

We'll figure something out, Inez. I promise.

Chapter 28

"**I** lied, Blake. I want you!"

Inez's words ring through Blake's bones and he throws his arms around her, lifting and spinning her into his room. Her laughter in his ear makes his heart race, and he stops to kiss her. They fall onto Blake's bed, and she moans as she makes herself comfortable on top of him. "I love you."

Blake opens his mouth to say the same, but Inez's face turns startled as a pointed blade pierces through the front of her chest, splashing warm red all over him. Blood pours from her head down the side of her face, and her body falls limp on his chest. The blade hits him, splitting his skin and sending a sharp pain through his torso.

Yelling and trembling, he looks up at the culprit, and Rex stands there, towering over them with an army of cobras upright at his sides, a sharp-toothed grin spreading across his face.

"Your turn, Pup," he says. Blake tries to wriggle himself out from under Inez's body, but he's surrounded by hissing cobras, one stopping at his face and lunging forward.

Blake jolts up in his bed and searches desperately for Inez before remembering the events of yesterday. He flops back down, lungs heaving, unable to shake the images of his nightmare. Inez's dreams must be even worse.

Inez!

He glances at his clock. It's still early, but she should be awake by now. He shoots out of bed to grab an outfit from the scattered pieces of clothing around his room. After fumbling to pull them all on, he rushes to Inez's door, banging furiously.

"Inez! Inez, please let me in!"

Silence.

He knocks harder. "Inez!"

"What are you doing?" the familiar voice calls from behind.

Blake whips around; Inez is holding a long fabric bag in one arm and a frown on her face.

"We need to talk."

"I have nothing to say to you. Get away from my room."

"Inez, I know you're scared, but please just talk to me."

"You don't know anything." Inez yells. "Stay away from my room and stay away from me. I have a boyfriend. If I catch you creeping around again, I'll have Allistair kick you out of here."

Good. Inez is looking at him head-on for the first time since that night. He swallows hard. "I know you didn't mean what you said yesterday."

"I meant every word. You're nothing. You're not a fool, you're a spoiled pup who can't take no for an answer. Get away from my room!"

"What's going on?" Xavier calls as he approaches the two. "Is everything okay?"

"No, it isn't. Pup here is blocking my bedroom, and I can't get in. I'm getting a little scared, actually."

Xavier shoots Blake an unimpressed look. "Let me guess, you like Inez, and she prefers Allistair, right? Come on, man. Don't push your feelings onto people like that."

"That's not what I'm doing!" Blake stops to take a deep breath and regain control of his volume. "She looked shaken up yesterday, and I want to know if she's doing alright, that's all. I swear. She's my friend, and I want to check in."

Xavier shifts his jaw and turns his attention to Inez. "I think that's fair. Are you doing okay?"

"I'm fine." Inez spits out her words, crossing her arms and turning her head away. "Thanks for asking."

"Good," says Blake. "So how did your meeting with Rex go?"

Inez rolls her eyes and lifts her nose to the side, ignoring the newfound curiosity on Xavier's face.

"Xavier, if you don't mind, Blake has a fitting appointment with my uncle in a few minutes. Could you make sure he gets there in time, please? I'm not sure he knows the way."

"Sure thing," says Xavier, smiling at Blake. "I'll show you where to go."

217

"Don't bother. I'll just read the plaques." Blake trudges off. His eyes flick to Inez in time to see her turn away.

He takes a deep breath, holding back every desire to turn around and beg Inez to talk to him. Fighting every urge to tell Xavier exactly what's going on. Resisting every instinct telling him to barge into Rex's room and beat him to the ground.

VICTOR'S ROOM IS TOO QUIET for comfort, and all Blake can do is stare at his reflection in the mirror. Shelves of books and trinkets line the walls behind him as black fabric covers his body. Light blue embroidery lines the cuffs and runs up both arms.

He hasn't seen the symbol on the back yet, and his mind wanders through various possibilities. Rex has a lion, and Mishkin probably has a cat. Is Blake going to get stuck with a fuzzy little poodle because of his nickname? That would be a good way for Victor to mess with him. What would Inez have? Probably a phoenix, or a dragon—something related to fire. A tiny jab gets him in the leg, making him flinch. Victor apologizes and fixes his needle, reminding Blake of the awkward silence that's been hanging between them.

He clears his throat. "So, are you glad Inez is going to the ball with Allistair?"

Victor's face lights up. "Is she really? Shit! Now their outfits don't match!"

"She didn't tell you?"

"She never tells me anything," says Victor, getting back to his sewing.

"I'm surprised too. She always told me she doesn't like Allistair that way."

"Did you tell her how you feel? Ask her to the dance?"

"Of course I did. She even said yes and that she felt the same way."

"Did she?" Victor raises a brow at him through the mirror.

Blake winces. "Sorry. I'm sure that's not what you want to hear from someone like me."

"Don't take it the wrong way," says Victor, his face softening. "It's a guardian thing. I want the best for my niece, and I know Allistair can provide that. Or at least I'd like to think so."

"Well, you got what you wanted. She chose him. I just wish I knew why she would say yes to me and then change her mind so suddenly."

"It is a mystery. She even swore to me she wasn't interested in him."

"Honestly, Victor, don't you think it's weird? I mean, she fought so hard to convince everyone that she doesn't feel that way, then she goes to see Rex, and suddenly Allistair's the love of her life?"

Victor's body goes still, and the color drains from his face. "She went to see Rex?"

"Yeah, he asked her to meet him yesterday morning, and that's when she started acting all weird. But see, the day before, Allistair seemed kinda suspicious. I think he might have said something to Rex, and that's why she's suddenly so gaga over him."

"It wasn't Allistair," Victor mumbles, standing from his spot.

"What?"

Victor locks his narrow eyes on Blake's wide ones. The frown on his face makes Blake shudder in his spot.

"You told Rex how you feel. You gave him your word that no matter what her decision was, you wouldn't push her to reconsider. You promised him that the choice was hers to make. All he had to do was sway her choice."

The room spins. Blake's chest is getting tight, making him fight for air.

Inez got hurt because of me. Allistair didn't make this happen, I did.

His eyes sting as his brain floods with memories of trying to kiss her in the theater, begging her to stay in his room, and all those tiny looks and comments he made with others around. *It wasn't Inez. It wasn't Allistair. It's my fault.*

I did this to her.

"It's too late for regret," says Victor, setting Blake's arm in place so he can sew the sleeve. "You need to learn to keep your mouth shut until you've thought your words through. Especially since you don't know what kind of person you're dealing with. More importantly, don't ever let Rex know you're against him."

"Why not? Rex is a monster and I'm sick of kissing his ass. Everyone here deserves to know what kind of danger they're in."

"Use your brain, Pup. Remember that Rex saved all of these people. And you're a stranger here. For all they know, you could be calling him evil just because he isn't promising you a lead role. They have no reason to believe that Rex is hiding anything."

Blake clenches his jaw and glares at his reflection as Victor moves to the next sleeve.

He bites his lip, resisting the urge to punch the idiot staring back at him. It's bad enough everyone believes in Rex, but this mess started because of his own mistakes.

I did this to her. It's my fault.

220

"All right, you're all set. What do you think?"

Blake turns to check the back, and his jaw drops. A set of juggling clubs sprawl over his back with swirls twisting and turning around them.

"This is incredible! Thank you!"

"It won't be cheap," Victor chuckles. "I do all the embroidery myself."

"Take my money! I couldn't ask for anything better!"

"Glad to hear it. It's yours to keep and wear as you please. Though it will be mandatory for formal events."

Victor grabs and folds a black handkerchief from his supplies and tucks it into the pocket on Blake's chest, pressing his hand to it. "Do me a favor. Don't forget this is here. And don't touch it unless you need it."

"Okay. Why? Is it important?"

"Nah, just a little gamble."

"A gamble?"

Victor takes a few steps away, his back to Blake as he stares into a shelf of black-and-white movies. His hands are behind his back, pushing out his plump stomach.

"You ever seen those old movies where a man lends a woman his handkerchief when she's crying or caught in the rain? I always thought it was romantic. A tiny sign of trust and caring that usually leads to something much grander."

Blake's eyes shift through the movies on his shelf before he shakes his head. "Sorry, Vic, you lost me."

"You know, sometimes when things seem uncertain, it helps to look for a sign; Some signal to point you in the right direction. I always said that to Inez, too. But she never believed it, of course."

Blake furrows his brow, trying to put the pieces of this odd riddle together, but they make little sense. Is he trying to tell him that something will happen at the ball? That someone will cry?

"Well, you have your suit. Get out of my room."

Chapter 29

"**Y**ou promised me he wouldn't let it go on for long!" Blake grumbles as he watches Allistair and Inez from the other end of the table, giggling and fawning over each other. "I thought you said we could trust him. She won't even sit with us anymore!"

"We *can* trust him," says Mishkin. "He's probably just enjoying her attention while he can before she inevitably rejects him again. I talked to her last night, and nothing dirty has even happened with them. And it's you, by the way. She won't sit with *you*."

"That helps," Blake grumbles. "What if they don't split up before the ball?"

"Don't worry about it. Vladik and I have a plan B."

"Great, and what's plan B?"

"You'll know it if we need it."

Blake groans as he takes a bite of his pork roast, trying not to watch Inez anymore. He focuses on the lemon-pepper flavor dancing on his tongue. Before he can realize it, his eyes are back where they shouldn't be.

Inez's smile is so fake, he can almost see glue, and that's a bittersweet comfort. He's seen the eyes she has when she's truly enamored, when she's treated like the royalty she is. She's so quick to lean on Allistair, put her hand on his, and say some sort of romantic things without even a single blush. That's not newfound love. At least, that's not how it is for Inez.

Allistair says something to her, and Inez looks away to answer, much like she'd done to Blake before. *She's hiding something, Allistair. Make her look you in the eye. Wait, don't do that. Don't let her think she made the right decision. Please, dear God, just go with it.*

To his relief, Allistair seems to accept her answer without a second thought, and Blake scoffs to himself, his pride rebuilding.

I can read Inez better than you can. And I will never let her feel like she has to hide from me.

Inez stands and heads to the beverage table with her empty cup. Blake grabs his half-full cup and follows her. He hears Mishkin protesting but quickly drowns him out, keeping his steps slow and casual, without being slow enough to miss her.

He steps up to the table as she pours herself a glass of wine.

"Inez."

"What now?" She glares at him, and Blake notices that Xavier is raising a brow at him from the table. Not just Xavier, a few others are staring at them too, some whispering among themselves. So much for keeping this whole thing a secret.

"I just wanted to apologize for this morning," says Blake. "You're absolutely right. You are a beautiful, magical woman, and you deserve to be with whoever makes you happiest. If you say Allistair is the love of your life, I have no reason to argue. You have my support, and I wish you all the best."

Inez's eyes drop to the floor and her head turns away. "Thank you. I'm glad you understand."

"So, tell me. What did you lie to Allistair about?"

Her glare burns into his skin, and before he can react, Inez's arm swings across the air, splashing wine across his face and neck, dripping to his chest. She slams her glass down, shattering it against the carpet at his feet before turning away and storming off to sit next to Allistair. He asks if she's okay, but she quickly changes the subject.

Blake steps back toward the table, eyes down, but Xavier locks their stares together. He points to Blake, then flicks his hand to the side, directing him back to his seat.

With his jaw clenched, and enough of his pride shattered, he follows the silent command. Whispers of "poor guy" and "pretty harsh" and "he's kind of plain anyway" follow him until he sits back down.

Mishkin sits with his head on one hand, the other tapping his fingers on the table with his eyebrows raised.

"Yeah, I know," says Blake. "You told me so."

Chapter 30

Avoiding Inez is harder than he thought. The day creeps by as slowly as it can, taunting him with long hours of whispering and suspecting looks from the others. Not knowing what else to do with himself, he practices his juggling clubs outside until the chilly air numbs his fingers. He skips lunch, figuring he'd only put his foot in his mouth again. Lying on his bed, staring at the ceiling isn't any better, but it isn't making things worse.

Why does it even matter? He sighs. He joined the circus to perform with the people he admires. Not to fall in— *Wait. No, that can't be. Can it?*

He sits up and rubs his temples, contemplating. *I did, didn't I? I fell in love with her. I love you, Inez. And I can't even let you know.*

★ ★ ★

AT DINNER, INEZ EVADES HIM, pretending he isn't there. Blake's heart sinks as she fawns over Allistair, who is returning her affections with smiles and nuzzles to her temple.

Dishes are piled as everyone finishes. Blake gathers his utensils onto his half-empty plate and chugs the rest of his wine as he walks off. He's been having one glass at dinner since he arrived, but lately it's been three, and with less food in his stomach, he's already feeling the effects. A hand lands on his shoulder to stop him before he heads to the kitchen.

"Where are you going, Puppy Dog?" says Axel with a head tilt. Her tone and smile are friendly enough, but Blake's mind rattles. They haven't spoken so directly before.

"Um, I'm on cleaning duty."

"I don't think so." Axel grabs his dishes. "Mishkin, be a good kitty and take these to the kitchen for me, please. Pup and I need to have a word."

"Uh…" Mishkin blinks at the new dishes in his arms, then furrows his brow at Blake. "Sure."

Axel pecks Mishkin's cheek and wraps her elbow around Blake's to pull him away. "Thanks, Mishkin. Come on, Pup, let's walk and talk."

"Can this wait?" he asks, struggling to keep at her side. "I don't feel right about skipping cleanup."

"Everyone does it once in a while; it's no big deal. Besides, you're one of the more talented people here.

227

There's no reason you should stoop to doing petty chores like that."

"Does that mean you don't do any chores at all?"

"My responsibility is to myself. I'd rather spend my time doing things that improve my talents, so I can keep earning the lead role."

Blake isn't sure what to say as they head upstairs. The other members practice so often, and Axel being the lead every time seems unfair to the others. Then again, he hasn't seen their rehearsal process yet. He promised Inez he wouldn't be so quick to jump into judging things he didn't understand.

"My performance on stage has to stay PG because of all the kids. But you've seen a few of my more *passionate* pieces now, right?"

"Yeah." Blake's cheeks redden, remembering how transparent her underwear always was. And outside, no less.

"What do you think? Do you like what I do offstage?"

"Of course." Blake smiles. "We never spoke much before, so I hesitated to say anything, but you're beautiful and a thrill to watch."

"I'm glad to hear it." Axel smiles as they climb the next staircase.

His heart races as the third floor comes into view. Thick curtains cover the windows, darkening the halls, twisting Blake's stomach into a knot. "Where are we going?"

"I just want to talk in private for a minute." Axel leads him to a door and pulls a key from her pocket. Her name is on the plaque, and it occurs to Blake that he's never seen the other members lock their doors before.

Axel strolls in, pulling him along by his wrist and shutting the door quickly.

"What's this about?"

"You're not exactly subtle, Pup." Axel pulls a bottle of wine from a mini cooler and plucks two glasses from a shelf. "I see the way you look at the Fire Goddess."

"And you're going to tell me to give up, right?" He frowns as Axel fills both glasses. "You're going to say she's happier now, and I need to let her go."

"Well, yes, and no. Inez is even more transparent than you are. She's so fake it makes me sick. We can all tell she doesn't really like Allistair."

"Why do I need to let her go, then?" Blake grumbles, ignoring Axel's remark. *Remain neutral.*

She hands him a glass with a smirk on her face. "Because Inez doesn't like anybody." She clinks her glass against his and takes a sip.

"What do you mean?"

"She's not called the Fire Goddess just because of her talent. Her sharp tongue will do more damage than any flame I've seen her dance with. She messed with Ian's mind, she's messing with Allistair's *again*, and she's messing with yours. Play with a fire like hers, and you'll get burned in ways you can't even imagine."

"Maybe you only believe that because no one here understands her or her emotions. Ian took advantage of her as a teen while he was in his twenties, and you blame her, don't you? She isn't the one playing mind games around here."

Axel chuckles. "You're really sweet to have faith in such a minx." She puts a hand on his cheek and lifts his chin to look him in the eye. She's only a few inches shorter than him, but she's positioning herself to appear smaller. "Come on, you're smarter than that."

"I think I should go."

"No! I mean—" Axel sighs. "I'm sorry. I don't mean to talk trash about my friend. It's just that you're so talented, and you seem so intelligent. I can't see why someone like you would fall for her tricks like that."

Blake's lips shut tight; eyes focused on the floor.

"We'll change the subject, okay? I didn't bring you here to make you mad. We're just two friends getting to know each other. Have some wine."

He takes a small sip. Its sweet flavor begs him to take a second taste, as does the light spinning already in his head from the three glasses before, but he resists. "So how did you end up here?"

"I was Rex's first adoption. My father was sexually abusive, and my mom was too busy with work to care. I made friends with Allistair, and they took me in; rescued me. After about a year, I learned gymnastics and trapeze. Allistair was obsessed with magic, and he learned quickly. It's because of us Rex got the idea for a circus. We were struggling at the time, and it was his get-rich-quick scheme. Not that it was quick at all, but it worked out."

"If that's the case, it's kind of weird he doesn't want Allistair to marry you instead."

"I'm too much like family. Legally speaking, I am Allistair's sister. It doesn't help that I'm blonde like them too. Besides, Inez carries more value."

"How?"

Axel tightens her lips as if rethinking her words. "Doesn't matter. Let's talk about you. What kind of home did you run away from?"

"You never seemed interested before."

"I'm shier than I seem. It's easier to show your body instead of your heart. Especially around a handsome devil like you."

"Do you even know my name?"

"Blake," she laughs. "Calm down. I'm trying to help you."

"Why?"

"Because I like you, silly. Every time you perform in the yard, you have such an endearing energy about you. You're so handsome too. Stunning. And the fire suits your personality, so warm and inviting."

"You should avoid me then. So I don't burn you."

Knowing he shouldn't, Blake gulps down the rest of his wine to avoid saying anything else. His stomach is churning from Axel's sudden interest. Even with his head spinning, there's clearly something not right about all this. He pushes his empty glass into her hand and turns away, focusing hard on the floor to make sure he walks straight.

"Thanks for the drink, but I have chores to do."

"No!" Axel sets the glasses on her vanity and grabs his arm with both hands. "If you leave, I won't be able to help you!"

"How is any of this about me?"

Axel yanks him back and stands strong between him and the door. "Your feelings for the Fire Goddess did nothing but break your heart and get you on Rex's bad side. If you and I date, all of that can change. I can be faithful, I'll never lie, and Rex will favor you. We can be top stars together." She steps closer. "Owning the stage. Living our dreams."

"Pretty sure Allistair is the top lead, and if Inez marries him, she'll rise above you too. I don't think Rex's favor will help much."

"Allistair is training to be the next King. He won't be able to accept a lead role. He'll elect Inez as his Keeper, married or not, which means she won't have time to go on stage. You'll rise above everyone after next year, shining at my side. On the stage you've been watching all your life."

He drops his gaze to the floor as Axel closes in, placing her hands on his chest and sliding them up to his shoulders.

"I'm pretty adventurous, you know," Axel coos. "There's nothing I won't do for you. Tell me, what are your darkest fantasies?"

Blake's body threatens to react the way his mind shouldn't, but he keeps a straight face. She leans in with a tiny grin, and much to his own relief, he turns away.

She huffs and shoves him back. He wobbles backward as she steps closer until his legs stop short and he falls back onto soft fabric and pillows.

"My bed is more comfortable than hers." Axel crawls on top of him, and Blake scoots back until he's propped against the wall. "My word is more reliable." Her hand grips the brim of his pants. "And I can make much better use of my tongue."

Blake pulls her hand from his pants, but her lips press against his too quickly to let him react. Her tongue slithers into his mouth as her hands pin his wrists down. She rubs her warm slit against him, her breath getting heavier, and his dick betrays him after all, begging to be let out. He pulls his lips away from hers. "Get off!"

Axel jolts up with a scowl. "Why? You said I'm beautiful! Why would you say that if you don't want to fuck me?"

"I said I liked your performance. I didn't say I liked *you*."

Axel laughs, pulling her hand to her breast, continuing to rub her crotch against his. "Are you sure? Your cock isn't complaining. You feel pretty big too. It'd be a shame to hold it back."

Blake shoves Axel to the side and storms toward the door. Axel wraps her arms around him, her hand scrambling under his pants. "What's wrong, Pup? Could it be you're a virgin after all? No need to be shy. That's even sweeter."

She's grabbing his cock now, stroking, making him harder. A surge of desire pulses through his body, begging him to reconsider. With a hungry breath, he pulls her hands off of him, lacing his fingers through hers as he turns around, looking her in the eye and lowering his face. She closes her eyes and leans up.

"I said no," he says, despite his body's begging. His voice is low but strong, startling Axel. "You're pissing me off. In fact, you're toying with me worse than Inez ever could. Stay the hell away from me."

Blake drops her hands and storms off, leaving her frozen in shock. He expects more backlash, but he makes it to the hall and closes the door without any more interruptions. His body relaxes, and he takes a deep breath, his mind already flashing through everything.

What the fuck just happened?

As if knowing the answer, Blake's eyes dart to the end of the hall onto Rex's face, glaring at him through a crack in his bedroom door, but it closes before he can say anything. He glances at Axel's door and back at Rex's, growling as he makes his way back downstairs.

He isn't sure if Rex pushed Axel to do this, or if Rex thinks Blake intends to pursue Axel now. Neither situation is ideal, but he has to tell Inez what happened before she hears some twisted version of whatever the hell all that was.

On the second floor, Blake looks down the staircase to find Inez giggling and leading Allistair toward the front door by his arm. His heart twinges in his chest, but if she's

out of the mansion, it'll give him some time to cool off
and let the bulge in his pants die down.

Traitor.

He rushes to his room and flops onto his bed. The cold
sheets help him cool off, but they don't stop his mind from
racing. Inez won't listen to him, but he has to try to tell
her what happened.

★ ★ ★

"I KNOW IT'S YOU, PUP. GO AWAY," Inez calls from the
other side of her bedroom door.

Blake's lips tighten, but he doesn't answer, doesn't
move. He keeps his breath low, as if breathing too loudly
would wake the whole mansion. His heart surges. She and
Allistair got back well before everyone went to bed.
Could she have heard some kind of lie already? It's been
hours, but he didn't notice Rex or Axel downstairs for the
rest of the day.

He quickly scans the dark halls to make sure everyone
is still in bed. Seconds tick by before the doorknob makes
a slow, cautious turn. The door pulls back far enough for
Inez to peek out, gasp, and slam the door onto Blake's
arm. The impact shoots pain through his arm and up to his
shoulder, but he won't let her shut him out this time.

"Go away before I scream!" Inez whispers with a hiss.

"Just tell me what's going on, please."

"I told you, I lied!"

"Look me in the eye and say that. I won't believe it
until you do."

Inez gives up her push on the door and glares at him.
Blake's heart stops as Inez opens her mouth, and he
prepares himself to hear the words he's been dreading.

The sound of a door echoes from down the hall. Blake turns toward the sound, but his arm is yanked forward, and he stumbles into Inez's room as she carefully closes her door. She leans her ear against it.

"I'm listening for footsteps," she whispers. "As soon as the coast is clear, you go back to your room, got it?"

A smirk creeps onto his face, though Inez has turned away without another word. "I knew it. I knew you didn't mean it."

"Shut up. I meant every word. We're done, and you're leaving."

"Just tell me what you heard about me and Axel first."

Inez tenses. "You and," she straightens herself and gapes at him. "What do you mean?"

"Axel pulled me into her room after dinner. She kissed me and...grabbed my dick. She tried to get me to sleep with her, but I couldn't. I didn't let it go any further. Actually, I didn't want *any* of that to happen. She's fun to watch, but I'm not so sure I want to see her face again after today."

Pink forms on her cheeks as she crosses her arms, turning away. "You can do what you want. It's none of my business."

"I didn't want to. She wouldn't listen when I said no. It was pretty gross. I damn near puked when I left her room."

A tiny snicker escapes Inez's nose, and she covers her mouth. A tiny smile grows on his face, but Inez clears her throat and turns her back to him. "None of that matters. You still have to leave. You can fuck whoever you want."

He wraps his arms around her. She tenses in his arms, but he keeps his grip light. "I don't want to. There's only one woman I care about here. Can you guess who that is?"

"Blake," Inez whimpers with the smallest struggle, "let me go."

"I can hug you to death, or you can be honest with me. Do you still care or don't you?"

Inez drops her gaze to the floor as her body loosens in his clutches. She leans her head against his chest.

Blake presses his lips to hers, and lets out a relieved sigh when she doesn't pull away. He drops down to her neck. The heavy breath that escapes her sends hunger through his veins. He pulls her closer, teasing her skin with light nibbles and tiny tastes. He slides his hands around her back and along her waist as her breathing gets heavier, hungrier. Her hand grabs at his hair, and Blake pulls away to rest his forehead on hers, locking onto her gaze.

"Inez, I—"

Her hand covers his mouth. Her eyes seethe into his skin, more terrifying now than when they'd first met.

"Get out."

★ ★ ★

THAT WAS A TERRIBLE IDEA. Blake flops onto his bed. *I acted just like Ian. She was right to kick me out. But she really looked like she did before that morning. Like she cares.*

Blake rolls onto his back and growls at his ceiling. He can't keep pushing her like this. Tomorrow is the ball. His eyes land on the fabric bag that holds his suit.

If he gives Inez some distance, avoids her during the day, she can have some time to cool off and talk to him during the night. That's all he needs. A chance to talk. No kissing. No pressure.

On the bright side, he told Inez what happened before anyone else could lie to her. Even better, she seems to believe him. On the downside, he loves her, and he missed his chance to say it. Worse, she didn't let him say it.

His brain flashes back to what she almost said before she pulled him into her room. What was she about to say? He shudders at the thought. If she can say that to his face, he'd have no choice but to accept it. He's pushing his luck as it is.

If it weren't for the blood that dripped onto his hands, he'd have no reason to push for an answer. How long can he keep trying before the other members kick him out for being a stalker?

Axel's face floods his mind, and memories of her touch are still violating his body. He takes a deep breath and grabs a towel, hoping a hot shower will wash those memories away. He doesn't care about the reasons behind Axel's behavior anymore.

The scorching water relaxes his muscles, but his stomach continues to twist and tumble.

Tomorrow is the ball. Tomorrow he'll sort everything out or fail, knowing he did everything he could.

Chapter 31

The night of the ball arrives—Halloween night— and Blake puts on his embroidered suit and a pair of dress shoes that Victor dropped off this morning. He turns himself in his vanity mirror a few times and loves what he sees. It's a perfect fit, and the blue pattern feels like an extension of himself.

Straightening the black necktie, he takes a deep breath and eyes his determined reflection in the mirror.

He's avoided Inez all day, managed not to do or say anything stupid, and even practiced poi in his room for a while. Now he just needs the truth. To find out what happened while she was alone with Rex and get her to admit her feelings for Allistair are fake.

Even if she never goes back to Blake, he can't stand to see her lying to herself. Whatever she chooses, it has to make her happy. His phone rings in his pocket again, and Blake is surprised his mom waited so long. Her timing is still the worst. He sends her to voicemail and shoves his phone back in his pocket to recenter himself.

He nods at his reflection and rushes out the door to Mishkin and Vladik's room. He looks around the halls to the other members in their gowns and tuxedos. Most are black with brightly colored embroidery and unique symbols for each member.

Axel's gown is midnight blue with white patterns and Cinderella's glass slipper embroidered on the side of her waist. She narrows her eyes at Blake as he walks by, and he returns the gesture.

Good, at least they're on the same page. His eyes dart around the halls, searching for the strawberry-red hair. No surprise when he doesn't see her. She must have gone early with Allistair, since he's been helping his father with the planning.

He reaches the door he's looking for and knocks, opening it at Mishkin's call. He pokes his head in first. "Oh good, you're dressed this time."

Vladik chuckles as he adjusts his tie. His black suit is adorned with white embroidery and a short-handled sledgehammer with an oversized head on the back.

"Blake is lady killer in his suit, yes, darling?"

Mishkin looks away from his mirror and grins at Blake. The top of his gown has layers that look like the top of a suit, and white embroidery lines the bottom hems with star patterns, identical to Vladik's. A cat silhouette rests on the side on the skirt. Black and white eye makeup highlights Mishkin's eyes, emphasizing his catlike nature, and his lips grin under black lipstick.

He rushes over to straighten a few bits of Blake's suit. "He sure is! And it's a good thing too, because you are having your Midnight Dance with Inez tonight!"

"You sure about that?" Blake asks.

Mishkin crosses his arms as if offended. "If I wasn't sure, would I have slipped that condom into your pocket just now?"

Blake blinks as his hands pat both pants pockets. There *is* something in one of them. He yanks it from his pocket and gapes when he sees the small square package. "Mishkin!"

"What? Safety first!"

"You could've just given it to me!"

"I was hoping it'd be a convenient surprise," he says with a shrug. "But you don't seem to trust me."

"I *do* trust you." Blake chuckles, dropping the condom back into his pocket. "By the way, you both look great. And thanks for putting up with me lately. I know I haven't exactly been easy to deal with."

"Oh, shut up, mush ball," Mishkin scoffs. "It's time to go."

Vladik holds out an arm, and Mishkin takes it with grace. Vladik holds the other out for Blake, and he takes it with a smile. If nothing else, it helps to know he isn't going alone.

★ ★ ★

THEY ENTER THE BALLROOM, with heads held high, and arms still locked together. The event is in full swing, with lights, music, and a few caterers lining long tables with a colorful array of hors d'oeuvres.

Dresses and suits flood the ballroom, including designs that don't fit Victor's style. In fact, Blake doesn't recognize many of these faces at all.

"Hey, is it just me, or are there a lot more than fifty people here?"

"There's probably close to two hundred." Mishkin replies. "Rex invites his investors and business partners, along with the farmers and butchers who provide our food. He also invites his personal friends and other people of status or relevance. He likes to let everyone know how much he appreciates their help and contributions."

Blake nods as the three of them unlock arms and settle by the drink table.

Inez and Allistair are making friendly small talk with a caterer. Blake's heart almost leaps out of his chest. Inez's dress is black with red trim, and on the side of her waist is a red rose surrounded by wisps of fire and embroidered patterns that bleed into the bodice. The top of it lines the shape of her bust, thin straps sitting on her porcelain shoulders. On her neck is a thin scarf that hangs over her back.

Beautiful.

A smack ripples over Blake's shoulder, and he whimpers in pain as he turns to glare at the culprit. His jaw drops to see the familiar old face.

"Blake, my boy! How's Casa de Fool been treatin' ya?"

"Hartman! You're here too?"

"Of course! Rex owes me too much to shoo me away!"

"I have a serious question, sir, if you have a minute."

"Sure. Let's step out."

Mishkin and Vladik wave him off, assuring him they have time. Blake takes a quick glance at Inez, who is talking with Celia. His eyes flick to Rex on the other side of the ballroom, his glare piercing through him. Blake gathers himself and follows Hartman out of the ballroom and into the dark mansion hall.

"What's on your mind?" Hartman asks, flicking his lighter against a new cigarette.

"Sir, when you convinced Mishkin to help me get in, you said it would get things moving. Can you tell me what you meant?"

Hartman's eyes harden as they stare into Blake's, chilling his soul with a nice, long drag. The scent of the smoke burns his nose, but he resists the urge to cover it. Hartman turns his gaze up to the ceiling as he lets out the long breath, as if thinking of the right words to say.

"Tell me, what do you make of the King?"

Blake opens his mouth but hesitates, glancing over his shoulder at the open ballroom behind him.

"Be honest," says Hartman. "He can't hear you out here."

One deep breath, and Blake clenches his fists. "He's a fucking monster! He let Ian get away with harassment and throwing knives at his teammates! Then Mishkin almost died and he didn't even care, and now the woman of my dreams won't talk to me because he was alone with her, and I don't even know what happened!"

The corner of Hartman's mouth lifts into a smirk, and he chuckles. "Good, you aren't stupid, then. And who, dare I ask, is the woman of your dreams?"

Another hesitation, another quick glance over his shoulder, and Blake's heart sinks in his chest. "Inez Marquis. The Fire Goddess."

Hartman's eyes go wide but he keeps calm as he taps the ashes from his cigarette. "She like you back?"

"She said she did. Things were going well. But then Rex had a meeting alone with her, and now she won't talk to me."

Hartman's gaze burns into the floor. He takes another long drag.

"You didn't answer my question. Why am I here?"

"You're here because of that *fucking* King!" Hartman coughs out smoke and growls low in his throat. "I can't give you the details yet, boy. Sorry. But having you here is going to do a lot of good. In fact, it might be better than I imagined. If you and Inez are really an item."

Blake blinks hard at him. "What do you mean?"

"I'm trying to help her. Not just her—everyone. But right now, your cluelessness is my greatest weapon. Just don't fall for that King's tricks." His eyes harden again as they stare into Blake's. He holds his fingers out at him with the cigarette still burning. "And you'd better take damn good care of my granddaughter."

Blake freezes, almost afraid to breathe. "Wait, she's your—"

"Can I trust you?"

"Of course! I just don't know what you expect. But I swear, if I can just get her to talk to me again, if I know for sure that her feelings haven't changed, I will treat Inez like the royalty she is. I'll help everyone no matter what happens. They can't keep living with a leader like this."

Blake bites his tongue, opting to leave out the fact that he was ready to quit the circus and run away with Inez a while ago.

Hartman pats Blake's shoulder, his face still twisted in a frown. "This talk never happened. Now, go back in there and ask her to dance."

Blake wants to ask who else knows Inez is his granddaughter, but Hartman stomps away too quickly, grumbling under his breath.

With no idea how to handle everything, he returns to the ballroom. His feet threaten to wobble from the whirlwind in his mind. His eyes scan the dance floor and tables until he sees Inez at a snack table, alone. Perfect.

He breathes to recenter himself, then glides her way, doing his best not to rush over like a lovestruck puppy. He smiles when she notices him.

"Hi."

"Hi." She says flatly, turning her gaze to the dance floor.

"You look great."

"Thanks."

"So, uh…would you care to dan—"

"No." She turns and walks off.

Blake scrambles to her side. "Inez, please, talk to me."

"Last time you wanted to talk, you held me there, and kissed me without asking; even knowing I have a boyfriend."

"I did, and I'm sorry. I know that was wrong and I have no excuse. But I mean it this time. We don't have to be in private either. Right here, let's talk."

"There's nothing to talk about."

"There's a lot to talk about. I remember, Inez, and I know you do too. I remember how you looked at me when I kissed you, and how soundly you slept in my arms. I remember how you blushed when you told me you never enjoyed being touched before. I remember your smile and laugh when you're actually enjoying yourself. And that's not just with me, but when we're with Mishkin and Vladik too. I see it with Celia, and I even saw it with Allistair

244

before all this started. I don't see any of that when you look at him now."

Inez's gaze drops to the floor for a moment before she turns her head to the side. "I don't know what you're talking about."

"Yes, you do."

"Blake!" Allistair wraps his arm around his shoulders. His suit is black with gold and lavender embroidery, and he's wearing purple and black eye makeup to match. "So good to see you, man! We've barely talked these past few days!"

"Yeah." Blake looks away to roll his eyes. "Real pity."

A tiny snicker escapes Inez, and Blake raises a brow at her. She clears her throat and straightens her posture.

"Actually, Allistair, Pup and I were just wrapping up a brief chat. Now that we're done, can you and I dance?"

"Of course," says Allistair, patting Blake's shoulder. "Excuse us, will you? We'll catch up later."

Blake's glare burns through the two, and he takes a few steps back before turning to find Vladik and Mishkin. *Wait, where'd they go?*

His eyes scan through the crowd until a force pulls on his arm with a light giggle.

"Care to dance, sugar?"

"Celia! Absolutely." Blake smiles, taking a moment to admire her yellow gown with a black embroidered bird on the lower side. "Wow. You look absolutely beautiful."

"Well, so do you!" Celia rests her hands on his shoulders while Blake rests his on her waist.

The two swing themselves around the dance floor. He's surprised that Celia still seems to like him. He imagined Inez trying to sway Celia's opinion. Either she didn't try, or it didn't work. But he's happy to see Celia so full of life again.

245

"Have you been doing okay since Ian left?" he asks.

"I can rest much easier, that's for sure. I saw how he treated Inez too. Terrible."

"Why do you think Rex waited so long to fire him?"

Celia's eyes turn upward as she ponders his question. "I think Rex is just so pure-hearted that he can't bring himself to think badly of people. My daddy was the same way. He had so much faith in the good of this world."

Blake bites his tongue, forcing himself to nod as if she were right. Celia's dad sounds like he was a truly good man. It makes him sick to think Celia could compare him to such a monster. Would it be smart to tell her? Would she even believe him?

"I wonder about Inez, though," Celia continues.

"What do you mean?"

Celia drops her gaze to the floor, a light blush on her cheeks. "Honestly, I kind of like Allistair. Always have. Something about Inez changing her mind doesn't sit right with me. If I find out she's just mooching off the prince, there will be hell to pay."

A smirk forms on Blake's face as he twirls Celia under his arm. "You're jealous!"

"No! I'm protective! Allistair can turn me down if he wants to, but I won't let anyone use him like that."

"Well, you can relax. Inez is lying, but probably not for the reasons you're thinking."

"Why then? Whose ass do I need to kick?"

"I'll tell you everything as soon as I know. Right now, I'm still trying to get her to tell me what's going on."

"Why would she tell you? She never tells you anything."

Blake tightens his lips, and his eyes shift around the ballroom as they move around the dance floor. He forgot that he never told Celia what's been going on. Her jaw drops as if reading his mind.

"You're dating!" she barks. Blake shushes her, and Celia shrinks in her spot, lowering her voice just enough. "What happened?"

Blake shrugs. "Not sure. She's just been acting weird. I'm trying to figure out why."

"Then what are you dancing with me for, fool? Go get your girl!" Celia spins him around and shoves him away. "And if it doesn't work, come find me and I'll nag her myself!"

He smiles at her over his shoulder, and she winks at him before wandering off toward Knox and Melody.

You're the one who's pure hearted, Celia. Please don't ever change.

His smile vanishes when he turns around. He forgot to tell her it isn't so simple.

Chapter 32

It's hopeless.
    Blake leans against the wall, munching a handful of popcorn piece by piece, watching everyone, including Inez, dance in couples and groups, lost in the music. A few others are scattered around snack and drink tables, but he made a point to stand in a corner away from the whispers that have been following him around the halls.

Mishkin and Vladik are dancing too, and Blake grins at the sight. *They deserve to have fun after dealing with my stupidity.* Though it isn't long before they spot him, exchange looks, and hurry over. Blake hurries to finish the rest of his popcorn before they get to him.

"What's going on?" Mishkin asks.

"Celia knows. And Inez still won't talk to me."

"Right," says Mishkin, looking up at Vladik. "Plan B, then!"

Vladik nods, and they shuffle across the dance floor, Vladik dragging Blake by the arm. He lets go in the middle of the dance floor.

"Wait for the signal!" says Mishkin.

"Okay, what's the signal?" Blake asks.

Mishkin and Vladik scurry off, and Blake throws his arms up at the lack of response.

He does his best to keep sight of them as they scurry around the other moving bodies. Eventually, he's able to make out Vladik's form. He's about to head over when Mishkin plunges through the crowd, his arm linked with Allistair's.

"It's over here. You have to see what I'm talking about to understand." Mishkin winks over his shoulder at Blake as he continues to lead Allistair off.

Blake turns back to Vladik and sees him dancing with Inez. *Wait for the signal.* Blake shuffles his feet in place, awkwardly bopping along to the music as their dance gets closer. He tries to step around and hide within the crowd so she can't see him. Vladik catches a glimpse and spins Inez, giving Blake a quick nod.

Wait, was that the signal? But what do I do? Blake takes a few steps over, waiting, hoping that there will be another cue.

Inez is smiling when Vladik leans in and whispers something in her ear. Her smile drops to worry before Vladik spins her again. She's so surprised that she stumbles a bit, and Blake steps over to catch her in his arms.

"Blake!" she says, pushing him away. "I can't be here with you. Let me go."

"Why not?" Blake holds her waist as gently as possible without letting her get away.

"I have a boyfriend!"

"So, dance with me as a friend. It's not like this is the Midnight Dance. We still have time."

Inez stops struggling and stares into space. He runs his fingers through her hair, and Inez seems to melt at his touch.

"I can't," she says, eyes watering. "Please, just leave me alone."

Blake locks his eyes onto hers and runs his fingers along her scalp. He finds a swollen spot that feels like a scab and Inez pulls herself away with a whimper.

He grits his teeth and takes a slow breath. "I knew it. Rex hurt you, didn't he?"

"Quiet down! Just stay away from me. I'm fine."

"Talk to me, Inez, I'm begging you. If you still want me to leave you alone after that, I will. I just want to know why. Please."

Inez trembles in his arms, and her lip quivers. She turns her head to the side, this time with intent rather than to hide. Blake follows her sight line to the far wall where the Fools' King stands with Victor. He's rapt in conversation, almost oblivious to the rest of the dance floor.

Blake's gaze hardens as the King laughs with his peers, so at peace with his actions, while Inez is left to tremble in his presence. Worse, Victor doesn't seem fazed either. He's laughing along, as if his conversation with Blake never happened.

A hand grabs at Blake's wrist, and in the blink of an eye, Inez is pulling on his arm, leading him out of the ballroom. They rush through the hall, with only their

250

echoing footsteps breaking the silence until they reach the back door and step out into the frigid October night.

"Yes, okay? Yes!" Inez shouts, tears pouring down her cheeks. "He hurt me! Rex saw you leave my room, and it pissed him off. That's why he asked me to meet him, so he could beat it out of me and make me marry Allistair. It still hurts." She puts a hand over the sore spot on her head, taking short, choppy breaths between her tears. "He made me say those things. He hit me, threw me, threatened me until I agreed. He told me that if I didn't do what he said, he'd kill you. *Kill* you, Blake! I hid the blood so you wouldn't see. How did you know about it?"

"I touched your face when you came in, remember? I didn't see the blood on my fingers until after I left. I wanted to comfort you, but you kicked me out."

"I'm trying to protect you. We'll both be safe if you just go along with it."

"I can't do that, and neither can you. Going along with Rex's plan won't make either of us happy."

"What if it will? Allistair's a good man. He never forced me to do anything; he wouldn't even let me kiss him because he knew I was lying."

"Wait, really?"

Inez nods, wiping away tears, only for more to fall immediately. "I didn't try that much, but I wanted it to be true. I told myself it *could* be true. I could learn to love him, and it would be okay because I already enjoy his company."

"But it didn't work, did it? Because love doesn't work that way. It's not something you can force yourself to learn."

"I tried. I stared at my door every night, waiting for a knock. I whispered for Allistair to come in, but I...I always imagined you. I imagined you coming in, kissing me, holding me in your arms and refusing to let go. And then, I let you into my room, and you did. You held on to me, but I couldn't give in because I was so afraid. The whole reason I'm here is because everyone I cared about is dead. And when Rex threatened to kill you, I..."

Inez's voice trails off into a whimper as she covers her face. Blake puts a hand on her trembling shoulder, carefully, gently, as if his touch could shatter her. "I understand. Thank you for telling me."

"Please," Inez's voice falters. "For your own safety, stay away from me. You said you would if I told you everything, now go!"

"You haven't told me everything."

"What else is there?"

"You haven't told me what you want."

She turns her head to the side, sniffling. "I want you to leave."

Blake puts his hand on her jawline and carefully turns her head back to him. Her eyes gaze into his, tears spilling out again.

"Try that again, Inez. Tell me what you want."

Her lip quivers. "I want you to kiss me."

A smile spreads on Blake's face, and he places his lips on hers as gently as possible. Soft and sweet. He wraps his arms around her, and she melts in his embrace, their kisses becoming deeper.

More and more. Blake quietly begs her not to pull away, but she does, and far too soon.

"Blake, I mean it when I say I want to be with you. But I can't let you get hurt for it. I can't stand to lose anyone else."

"Can we at least try to figure something out? I'll be discreet about it, I'll lie if I have to, but I don't want to lose what we have. Nothing will happen to me, I promise."

Inez leans her head on his shoulder. "I'm not sure I could live with myself if anything bad happened to you."

"And I couldn't live with myself if I let you go. I love you, Inez. I'll risk it all if it means I can stay by your side."

Inez leaps at his words. Her tears are slowing down, but her breath is still quivering. She drops her eyes to the grass, and her silence is making Blake's heart race.

You know, when things seem uncertain, I...

"Wait for a sign," Blake whispers as Victor's voice rings through his mind.

"What?"

Blake furrows his brow toward Inez, but his focus is somewhere else. "A gamble."

He pulls the handkerchief from his suit pocket and whips out the neat folds. Black fabric with an embroidered red rose surrounded by flames. "Inez."

Inez's jaw drops. "Wh-where did you get that?"

"I've had it this whole time. Right next to my heart."

Inez's tears pour down her cheeks again, and she laughs as if she can't believe the absurdity of it all.

"Looks like we have an answer. Must be written in the stars."

"Stop." Inez smiles, but she closes her arms around her chest. "I don't believe in the stars."

"Maybe the stars believe in us. I don't blame you for being afraid, but I know you're brave enough to fight for what you want."

Inez shakes her head with a smile. "You make me sound so noble. We're not in a fantasy book, you know. We're not guaranteed a happy ending just because we fight back."

"No, but we aren't guaranteed a sad one either."

Inez shakes her head again, this time frowning. "Please stop. It sounds like you have an answer for everything, but life isn't so simple. It never has been."

Blake lets out a heavy breath, heart sinking. "So we're done then? Is that really what you want?"

"It's not what I want at all. But it's the safest option."

Blake wraps his arms around her, resting his forehead against hers. He takes a deep breath and swallows down the lump in his throat.

"Alright. You win. I'll leave you alone. Would one last kiss be okay?"

With tears in her eyes, Inez presses her lips to his, and he never imagined the sensation could be so heartbreaking. He tightens his grip with one hand stroking her hair, hoping to make this last as long as he can.

"Inez!" calls a familiar voice, startling the two. They look over to see the dumbfounded Prince, close enough to have heard everything.

"Allistair!" Inez calls. "We were, um—"

"Don't." Allistair puts up a hand, stepping closer. "I knew there was something going on." His eyes dart back and forth between the two. "Why did you guys lie to me?"

"Why?" Blake steps in front of Inez. "Your father almost gets Mishkin killed and beats her up, and you're asking why?"

"That wasn't my father!" Allistair barks. "He wouldn't hurt a fly!"

"Why do you think Inez pretended to date you? If you knew she was lying, you should've asked why a long time ago!"

"I did ask, and she never told me!" Allistair looks to Inez with a tremble in his eyes. "Inez, did you fake all of this because of my father?"

Inez hesitates, then nods her head.

"What did he do?"

Inez opens her mouth to answer, then closes it again. She lifts her hand and gently pulls off her silk scarf to reveal dark bruises on one side of her neck.

Blake's eyes fill with rage, and he grabs Allistair by the shirt. "You fucking asshole! You've been with her this whole time, and you didn't even notice?"

"How could I? She hid it from me!"

"Have you even been trying to figure out what's been going on? Can you even tell when she's lying?"

"You didn't see it either! So that makes us even!"

Blake shoves Allistair back, fists trembling as he remembers when she pulled him into her room. That was his chance to find the clues, the bruises, the head wound, and he let his lust take over. He growls, pushing aside his self-loathing.

"You had more of a chance than I did! She spoke to you. You knew she was faking it, and you didn't dig for an answer. I tried. I did everything I could to make Inez tell me." He points to the closed door of the mansion. "Everyone in there thinks I'm an obsessive stalker. But here I am, trying again, and it worked! She told me. What the *fuck* have you done to figure it out?"

Allistair's head hangs low, and his shoulders slump. "You're right. I didn't try as hard as I could've. I just wanted to believe it could be real—that Inez had really changed her mind."

"How could you not see the bruises?"

"She wore scarves and turtlenecks. I never would've seen."

"Blake," Inez grabs his arm. "I told you, Allistair wouldn't even let me kiss him until he knew for sure. There's no way he would've seen anything."

255

"What were you planning on doing tonight?" Blake's glare burns into Inez's face, making her eyes wide. "Would you have let him see then?"

"Blake, of course not."

"Then what would've happened?" Blake glares between the two. "What if I had given up and danced with Celia or Axel all night? What would've happened then?"

"I," Inez trembles. "I don't know."

"You don't know?"

"Blake, stop." Allistair pushes Blake's shoulder to turn him his way. "She was acting out of fear. She probably had no idea what would happen this entire time."

"And what would you have done?" Blake yells. "If she gave you consent, can you honestly say you would've refused?"

Allistair sighs and shakes his head. "No. No, I can't. But if that happened, I would've seen the bruises, and she would've *had* to tell me. There's no way this could've stayed hidden much longer. I wouldn't let anything happen if I knew she was hurt."

Blake huffs, taking a few steps back to process everything.

"Inez," says Allistair, "if you and Blake want to be together, you have my blessing. But please, stop hiding from me. From us. If people are getting hurt, I need to know about it. And if my father is really the one at fault, I'm the only chance we have at stopping him."

"How can we trust you?" Blake barks, storming to stand in his face. "We've been trying to tell you that Rex is terrible, and you didn't believe us!"

"I believe you now!" Allistair yells, before taking in a breath to recenter himself. "I'm sorry I didn't listen before. I watched my father go hungry just to feed me and

256

Axel. It's hard not to see someone like that as anything less than heroic."

Blake's heart twinges, and he stares at the ground.

"Allistair—" Inez grabs his hand. "I'm so sorry I lied to you. I'm sorry for hiding. I made a mess of things."

"I'm sorry too." Allistair squeezes her hand and looks over at Blake. "To both of you. If I were determined enough to find an answer, this wouldn't have gone on for so long. I guess part of me got lost in hoping."

"So, what now?" Blake asks.

"For now, you two enjoy the rest of the ball. Don't hide anymore. One thing I know is that my father loves his position of power, so don't show him he can control you. Let him see your Midnight Dance. He'll go looking for me, so I'll wait for him in my room. I'll find you guys at breakfast tomorrow. Maybe lunch if I sleep in. I'll let you know what he says, and we'll work around his commands without lying to each other. We can make sure everyone else stays safe."

"Is it that easy?" Blake asks.

"Not at all." Allistair shakes his head. "I'll take a huge ration of shit, of course. But if I'm going to be the next in charge, then the safety of my fools comes first." Allistair walks to the door and turns back to them once he steps inside. "There's only a few minutes until the Midnight Dance. Remember, don't hide."

The door closes behind him, leaving them under the starry sky. Blake lets out a heavy breath, unclenching his fists and allowing the night breeze to cool off the rest of his frustration.

Nothing happened. Inez is safe. I love her. I love you, Inez. He lifts his gaze to her and lets a tiny grin form on his face. Inez grins back as she takes a step closer.

"I know you don't believe in the Midnight Dance," he mutters. "Want to go up to the patio? We can keep this a secret if it makes you feel safer."

"No. Allistair's right, I can't give Rex power by running away. Fuck him. I've done too much for him out of fear. I'm taking my life back."

She grabs his hands. "I'm taking my love back."

Blake smiles and caresses her cheek with his free hand. "It's okay to be scared, Inez. Especially after what you've been through. I'm proud of you for every ounce of bravery you can muster, but it is okay if it's just one ounce at a time."

"Some days it will be, but not tonight. Besides, I'm more worried about you. He said he'd kill you, and considering what he did to me, I can't put it past him."

Blake shrugs. "Love has always been a risk. We may as well take it like true fools."

"Are you sure I'm worth it? You could date anyone else in here without all these problems."

"I've never been more certain of anything in my life."

Inez smirks. "Is that just because of the handkerchief?"

"What? No. Pretty sure it was you who lost your mind over a handkerchief. I know how superstitious you are."

Inez laughs as Blake pulls her into his arms and presses his lips to hers.

"You don't have to, you know."

"Yes, I do. It's not just about me. It never was. You've been dragged into it too, and Mishkin nearly died. I can't let this go on."

"You're amazing." Blake plants a soft kiss on her forehead.

She smiles and squeezes his hand as she leads the way back inside. Their footsteps echo in the hallway, and despite her determination, her hand is still quivering in his.

Her feet freeze just outside the ballroom. Blake follows her eyeline to Rex, who is chatting away with men in black suits. All of them hold glasses of wine or champagne and laugh in unison.

"It's not too late," Blake whispers. "We can still slip away."

"I know, but we can't hide forever."

Inez takes a deep breath and a slow step forward. Blake follows her lead, making sure to keep her pace.

Mishkin and Vladik spot them, and grins line their faces. Inez forces a smile, but her puffy eyes don't do much to hide her fear.

They settle in the center of the dance floor as the music shifts from upbeat to calm. Couples form all over the dance floor, while a few strays litter the walls and food tables, idling in conversation or downing another drink.

Blake rests his hands on her waist as her arms wrap around his neck. The two lock eyes as the music plays.

He rests his forehead on hers. "I meant it you know. I love you. So much."

"I know, I love you too."

"I'm not happy with you though," he smirks. "I was really worried. I had nightmares and everything."

"I'm sorry."

"Sorry doesn't cut it."

"What do you want me to do?"

"Kiss me. You owe me unlimited kisses until I forgive you."

A grin creeps onto Inez's face, and her eyes shift around as if she's trying to hide it. "And when you forgive me, then what?"

"Then I'll kiss you as a reward."

259

Inez giggles and presses her lips to his, soft at first, then adding more pressure, more tongue, more passion. Blake wraps his arms around her, pulling her close to him.

He opens his eyes to peek toward the wall behind Inez, where Rex's rage is blazing. Blake can't help but grin at the sight as he combs his fingers through Inez's hair, trailing his lips down her neck, carefully kissing each bruise, his confident gaze not leaving Rex for a second.

Inez's arms pull him closer, prompting him to continue as she presses her own lips down his neck as well. Blake's heart is melting, and his grin is glowing. *See that, King? Even you can't keep her from me.*

Rex narrows his eyes before he quickly but calmly exits the ballroom. Blake returns his gaze to the sparkling brown eyes in front of him.

"Do you think Rex saw us?" she asks.

"I think he got the message."

★ ★ ★

BLAKE SHUTS INEZ'S BEDROOM DOOR with his foot as their hungry kisses continue. He takes off his jacket and undoes his tie as they make their way across the room. He guides her onto the bed, hovering over her, lips lowering to her neck as his hands explore her curves through her gown. Her moans and heavy breaths heat up every inch of him as the bulge grows in his pants.

Inez sits up to kiss his neck as Blake's hand finds the zipper on the back of her dress. He tugs it a tiny bit but doesn't pull it down just yet.

"May I?" he whispers.

"Please do," Inez breathes as her kisses line his collarbone.

He trails his kisses down her neck, spotting the bruises, and freezes, prompting Inez to do the same.

"What's wrong?" she asks.

"A lot's been happening, and you said your head still hurts. Are you sure you're up for this?"

"Everything that's happened has made me *need* this." She presses her lips hard against his. "I want you to fuck me. Don't make me beg."

A hungry growl escapes his throat as he pulls the zipper down and guides the straps down her smooth shoulders. Her breasts are braless, and her pink nipples look delicious. He kisses down her chest, then grabs one breast in his hand and teases the opposite nipple with his tongue. Inez arches her back, pulling at the front of his shirt.

She gets the buttons open, and Blake yanks it off as quickly as he can. Inez scoots herself out of her dress, her pink panties whetting his appetite. His hands caress her hips then reach around to grip her ass, pulling a small sound of pleasure from her lips. Her skin is so smooth, every part of her fits perfectly into his hands, and he can't wait to feel and taste every inch.

Blake grips at the hem of her panties as Inez lies back, and he pulls them down, licking his lips. Her pussy is shaved, smooth, and he's about to taste when he notices Inez is hiding her face in her hands. He guides one off and presses his lips to hers.

"Please don't hide," he whispers. "You're beautiful. All of you is beautiful."

Inez smiles and kisses him again before he trails kisses down her cheek to her neck, teasing her skin with his lips and teeth. Her heavy breathing sends hot chills through his body as his lips and tongue trace down her stomach. He opens her legs and trails more kisses from her knee

261

down the inside of her thigh, reveling in every soft moan from her lips, every hungry breath, every squirm that begs him for more.

He takes a second to glance up at her blushing face before he gently places a kiss just above her slit, then moving down to stroke her clit with his tongue, and she tastes as sweet as she looks. Her back arches, and he brings one hand up to cup her breast and the other to tease her entrance before gently pushing a finger inside. Inez's soft moans get louder, more and more as Blake's pushes in a second finger. Her hand grips at his hair.

"Yes, Blake. Please, yes."

His movements become faster and harder, but he slows down before he stops, trailing wet kisses back up her body, up her neck, then finally back to her lips, enjoying every second, every taste, every sound he'd been wanting for so long.

He pulls off his pants and boxers, grabbing the condom from the pocket and holding onto it while Inez grabs at his cock. Her grip alone is enough to send him reeling, but she pulls it into her mouth, and he growls low in his throat. Her tongue, like silk, sends a wave of euphoria through his body as he grabs her hair, being careful to avoid the bump he found before.

"Ugh, fuck, yes," he groans.

After a short while, Inez pulls away, and Blake slides the condom on before he drops himself between her legs, pushing his tongue into her mouth again as his cock slides itself up and down the wet slit. He nibbles at her ear as she presses her chest against him. His grin grows at her hunger.

"Do you still want to?" he asks.

"God, yes."

Blake grins as he pushes himself inside, her walls tight against him. Inez's gasps fill his ears, and he pauses to let her adjust to him. Ecstasy pulses through his veins as he slowly pulls out and back in again. He continues the motion, his hip teasing her clit. Slowly at first, then gradually getting faster, harder. His hands grip her hips while his teeth nibble her neck. Inez's hands claw at his back and hair, pulling him as close as she can.

Inez's body bursts into a fit of quakes and moans; beautiful, unbridled pleasure painted all over her face. Her walls tighten around him, and the euphoria pulses through him as well, thrusting harder and faster until he trembles, pushing deeper inside as his own pleasure is released.

He stares down at her hot, panting body, lowering himself to rest his forehead on hers. He kisses her again before he drops to her side, catching his breath.

He carefully removes the condom and settles himself at her side. She scoots closer, her head against his chest as his arms wrap around her. He massages her scalp and neck while he steals a few more kisses. It isn't long before she's sound asleep, and he plants a gentle kiss on her forehead.

This is where I belong. By your side. Forever.

Chapter 33

Blake's eyes blink open to a mess of red hair. Sunlight creeps in through the window, glowing against the smooth skin that has shifted out of the blanket. He pulls the covers over her shoulder, and she shifts closer to him. He wraps an arm around her, and she lets out a soft, content moan.

They go still again, and Blake closes his eyes to take in everything. The warmth of her body, her silky-smooth skin, the scent of her hair. It's all too perfect. This is how he should wake up every morning. Just like this.

His heart races when Inez turns herself around to kiss him.

"I love you," he whispers. "I know I've said it a lot, but damn, do I mean it. I love you so much."

Inez giggles. "I know. I love you too."

She presses a hand against his chest, pulling the blankets from hers. Her body practically shines in the morning glow, and she grabs his hair again. He grins and climbs over her, and she giggles through heavy breaths as he trails his kisses down her neck and to her chest.

A knock on the door startles them both, and Blake glares at the door.

Go away. Go away. Go away.

"Blake, I know you're in there," Allistair's voice calls, much more stern than last night. "Get to the office right now."

"In a minute," Blake growls, regretting that he responded at all. Even Inez raises her brows as if asking him why he said anything.

"Now!"

BLAKE BURSTS INTO THE OFFICE without knocking, but he pauses when he sees the room empty.

Crack!

A weight at the back of his skull makes the room spin and his body go limp. He turns his head, and barely catches a glimpse of a dragon tattoo before everything goes black.

Chapter 34

Angry ringing fills Blake's ears, dulling down as his vision clears up. He's on his side, on some kind of leather seat, and a small bump under his body sends a shooting pain through his skull, threatening to make him sick. His hands are tied behind him, and he struggles to sit, eyes widening at the passing scenery of trees and rock walls.

"Hey look, boss, he's awake!"

The voice sends a chill over Blake's skin, and he turns to glare at the bald-headed asshole on the seat next to him. He smiles at Blake as if greeting an old friend. "Hey, sweetheart. Did you miss me?"

"Ian!" Blake barks, sitting as upright as possible in his restraints. "What the *fuck* is going on?"

"I think it's safe to say you're fired. Ain't that right, King?"

Blake catches his breath as he turns to see Rex in the driver's seat, a metal cage protecting him from both of them. "What the hell?"

"You swore to me, Blake. You promised to live under my command at the mercy of the stage. You signed the contract, now it's liable to termination or worse."

"The 'or worse' is the fun part!" Ian grins.

"I tried to be fair," Rex says with a calm, blank voice, eyes glued to the road ahead. "I tried to warn you that Inez wasn't interested, and then you went and hurt her so badly."

"What?" Blake sits up in his spot. "What the hell are you talking about?"

"I'm talking about what you did to our Fire Goddess. Everyone saw the bruises on her neck. I can't imagine what she's been going through in your presence. I won't have an abusive tyrant in my home."

"That was *you*!" Blake growls, fighting the ropes at his wrists and ankles. "I know it was! Inez came down from your room with blood dripping down her face!"

"How is that possible? I can't recall a time Inez was ever in my room. At least," Rex shoots a sly grin to Blake through the rearview mirror. "Not when anyone else could see."

"You bastard!" Blake kicks the cage.

"Ooh, that pissed him off!" Ian laughs.

"You fucking monster!" Blake yells. "You know what you did to her! And why is *he* here?"

"Well, that's not a friendly tone," Ian says. "King here called me up with a deal."

"As I was saying," Rex continues in a raised voice, "I tried to be fair. I even offered you my daughter and the limelight as a peace offering. I handed you your dream, as well as any sexual fantasy you could have, on a silver platter. I considered it a win-win, and was certain you would, too. But since you're *so* willing to give it all up, I can't afford to have you causing any more trouble in my mansion."

"That's why I'm here, Pup. I take care of one little pest, and I get my job back. Inez will still have to marry Allistair, but I can find time to sneak her away."

"I can't fucking believe this!" Blake kicks at the cage again. "You offered me your *daughter* like a piece of property? What the *fuck* is your problem?"

"Ian, cease his kicking, please."

"Yes, sir!" Ian pulls out a switchblade and sinks it into Blake's leg faster than he can react.

He screams as the pain shoots through him, and warm red oozes from the wound and soaks his pants, turning the blue embroidery into an angry shade of violet.

"Now, be a good boy, or I'll have to get the other leg too."

Blake's body trembles, and the pain continues to throb up his leg to his hip and down to his knee.

"They'll notice I'm gone. What do you plan to tell them?"

"Exactly what I told you," Rex says. "You've been fired for abusing one of your colleagues."

"You really think they'll believe that crap?"

"Considering the evidence, I'd say so. Inez begins avoiding you shortly before the ball and won't tell anyone why. She goes back to Allistair because he's her best friend and soulmate, and they attend the ball together. Then suddenly, she's bruised and dancing with you, of all people. You, who came after me when Mishkin collapsed

268

from his unpredictable heart condition. You, who threatened to steal her away from Allistair."

Blake grits his teeth, glaring at Rex's soft, calm expression through the rear-view mirror.

"Well, she isn't my child," Rex continues. "So I try not to pester her, but her safety is just as important to me as everyone else's. She is our beloved Fire Goddess, after all, and you're just a runaway pup. I'm sure the evidence speaks for itself. Even now, you're still in last night's clothes. You spent the entire night in Inez's room, filling the walls of her safe space with lustful nightmares."

"Oh, so you *did* fuck her!" Ian sneers, twisting the knife in his leg.

Blake's screaming scratches his throat, but he can't hold it back.

Ian leans in with a grin. "That pisses me off, but I'm a little turned on, too. Tell me, what did that bitch do with that velvet tongue of hers?"

Blake growls and twists himself to ram his head into Ian's mouth, the pain in his leg is dull in his rage.

Ian yells out in pain as a tooth digs into Blake's skull.

"Keep talking about Inez like that and I'll *fucking* kill you!"

Ian touches his bloody mouth and glares at the blood on his fingers. His eyes flit to Blake and lunges his fist into his jaw, sending more pain through his already splitting skull. He falls back, shaking, his leg still throbbing as his blood stains the leather seat.

"My, what a temper." Rex smiles. "It's no wonder Inez was so afraid. I can't have you threatening my circus. I believe we all know what happens to violent dogs."

"And what about Ian here? He's been threatening them forever and even took advantage of Inez! Then you hurt her in order to frame me? I'm not the one who needs to leave the mansion!"

"Not giving up, are you?" Ian twists the knife, and Blake screams out again.

"That's enough!" Rex shouts. "We're here."

The car swerves off the road, bouncing and swaying back and forth as it drives over rocks, bushes, and fallen trees. They stop short, and Blake is thrown against the cage, then dropped onto the car floor. The knife is still in his leg, making him groan through gritted teeth.

Ian and Rex step out of the car. Blake curls into a ball, pain shooting into every crevice of his body. When he doesn't move quickly enough, Ian yanks Blake out by his elbow. His hip, knee, and ankle bump the bottom of the car on the way out. Ian drops him onto the ground, and another pang shoots through his head, the stab wound in his leg, and a rock digs into his shoulder.

Blake winces, doing his best to ignore the pain as he struggles to sit. "So, you're just going to kill me out here, and all your problems will be solved?"

"Of course not," says Rex. "My status is far too high to put any more blood on my hands. Ian here will do it for me, and I'll handle that pesky Fire Goddess when I get back."

"Why kill me at all? Why not just void my contract and make me leave?"

"Inez has been sneaking out of this mansion for a while now. She's been looking for work and building connections outside. If I let you live, she has more reason to leave. And of course, I cannot risk you revealing our secrets. In truth, your contract was life or death from the beginning. I could renew, or you could disappear, but you were never going back home."

"You loathsome piece of shit!" Blake struggles to stand, pain shooting through his leg. "Your high status is nothing but a lie! You're a pathetic, worthless excuse for a leader! You'll never be anything more than a lowlife, disgusting psychopa—"

Rex's ringed fist slams into Blake's gut, forcing the air from his lungs. Blake falls back, body convulsing, begging for a breath of air.

"It's tragic, really. I planned to hire you when you were young, but your late mother wouldn't trade you in for any amount of money in the world. Then years later, like a dream come true, you came straight to me of your own free will, so eager to join. But I was unaware of your true nature. You're nothing but a pest, and you'll be exterminated as such."

A breath of air finally makes its way into Blake's chest, and he coughs, spitting out whatever raspy curse words and threats he can manage. Ian presses his foot to Blake's head and pushes his ear into the soil. Pain shoots into every inch of his body, but Ian is frowning at Rex, and Blake struggles to listen.

"Did I hear that right?" Ian asks. "*You* will deal with the Fire Goddess?"

"My children will never accept your return," Rex responds. "Give me ten minutes to remove myself from the area, then finish the work. When it's done, you will receive payment. However, you may not return to the mansion."

"You promised I could!" Ian removes his foot, but everything hurts too much for Blake to move. "You swore it!"

"You wouldn't have helped me otherwise." Rex struts to the car, and Blake trembles as Ian and Rex continue arguing.

271

Memories flood his mind, of his time before joining the circus. His run-down apartment, his dead-end job, his parents who always pressured him, but they loved him. His life wasn't perfect, but it was fine. He gave it all up to end up here. Judy tried to warn him that something was off about this troupe, and he ignored her.

He gave it all up to end up here. Judy tried to warn him that something was off about this troupe, and he ignored her. Was it really worth this?

Yes, because I got to meet her.

Memories with Inez replace the others and tears flood his eyes.

So this is it. I took the risk, and I'm paying for it. But I got to stay by your side. I got to hear you say you loved me. And I'll always love you, Inez. I know you won't let yourself be overpowered by Rex. You'll be okay. I know you can escape that place with your own strength. You will move forward, and I'll be watching, proud of every step.

And when you do find someone else to trust and open up to, I hope it'll never come to this for either of you.

"In any case," Rex barks, snapping Blake back to the present. "Now that you have the filthy dog who slept with your woman, it's a matter of personal pleasure for you, isn't it? Think of it as a labor of passion."

He slips into the driver's seat, backs onto the road, then zooms off at top speed, leaving the two in silent stillness.

"*Fucking* King!" Ian kicks a rock in the disappearing car's direction. He yells at the empty road, then turns and grabs Blake's elbow and shoves him against a nearby tree with a grin. "He's got a point, though." He pulls a fresh switchblade from his pocket and holds it to Blake's face. "I could give you a nice revenge fuck before I kill you. Then I'll go after the King and take Inez back myself."

"And what'll you get from it?" Blake asks. "Rex is using you. If you kill me, you'll just prove that you're nothing but his mindless pawn."

Ian laughs. "Nice try, you just want to stay alive."

"Obviously, but what good will it do you to kill me if you're not getting your job back anyway? He dropped his end of the bargain, why bother keeping up yours? He's going to pay you in ten, twenty minutes, anyway. You can take the money and run. No need to put blood on your hands over that piece of trash."

"You think you're my first kill, Pup? I'm gonna finish you off because I want to."

He presses the knife to Blake's throat. "Too bad, you're pretty damn cute, but you talk too much, so I'll make this quick." Sharp pains burn through Blake's neck as he yells out in pain.

Bang.

A shot rings through the air, and Ian whips around to face the road. A man in a tan suit and black ski mask holds a gun toward them, standing tall and statuesque. Ian steps back with his hands up.

"Get back!" calls a strong voice, and Blake can't recognize who it belongs to.

Ian chuckles before he focuses on Blake. "One shot, then."

He raises his knife, grinning back at the shooter as his wrist twists to adjust its aim. Blake squeezes his eyes shut, readying himself for the final throw that will end him before he's rescued.

Bang.

Ian screams, and Blake opens his eyes to find the knife at hiss feet. Ian grips his wrist and yells out in pain at his bloodied hand, then at the shooter. Scarlet streams drip down and stain the dirt. Ian stares the shooter down before running off in the opposite direction as Rex.

The shooter keeps his gun aimed at Ian, stepping over to Blake but never once looking over. Soon Ian is out of sight, and the shooter puts his gun away before collapsing to his knees.

"Hey!" Blake calls. "Are you okay?"

"Damn it, that was killer on my back," the shooter says in a much more familiar voice, and Blake's eyes go wide.

"Hartman?"

The shooter pulls off his ski mask and smiles through his white beard, his hair a tangled mess around his face. "Didn't expect me, did you?" He chuckles.

"You Shit Head!" Blake's eyes tear up as he laughs. "I thought I was on someone else's hit list!"

Hartman chuckles as he hobbles over to untie Blake's wrists and ankles, cringing at the knife in his leg.

"We can't take you to a hospital, they'll want to investigate. If they do that, Rex will just bribe his way out of justice. Again. And he'll likely find a way to get *you* locked up instead."

"So, what do we do?" Blake asks as the two help each other stand and hobble to the car.

"I have a private doctor. I'll give her a call."

Chapter 35

* * *

Removing the dagger hurts more than having it stabbed, and Blake clenches his teeth on a leather belt he was offered.

Hartman's private doctor couldn't bring an anesthetic on such short notice, but Hartman graciously pours wine into the wound while the doctor gets stitches, much to her disdain.

After an hour of cleaning, stitching, and disinfecting, Blake can finally take a breath as he relaxes on the couch. Hartman writes a check for the doctor, an even larger sum for keeping the incident quiet. The doctor looks unsure, but she agrees and accepts her payment.

The ache in his leg is persistent, but the doctor assures him there's little chance of permanent damage, and he's grateful.

She helps him sit up to take a painkiller with a cup of water and demands that Hartman give him something to eat before she takes her leave.

Hartman hobbles over to Blake with his cane and a lit cigarette, tossing a small pack of cookies onto his chest.

"All right, you're well enough. Now let's go."

"Go where?"

"Back to the mansion. I got a bone to pick with a King."

★ ★ ★

IN THE FRONT SEAT, Blake stares blankly at the passing scenery. The events of this morning seem so distant, almost like a dream. If his leg weren't sore from limping to the car, he'd almost believe it was. He's grateful the clothes Hartman lent him are presentable, albeit a bit loose, but a blue button-up and black slacks are hardly embarrassing.

"How did you know where to find me?" he asks, munching on another cookie and trying not to cringe. *And how does a rich bastard like you have such stale snacks?*

"Victor called me," Hartman responds. "I guess he knew Rex was up to something and couldn't stop it. He gave me the coordinates from Rex's phone, and I just had to hide before he left the spot. Lucky for us, Rex won't get his hands dirty anymore. I knew he'd have someone else doing his dirty work, so I wasn't too worried. And it's nice to know Victor isn't as useless as he seems."

"So, what's the plan?"

"For now, just follow my lead. Stay quiet until I tell you to speak. Victor warned me you don't think things through."

Blake slouches in his seat with a heavy breath, crumpling the package as he chews the last cookie. Hartman isn't wrong, and it's weighing his chest down. All of this could've been avoided if he just knew how to keep his mouth shut. It could've saved him a few stitches and Inez a few bruises.

Inez. His heart races at the thought of her, in Victor's office, hearing news of his death. Or being told nothing and running through the mansion halls, looking for him, scared out of her mind.

He shakes away the images, trying to assure himself that she'll be okay. He's on his way back. She won't have to be scared for long. Even better, Rex isn't taking Ian back after all, so at least he won't be there to make things worse. Still, his heartbeat isn't slowing.

"So," he says, hoping to distract his mind. "Where did you learn to shoot?"

"I joined the army after high school. Hurt my back in battle and buried myself in office work when I got better. It wasn't until years later that I invested in The Fools' Circus because I heard some evil bullshit was going down. Now I need to make sure that damned Rex gets what he fucking deserves."

"Speaking of Rex," says Blake through gritting teeth. "He mentioned that he wanted to adopt me when I was young. Do you know what that's about?"

Hartman's glare softens to concern with a brief glance in Blake's direction. "You've performed at parks and in front of shows since you were small. Did you really think Rex wouldn't notice? He offered your mom quite the large sum in exchange for your adoption."

277

Blake tenses. "So that was true? He tried to *buy* me?"

"Your mother refused, of course. But if you hadn't been adopted so quickly after her death, you would've been at that mansion much sooner."

Blake bites his lip as he glares at the road ahead. *When did Rex make that offer?* A pang in his chest makes his blood run cold.

If Ian kills for Rex, does that mean...? No, it had to be an accident. If Rex hired someone to kill her, he would've been able to adopt Blake right off the bat, right?

He takes a deep breath to calm himself. *Rex is a monster. An evil piece of trash. But even he can't control everything.*

"Keep yourself together," says Hartman. "That fucking King can smell fear. Hold your head high, and your back straight. Poker face."

"Got it." Blake's mind flashes to Inez's story, and how both of her parents died. "So, does Inez being your granddaughter have any significance in all this?"

Hartman lets out a heavy breath, and blinks as if holding back tears. "As far as you're concerned, no. For us, that's just the tip of the iceberg. But that talk never happened, remember? Inez doesn't know, and right now that's helpful. Don't say another word about it. Not until I can finally back Rex into a fucking corner."

"Got it." Blake smirks to himself as they pull up to the mansion. *I see where Inez gets her potty mouth from.* He searches the windows for a face. Any face, really, but Inez's face in particular.

When they reach the front door, Blake raises a hand to knock, but Hartman pushes it open without hesitating, and Blake follows close behind. A few members stare at the duo with wide eyes, as if they're staring at ghosts.

"Where's your King?" Hartman asks.

"In the office, sir." Ronan gestures down the hall. "He just called Inez in for a conference."

"Perfect." Hartman nods, making his way over. "Follow me, Blake. And Ronan, you come too. It's time you spoke up."

Ronan tenses. "I don't think that's a good idea, sir."

Hartman glares back at him and slams the base of his cane against the floor. "Never settle for silence! Silence gives power to the oppressor and keeps you under their foot. Get your ass in that office and speak the fuck up!"

Blake's jaw drops as Hartman continues on his way, calling for Blake to follow him. Ronan stares at the floor. Blake puts a hand on his shoulder and offers a comforting nod. Ronan's lips form a tight line, but he nods back, and the two follow Hartman down the hall.

Hartman opens the door without knocking. "Good afternoon, Rex. The ball was lovely! Thank you for having me!"

"Hartman!" Rex growls. "Why are you here?"

His face goes pale when he notices Blake and Ronan strolling in behind him.

Inez gasps when she sees Blake and runs over to squeeze him. Blake puts a hand on her cheek and presses his lips to hers; so sweet he might cry.

You're alright! I'm so glad!

"I found Blake here on the side of the road and decided to give him a ride home. Was curious to see how he's fitting in."

"He isn't," Rex hisses. "He abused my Fire Goddess to the point where she refuses to admit the trauma she endured!"

"Trauma? From Blake?" Hartman glances over at Inez, still in Blake's arms. "She ran up to hug him. I hardly think that's the reaction of someone who's been abused.

279

Though come to think of it, Blake was injured when I found him. I can't help wondering who the real culprit is."

Inez catches her breath and grips his shirt. She stares at Blake with wide eyes while Rex and Hartman continue arguing.

"What happened?" she whispers. Her eyes fall to the large band aid on his neck and she looks ready to scream.

Blake puts a finger to her lips and gently shushes her. "I'll explain later."

She trembles in her spot but shuts her mouth tight and nods.

"He hurt one of my children!" Rex exclaims. "I refuse to stand by and allow it!"

"Last I checked," Hartman grumbles, "Inez wasn't *your* child."

"That's not the point!" Rex snarls. "He's leaving, and I won't follow along with any more of your nonsensical whims!"

"What a shame." Hartman steps closer to Inez and grabs her chin, turning her head to see the bruises on her neck.

Red fills his eyes, and his nostrils flare, but he keeps his voice calm. "Tell me, dear. Who did this to you? Was it Blake?"

Inez hesitates, glancing over at Rex, whose glare burns in her direction. She takes a deep breath and stands tall, glaring back at the King. "No sir, it wasn't. It was—"

"That's what I thought." Hartman releases Inez and turns back to Rex. "You see, Rex, Blake is actually an old friend of mine, and I happen to know that violence is completely out of the question for him."

"How dare you!" Rex hisses. "You're questioning *me*?"

"Of course not." Hartman raises a hand in defense. "I'm just saying that someone else hurt her, and you need to fire the true culprit, whoever it may be."

Rex pulls back his lips, hissing at the old man. "It's not your decision to make!"

"No, but it *is* my money." Hartman frowns. "And I was *so* looking forward to seeing Blake on stage. Matter of fact, if you keep him, I can double your budget. Triple if he gets a lead."

"Corruption!" Rex shouts, slamming his hands on the desk. "You biased old man! Using your money to have things your way! Admit it, you're just using that boy!"

"And what do you call what you're doing? Adopting children for your personal circus. Shall I inform everyone how you found them all?"

"Everyone knows how I found them! They were lost and I saved them! I'm a hero! I gave them a choice, and they chose me! They owe me their *lives*!"

"Is that why you nearly killed Ronan here?"

Silence fills the office, and Blake is holding his breath. Rex's kingly façade is slipping to madness. Blake nearly forgot about Ronan, who's had his back to the side wall the entire time, as if trying to blend in with the reds and golds of the wallpaper. His eyes are wide, glued to the floor as if begging to disappear.

Hartman's gaze softens at him, and he gestures toward Rex. "Go on."

Ronan lifts his eyes to Hartman, then to Rex, and pulls his back from the wall. He takes a deep breath and steps forward to look Rex in the eye.

"Rex, we both know you have a twisted way of running things, and I'm sure I'm not the only one of your children aware of that fact."

"What are you going on about?" Rex sneers. "That time you fell from the balcony? That was your own mistake."

"No, it was yours. You didn't think I was good enough to be on stage anymore. When I begged you to let me keep trying, you proposed a challenge. You told me that if I could walk on my hands along the balcony rail, you'd let me perform. You took advantage of the fact that I was only fifteen and wouldn't see that as anything other than a genuine promise. And as soon as I was on the rail, you kicked me off the edge! I fell onto the first-floor roof, hit my head, and got this scar." Ronan turns his face to display the line tracing his cheek.

"And then you left me, bleeding and broken. I was out there for two hours, yelling for help before Mishkin and Vladik found me. I cried in their arms. My lungs ached, and I couldn't stop shaking. I was freezing, starving, and terrified. I almost ran away. I didn't want to come back. But then I heard you wanted Melody off stage next. She was only twelve, I had to protect her!" Ronan pauses to catch his breath as his eyes water.

"I stayed to protect the others because I knew what you were before they did. I saw what you were willing to do before your status went up. You're a fucking monster, Rex. And I won't let you get away with this shit anymore."

"So that's it." Inez steps to Ronan's side, glaring at Rex. "That's why Knox and Melody had Allistair minister the wedding instead of you, isn't it? You were threatening Melody, and they don't want anything to do with you either. She was lucky, but I wasn't. Neither was Ronan or Mishkin. In fact, I'm curious to know how many others would love to speak up right now."

"Everyone is beginning to see what you are." Blake steps to Ronan's other side. "You won't be in power much longer."

Rex stares at the group with a blank expression, and the silence in the air hangs heavy around them. He strolls around the desk, keeping deadpan eyes straight ahead and stopping at the door.

"The Pup's contract ends in a year. But I expect a large budget for these ridiculous accusations. It's a shame you all have to sink to such a distasteful level. Lying, and pointing fingers. But that's all right. I forgive you. Everyone will see the truth soon enough."

Blake holds his breath as Rex steps out, slamming the office door behind him. Moments of silence tick by in slow motion until a chuckle escapes Hartman's throat.

"What a damn baby!" Hartman pulls a cigarette and lighter from his pocket. "Hey, Fire Goddess."

Inez snaps to attention "Yes, sir?"

Hartman takes a step toward her, turning his head to let out a puff of smoke before turning to look her in the eye. "I know what you want, and I promise it's coming. It just can't happen yet."

Inez's jaw drops, and her body tenses. "I, um, I'm sorry, sir, I don't know what you mean."

"That's enough of this 'sir' nonsense out of you. Call me Gramps!"

"Um," Inez's eyes dart around the room, as if someone else might know what's going on. "Okay, Gramps. I don't know what you mean, but it was Rex who hurt me. Not Blake."

"I'm well aware. Believe me, I've turned him in to the police many times, and each time he manages to buy or charm his way out. He may need my money for the show, but he's far from broke without it. Don't worry, he'll get what he has coming."

"Why support him then?" Blake asks. "Why not withdraw your funding?"

"This damned country is full of rotten pigs like him. If I withdraw my support, someone else will step in, and there's a good chance the next guy won't care so much. Besides, Rex is right. I am using you, boy, and you're exceeding my expectations."

"Using me for what? To expose Rex?"

Hartman's eyes drop to the floor, and his jaw shifts. It isn't just Rex. *For us it's just the tip of the iceberg.*

Blake gives him an understanding nod, but his chest twinges. Does he have to keep this a secret from Inez? She might never forgive him, but there's likely some other reason for it.

"At any rate," Hartman continues, snapping Blake back to the present. "There's an even bigger storm coming, and I'm going to need you all to stay on your toes."

"So that's it?" Ronan says. "I faced my fear and called out a man who could kill me just to stay on my toes?"

"Your bravery today won the battle, but the war is far from over." He saunters toward the door before anyone else can say anything. "Have Victor call me if you need anything else."

The door closes, and Ronan and Inez look to Blake.

"So, you're just," Ronan shrugs. "Okay with being used?"

"If it means protecting you, Inez, and the others, I won't lose any sleep over it."

"Well, so far it got you a busted lip and a cut on your neck. And did I see you limping? What the hell happened to you?"

"I'll tell Hartman he owes me later. Right now, I'm really sick of this damned office."

Ronan nods and shakes Blake's hand. Inez gives Ronan a comforting hug, and they all leave in a silence that weighs heavy on their shoulders.

In the hall, Allistair waits by the staircase with his arms crossed.

"There you two are," he mutters. "Ronan, may I speak to Inez and Blake alone, please?"

Ronan looks to the two as if unsure. With their assurance, he heads down the hall, and the remaining three wait until he's out of earshot.

"Nice going, Pup," Allistair mutters. "You almost had me fooled."

"What are you talking about?" Blake asks.

"My father has seen you leave Inez's room with blood on your hands. I know you were lying."

Blake clutches his breath, but Inez steps in front of him before he can retaliate.

"You're fucking kidding, right?" She exclaims. "Did you hear anything that we all said in there?"

"I don't eavesdrop," says Allistair. "But I watched my father starve himself, work his hands to the bone, and still manage to give us an opportunity he never had. I'm sick of the lies."

"The only one lying is Rex!" Blake exclaims.

"You're a worthless, untrustworthy dog!" Allistair yells. "Everything was fine before you showed up! I know Inez would've turned down my love anyway, but she never kept secrets from me before! She never had to hide until you came in and forced her to lie on your behalf!"

Smack.

285

Inez's hand slams into Allistair's cheek, and his head is turned away. His eyes wide, as if his heart is hurting more than his jaw.

"That's enough!" Inez yells. "You have no idea what either of us has been through this whole time. I did hide, but it was because of Rex, not Blake. You're hiding from the truth because it hurts, but if you don't open your fucking eyes, then you're on the same path of corruption that Ian said you were!

"I did trust you, Allistair. That never changed. But if you're not going to trust me, then I'm not sure what to think of you anymore."

Allistair remains motionless as Inez shoves past him and makes her way upstairs. Blake moves to do the same, but Allistair grabs his arm.

"I love her too you know," he whispers. "And I'll be watching. I don't care if she never loves me back, but I won't let her get hurt again."

"I'm glad to hear that," Blake frowns. "But you're watching the wrong man. I hate to say that Ian had a point back then, but your father isn't who you think he is. If you really want to protect her, you can't stay blind forever."

BLAKE CLOSES INEZ'S BEDROOM door behind him while she reaches under her bed. He grins at the cute bum in the air and gives it a gentle tap. Inez kicks her leg out with a playful grumble and Blake laughs.

He takes in the view of Inez's room as if it's the first time. Memories of the night before seem so distant, as if he hadn't been here for days.

Inez pops back out from under her bed with a box in her hands. "This is for you! But before you open it, you have to tell me why you're limping. What the hell happened to you?"

Blake gestures toward the bed. They sit side by side, and Blake tells Inez about getting hit in the head when he entered the office. He describes the car ride, how Axel's advances were due to Rex's prompting, and how Ian decided to go along.

He tells her about the stab in his leg, and she gapes when he shows her the stitches. He explains how Hartman rescued him and had a private doctor fix him up. He tells her everything except Hartman being her grandpa. *That conversation never happened.*

"What the fuck," Inez whispers, eyes watering. "I waited almost an hour for you to get back from the office. When I went to find you, no one was there. You weren't in your room or out in the yard. I ran through the whole mansion, but no one had seen you all morning. I was terrified."

"I'm okay."

"Allistair kept you on the stairs just now, didn't he? What did he say?"

"He said he still cares about you and wants you safe. I know he's got the wrong idea, but I don't think he'll stay blind for much longer."

"What makes you say that?"

"I gave him the same warning you did, and I really thought he'd get angrier, maybe even try to fight me. But he just walked off, like he wasn't sure what to think."

Inez sighs and twiddles her fingers. "He was my best friend this whole time. I confided in him. If he lets his father brainwash him..."

"That won't happen." Blake rubs her back. "Take it from his angle. If someone tried to convince you that your father was evil, would you be willing to accept it so easily? Even with evidence?"

"I guess not. But if you really think he'll come around, will you help me convince him?"

"I'll do what I can."

Inez rests her head on his shoulder with a sigh. He wraps an arm around her and kisses her head. Inez smiles at him and presses her lips to his.

"All right, I guess you've earned your present."

Blake rubs his hands together with a grin, and Inez places the box on his lap. She grabs a small knife from her nightstand drawer and holds it out with the blade pointing down. Blake blinks hard at it.

"You just...keep a knife at your bedside?"

"I lived with Ian for years! What would you do?"

Blake nods his head with his lip between his teeth. "Fair point."

He accepts the knife and cuts through the tape. He opens the flaps, pulls out the air cushions, and he gasps. His eyes shoot to Inez, then back to the contents.

Rubber handles similar to his juggling clubs, but the top is a metal bar with a wad of fresh, rolled Kevlar at the top.

"Are these..."

"Fire clubs!" Inez exclaims. "You wanted to juggle fire, so I got you something a little more suited to your style. You can still borrow some of my other props to learn, but these are yours to keep."

Blake looks at Inez again, and grabs her head to pull her into a kiss. "This is amazing. Thank you."

"Of course! Believe it or not, I ordered it the day after your test, to congratulate you for passing. Then, I started falling for you, and it made me even more excited to see your face when you opened it. But it arrived the day I had to kick you out of my room, and having it was torture. I almost sent it back. I'm really glad I didn't."

Blake sets the box aside and pulls her into his arms. "This gift is just the cherry on top. When I was stuck in Rex's car, I really thought I'd never see you again. I was terrified of what Rex would do next and what might happen to you. The fact that you're alright and that you were so happy to see me; the fact that you love me the way I love you, that's the greatest gift I could ever ask for."

"I do love you. More than I ever thought possible." Inez smiles at him, and he presses his lips to hers, slipping his tongue in and pushing her onto the bed, climbing on top of her. His breathing grows heavier, relighting a hunger he wasn't able to satisfy this morning.

Her knee bends and hits the stitches on Blake's leg, and he grunts in pain. Inez covers her mouth.

"I'm sorry!" she whimpers.

"Not your fault." Blake sits up. "But I think it's safer if I stay upright for a while. Damn it."

Inez giggles and rises to her knees to kiss his cheek. "That's okay. If it won't hurt too much to stand, I'd like to see you try out your new clubs."

Blake smiles and pulls the clubs from the box, admiring how they feel in his hands and giving a light practice toss to get a feel for their weight. Standing sends a shooting pain through his leg, but he's thrilled to accept a request from his princess.

He tosses up a club and catches it by the handle with the other two, then flips it up and catches it on his forehead to balance it. Inez applauds as he drops it and goes into a basic cascade. He switches up his patterns and tricks, creating corners and zigzags in the air, but his heart twinges in his chest as he stares past the shapes at the woman cheering him on.

She trusts him, and he's keeping Hartman's identity a secret from her. Her confusion when he said to call him Gramps was proof that she has no idea. Why would he have to tell Blake something like that? And what will Inez say when she inevitably finds out that he knew? Why is this even a secret to begin with? Would telling her really ruin anything?

He shakes the thoughts from his head as he finishes his impromptu routine. Inez leaps up to wrap her arms around his neck to plant her lips on his, and he wraps his arms tight around her.

For all he knows, keeping the secret might end up protecting her. Spilling his guts on impulse is exactly what prompted Rex to attack her in the first place. He'll keep the secret for now and pray in his heart that she'll be able to forgive him. When she pulls away, her smile is beautiful enough to wash away any doubt in his mind.

We'll be okay.

Epilogue

January sneaks up on the cast and crew, and auditions are more intense than Blake anticipated, considering the lead roles are always the same. But this time, Allistair is directing the show under his father's guidance, so he can learn to be King.

Everyone seems to be fighting hard, and Blake has never juggled so intensely in his life. The fire clubs work beautifully, and he's able to create trails of light with the flames as well as shapes from his throws, though a lead role isn't his main goal. As long as he can go on stage, he'll be grateful.

The cast gathers the next day in the lobby to hear Allistair announce the roles, while the crew sits behind him to hear their assignments. Rex stands at his side, but Axel sits with the others, at the farthest point from Blake as possible without leaving the crowd. *Thank God.*

"Thank you all for your hard work," Allistair begins. "Our *Hunchback of Notre Dame* show will be nothing short of inspiring, thanks to you guys. I expect everyone, including the ensemble roles, to make this the best show thus far."

Everyone cheers, and Allistair smiles as he lifts his clipboard.

"The leading role of Quasimodo will be played by Vladik. Your build and strength will be perfect for scenes where he assists Esmeralda, who will be played by Celia Hannon. The role of Pheobus will go to Blake Avery."

"What are you doing?" Rex interrupts before he can get much further. "Why cast Celia as the leading lady? And why is that Pup playing such an important role?"

"I can't be the ringleader *and* a leading role," Allistair responds without flinching, projecting his voice as if announcing it to everyone. "And Celia showed us all what she's capable of during the challenge and her tryouts. She's a star waiting for her chance to shine, and I intend to give that to her."

Everyone cheers except Axel, who slow claps with a scowl. Rex clenches his jaw as Allistair announces the remaining roles.

The members disperse as soon as he's finished, and Rex leaves in a huff. Celia rushes right over to Allistair, expressing her thanks with fast paced words and a giant hug. Allistair chuckles and assures her that she can't slack off. She saunters off with her head high, and Blake flashes her a knowing grin.

"Hey," says Blake. The smile Allistair had for Celia quickly fades as Blake approaches him.

"Thanks for casting me. Does that mean there are no hard feelings?"

"My personal feelings are irrelevant," Allistair snaps. "I still don't trust you, but Hartman promised a larger budget if you were a lead. Congratulations, you're the new dollar sign of the troupe. We're not friends."

"You don't still think I hurt Inez, do you?"

"I don't know what to think. What I do know is that you and Hartman are planning to undermine my father somehow, and you've sucked my best friend into your game."

Blake bites his tongue. It's been months since Rex tried to kill him, and Blake's kept himself as vigilant as possible to avoid anything further. But nothing has happened, no one else appears to have been hurt, so there's little evidence to prove to Allistair of what his father really is. How can they convince him?

"I have a meeting with our investors. Be ready to learn aerials tomorrow. Xavier will teach you."

He turns toward Inez, who's smiling with Celia.

"I got a lead role!" Celia cheers as she leaps into the air.

"I know!" Inez cheers. "I'm so proud of you!"

She's Hartman's granddaughter, and Victor's niece. She took Rex's abuse and was ready to face him head on. She's more than an incredible woman. She just might be the answer.

The adventure continues in book two!

The Fools' Circus: Fire Goddess

Follow DaniReiAuthor on Instagram and Facebook for updates!

Glossary

The props in this book that are described as fire props all have LED and day (or practice) alternatives. Most professionals have all three options and interchange them based on the setting and goal of their performance.

Levi wand –A wand that's tied with a string to look like it's floating. Most fire wands have a wick on each end, but some only have one on top, while others have wicking all the way down the wand. The string can be long or short, depending on the performer's preference.

Poi – A short rope with a fairly large wick on one end, and usually a small knob on the other. Some poi spinners prefer loop handles, and the length of the rope can vary.

Fans – A wire frame, some with one long wick along the curve, but most have individual wicks to look like multiple floating orbs. The handle is a ring that comes in various sizes but are usually identified as Russian or tech grips. Each size has its own benefit based on the desired style of performance.

Kettlebells – Most often described as a cannon ball with a handle. Juggling these is a great display of physical strength and coordination.

Aerial Hoop – Or "lyra" is a metal ring where performers twist and hang to create unique poses and movements.

Silks – Fabric drapes that hang from an aerial rig. Performers can weave themselves into the fabric, climb it, or twist around it.

Basic Cascade – This is the first trick most jugglers learn and is the basis for more advanced patterns.

Kevlar – A thick fabric made to be fire resistant, also used on fire fighter jackets as protection. They only hold flame when covered in fuel.

About the Author

Dani Rei hails from Providence, a city with a rich art community. She is a flow artist and loves to dabble in shapes and colors whenever possible. She teaches flow arts on her YouTube channel, and occasionally performs for events in her area. When she isn't stuck on whatever new endeavor seems interesting this week, she can be found playing and enjoying life with her little one and life partner.

CPSIA information can be obtained
at www.ICGtesting.com
Printed in the USA
LVHW041229050222
710327LV00012B/259

9 781736 724637